To Barbara,

thank you to Chris

I hope you enjoy
this Aussie book

CONFESSIONS
OF A
FLOOR WALKER

RJ Qureshi

PAUL SMITH PUBLISHING
London

Published by Paul Smith Publishing

This paperback edition published in 2018

Copyright © RJ Qureshi 2018

Cover design Cody VandeZande & Zero Due Design

ISBN PB 978-1-912597-02-4

Paul Smith Publishing

www.paulsmithpublishing.co.uk

To my husband Manny, for believing in me, when sometimes I didn't believe in myself. You are my everything.

Also, to my children who I often "shushed" while I was writing, and glared at during the final stages when I needed complete silence. I hope I inspired you all not to just follow your dreams, but to grab them with both hands and your feet!

"We are not, by nature, deserving of all that we want. When we think that we are automatically entitled to something; that is when we start walking all over others to get it."

Unknown

PROLOGUE

It is truly surprising how many people have never heard of a Loss Prevention Officer, commonly known to well-seasoned thieves as floor walkers, or even know what it is that they do.

I must admit that until I became a floor walker I didn't fully understand what they did. I'd heard of them during my years in Corporate Investigations but back then I believed that they were a myth (much like the Lochness monster), a made-up tale used to frighten people or, in this case, to deter people from stealing.

Floor walkers are very real though, they are a thief's worst nightmare. They wander around shops pretending to be interested in the products but are really following people hoping…, well, most days praying for some low life down and out individual to steal something. Good Loss Prevention Officers or, LPO'S as we are called for short, blend in well.., looking like a regular shopper and you don't notice they are there until they approach you outside the store and escort you to the dreaded back office.

They look just like your mom, dad, brother, sister, aunt, uncle or even your grandma!

Eliza Raine Fox
A Journey to a Floor Walker

At just twenty-four years of age, I was already divorced and I'd had more bad boys than Hugh Hefner had had playboy bunnies (well, maybe a slight exaggeration, but nonetheless I was certainly no angel). I was fed up with my party girl lifestyle, poor choices in men and I knew I had to change before I completely derailed and became a total train wreck.

A former client (and old friend of my late father), William Greeley, had contacted me to ask if I knew anyone interested in a career opportunity in Australia. There was a staff shortage in a big box retail chain in their Loss Prevention department, both as a covert and as an investigator. I didn't have to think twice about it, this was exactly what I needed. A change is as good as a holiday they say, and what better place to change than in Australia. The land down under, seven seas and 7,400 miles away from my current shitty life. I'd always wanted to visit there, but just never found the time.

William wasn't at all surprised that I was interested, and deep down I knew he was hoping I would take this opportunity for my own sake. He had seen me in several night clubs very drunk, well…, if I were honest, completely wasted, and more than once he had dragged me out and put me in his car and sent me home. After a week-long binge, he finally convinced me to spend a few weeks in a 'retreat' to sober up and get some help. He knew (from when I was on top of my game) I had the same work ethic as my father and may have felt like he 'owed me one' for all the extra unpaid work I'd done for him during his messy divorce, and subsequent custody battle.

This was his way of paying what he considered his debt, as well as helping his late friend's only child get out of a very dark place.

William knew Australia's National Loss Prevention manager, Timothy Bell, and after speaking with him on the phone, a Skype interview was set up with the Queensland state Loss Prevention manager, Simon Green. I'm not sure if it was my confidence or my ample cleavage, but after half an hour of answering questions I was offered a full-time position as a Loss Prevention Officer and told that I'd also be assisting on internal investigations as well.

So, with my inheritance and both businesses and property settlements in the bank, *and* after jumping through all the necessary immigration hoops, my life was packed into a storage unit and with just two suitcases and a carry-on bag, I left Sin City, aka Las Vegas to begin my new life in Sunny Brisbane, Queensland Australia.

***

Simon had said via email that one of his coverts had a one bedroom apartment for rent and gave me her details. A series of long emails were exchanged between Covert Alexis Keeley and myself and by the time the plane touched down in Brisbane a few months later, Alexis and I had become great friends.

When I transferred a six month advance on the rent to Alexis, she had accidentally seen the balance of my bank account and had exclaimed;

"Jesus Christ Eliza, you're loaded! What the fuck are you doing taking this shitty paying job? Why aren't you out traveling the world?!"

It was true, I had enough money in the bank to support a small country, but I'd always been a worker, and the idea of just living off of my inheritance didn't sit well with me. I needed to be busy, I enjoyed hard work. It was something that daddy had instilled in me, and something he felt strongly about. He had taught me in my teenage years the value of a dollar and made sure that I understood how hard it was to actually make decent money, and how to invest it wisely.

Growing up in Las Vegas I had seen millionaires lose everything they owned. It really was a dirty world. These gamblers were like junkies, chasing the high, looking for that rush, spending every last cent they owned, selling their possessions, even stealing from loved ones to get that fix, always believing they could win the next time around and make some money back. Families were torn apart, homes were lost and all too often people ended their lives as a result of their poor life choices.

Daddy had made me promise that I wouldn't waste my time or money gambling, because almost always the house won. It was a promise that was easy to keep. I saw how hard my father worked to provide for us, how many hours, days and sometimes even weeks he spent away from home to give me the life I had. There was no way I'd throw it all away over a game of cards or a pokie machine He had raised me to be a strong independent woman and, with the exception of the past few years, I had been.

But we are all entitled to fall apart and go a little crazy, aren't we? As my childhood live in nanny, Nanny Elva, put it; it's ok to feel depressed and sad, just don't pack up and live there, consider it character building! That was probably the best advice she ever gave me. I knew moving forward, that life would never be the same again. I had no one left alive who loved me, no family or close friends.

But it was time to quit the bullshit pity party and actually live life for me.., make my own way. I wanted to take on a role that was challenging and full of adrenalin, something to take my mind off of the shit storm my own life had become. Listening to Alexis recap her days via email (and then in person), I knew this job was exactly the rush I was looking for; she assured me it would be "all that and more". And as it turned out, she wasn't wrong!

With a background in investigations, Simon said I would be the perfect fit for the company. He also said that there were opportunities within the company for career growth, that they would soon be hiring two full-time investigators to focus on busting organized shop stealing gangs. I couldn't wait to get started. Standing at just 5ft 2 inches, with long blonde hair, emerald green eyes, a slim build and a pair of boobs that women envied and men admired, Simon's only concern was me not blending in with the average customer.

***

Simon was 54 years old and a bachelor, and he would tell anyone who'd ask that he had no time for a wife, because he was married to his career. He had been in the industry for 25 years and was very set in his ways. Some would refer to him as a bit of a control freak who liked to micromanage his staff.

Personally, I never had a problem with him and would even go as far as saying that we had a mutual respect for one another in our roles. In years to come, fellow Loss Prevention Officers and even managers would often remark that I was Simon's favorite, I strongly disagreed with them. I just went above and beyond what was required to get the job done. I was dedicated and hardworking and Simon admired me for that.

That's not to say that we didn't disagree on a number of things, my clothing choices being the main issue, because Simon, you see, had this theory that you could not get a pick up (apprehension) unless you were wearing plain colored clothing. A theory I would later prove wrong because I actually got a 'pinch' in a hot-pink gym suit.

I was on my day off and just dropped by the store to pick up a few things when I saw a group of boys stealing BONDS brand underwear and socks (I learned quickly that you were never really off duty). If you asked Simon though, he would say it was purely a coincidence or even fluke. One that he made very clear I was not to 'try out' whilst actually on duty. I couldn't help but be a bit of a rule breaker when it came to our dress code and I'm quite certain he never found out about my lucky red dress.

Training to be a Loss Prevention Officer was quite intense, and probably the only position within the company that you're not just thrown in at the deep end; you are properly trained. I guess you need to be, as there is little room for human error and can cost the company dearly if a mistake is made. Or so we were often told.

They say to catch a thief you have to think like one, and in the beginning, I was shocked at the inventive ways thieves removed stock (sometimes large quantities) from stores. But after a while, you've seen and heard it all, and you soon learn to be one step ahead of the crooks (well, as often as possible anyway).

We liaised quite closely with the police and soon learned the relevant terms of offenses. For example, when the amount was under $150 shoplifters were charged with UTAG (Unauthorised Taking Away Goods) this is generally a minor offense unless the person is a repeat offender. Often the amount well exceeded the $150 which then made it an indictable offense and they were charged with stealing, a much more serious charge.

Obviously, there were times when depending on the situation and how complaint the offender was, they were charged with extra offenses: fraud, public nuisance, assault, indecent exposure and even urinating in public were fairly common though.

ALEXIS
THE MASTER FLOOR WALKER

Alexis Keely is 38 years old, standing at 5ft 10 inches she is exactly eight inches taller than me. She has the craziest, curliest, unruly hair I've ever seen! With her chocolate brown eyes, slim athletic body and tanned skin it is surprising she doesn't have more admirers on the job than apprehensions.

She claims her amazing physique is all thanks to her husband Thomas, who owns a personal training business, and works her ass off every night.

Thomas is ruggedly handsome, and you'd never guess by looking at him that he is 40 years old. With his thick sandy brown hair (not a gray in sight) perfect hazel eyes on his unwrinkled face, a toned body that most 20-something lads would kill for he didn't look a day over 30. Seeing him and Alexis together in gym gear, they look like they just stepped off the cover of a health magazine.

Before I met Alexis in person, I knew from our constant emails back and forth that we would be great friends (corny I know) but our often dry sense of humor is so alike that we only have partial conversations because we know what the other is thinking so we spend a lot of the time mucking around laughing at unfinished sentences. At times her teenage son Tyson claims he isn't sure who is supposed to be the grown up in the house!

For the first few months, I worked very closely with Alexis as she taught me everything she could about the job. It can be quite unpredictable though, so you are never truly prepared and have to assess each situation as it arises. When it was time for me to go it alone, we both felt like someone had severed off a limb!

For as exciting as the job can be, at times it is also the loneliest one of all.

CHAPTER 1
SAY CHEESE, AND SMILE FOR THE CAMERA

It was a busy Thursday night and I was working the late shift. I knew as soon as I laid eyes on Tommy Peters and his pregnant girlfriend, Shelly Long, that they were going to steal something. They had that grub vibe oozing from them.

I thought for a moment that they were going to steal shoes, but judging by the soles of their filthy black feet, it had been a while since they'd both worn a pair. As they made their way left at home entertainment (the opposite direction of footwear) Tommy grabbed a very expensive hard drive from the end of an aisle.

"This will be good for piccies babe, and maybe even our pornos," Tommy called out loudly to Shelly who had continued walking toward the photo lab.

"Well, you'll have to get it Tommy coz I'm not," Shelly replied, sniffing loudly as she sat at the photo machine. She grabbed a flash drive from her bag, inserted it in the machine and began clicking through pictures.

Tommy stopped at a price scanner and scanned the hard drive.

"It's two hundred bucks, fuck that I ain't payin that!!" Tommy cursed loudly as he dropped the hard drive in the stack of shopping baskets underneath the scanner. He walked empty handed over to where Shelly was sitting.

I was about to walk away, thinking maybe I had misjudged them, when out the corner of my eye I saw Tommy walk back to the basket, retrieve the hard drive and head toward a quiet corner of the store. Oh, it was on, I thought excitedly.

Tommy ripped the hard drive from the packaging and stuffed it down the front of his grubby shorts. Discarding the empty box behind some cushions, he headed back to Shelly and paced around the area adjusting his shorts frequently.

Obviously, a $200 hard drive wasn't quite enough for greedy Tom, because he then went behind the counter and helped himself to a camera and a very expensive set of lenses from the unlocked cupboard. He walked to the fishing section where he used a knife to cut the packets open, he dumped the boxes and stuffed both the camera and lenses down the front of his shorts where he had the hard drive already.

I wondered if he had a Tardis in his shorts. How on earth did he have that much room down there?

Looking quite smug and pleased with himself he went back to Shelly, who by now was at the counter paying for her order. It was rather comical watching Tommy walk around the store so uncomfortably while Shelly helped herself to several baby items. Baby clothes were ripped from hangers, tags removed and the clothing folded and stuffed into her hand bag.

She even tried to make Tommy put a pack of baby bottles down the front of his pants. She was unaware that his shorts were already full of stolen property (until he literally showed her there was no more room).

I called the police but unfortunately, they were busy. Constable Dan Simpson advised me to keep the offenders under surveillance, and they would try to attend, but I knew by this point that I'd just have to apprehend them myself with a manager.

Tommy walked quite confidently to the front of the store and exited with Shelly. He began bragging about how easy that was, and how stupid the store was for leaving the cupboard unlocked.

He initially looked like a deflated balloon when I approached him outside of the store and introduced myself as the store's Loss Prevention Officer. But as his eyes darted about looking for a hint of police presence, I knew he was planning his escape, and that he was not going to come back.

"Just give me the stock back," I began, pointing at the front of his shorts.

Tommy removed the camera and lenses from the front of his shorts and threw them at me. But before I could say anything more, he pushed past me and ran off, leaving a pregnant Shelly to fend for herself.

After several failed attempts at coaxing Shelly back to the store, it was decided that we would just follow her from a distance until the police arrived. They arrived minutes later and Shelly claimed she had no idea who the other man was, or what we were talking about. She said she didn't know how the baby clothes had come to be in her bag, that they must've just fallen in there. Pregnancy brain must be quite a bitch!

Shelly was placed under arrest and taken to the watch-house. I returned to the store and went to the photo lab with Constable Dan Simpson who requested the photos for evidence. We opened the photo packet and could not believe our good luck, as inside was a perfect picture of Tommy Peters, beer in hand with Shelly by his side.

It gets better though.., because Shelly had also used Tommy's name and correct cell phone number on the order.

"Perhaps they could be in the running for Australia's dumbest criminal," I joked to Officer Simpson.

"Yeah, you have to be a six pack short of a carton to think you could get away with this one," he replied laughing as he pulled out his cell phone to call Tommy.

"Tommy Peters?" he asked.

"Yeah, who's this?" Tommy replied.

"It's Constable Dan Simpson," he smirked, "and we've arrested your girlfriend in relation to a shop stealing matter and we need to speak to you about it also, so if you could come down to the…"

"PISS OFF PIG!" Tommy yelled angrily over the top of Constable Simpson and then hung up.

"You didn't really think that would work did you?" I asked curiously.

"Nah not at all, but I just wanted him to know we're on to him," Constable Simpson laughed.

My cell rang, I picked up and recognized the voice immediately, it was the center security manager, Dylan Gaines.

"Hey Eliza, I'm pretty sure that grub you are looking for is sitting in the food court right now eating a burger," he said.

"You're kidding!" I laughed, "he must've worked up an appetite with all that running," I joked, "thanks Dylan we will go check it out, give me a call if he moves."

Hanging up, I relayed the conversation to Constable Simpson and we headed to the food court. Sure enough, there was Tommy…, head down munching away on a KFC burger. The hard drive was sitting on the table beside his box of fries.

"Hey Tommy, fancy seeing you here," Constable Simpson said while placing a hand on Tommy's shoulder.

Tommy looked up behind him and immediately jumped up, attempting to flee. Constable Simpson's grip tightened on Tommy.

"Can I at least finish me burger? Fuck, I spent me last ten bucks on this feed!" Tommy protested as he was led away.

I bagged up the hard drive as evidence and said I'd head back to the store to finish my report and burn footage.

I later heard that Tommy had been sent immediately back to jail. He was wanted on outstanding warrants for a home invasion, and was also in breach of a restraining order that Shelly had taken out on him.

CHAPTER 2
HI-HO AND OFF TO COURT WE GO

It's always the ones you least expect to be crazy, that turn out to be complete nutters! I was working with Alexis, and it started out like most floor walking days. We'd already had a few little pickups, teen girls with underwear and a teen boy with the ever-popular white canvas shoes.

As we lapped the store we came across Patricia Milne, she was tearing tags from what Alexis had named period undies, you know the ones you wouldn't be caught dead in unless it was *'that time of the month'*. As quickly as the tags were pulled off, the underwear disappeared into Milne's handbag.

Milne wasn't your usual run of the mill stereotypical thief, she actually looked like a nice old lady, perhaps how you would expect your grandma to look. So, you can imagine our surprise when we approached her outside only to be told quite loudly, "FUCK OFF, SLUTS!" and then shoved out of the way as she made her escape from the complex.

Alexis whipped her phone out and began recording, I tried to reason with a very unreasonable, and out of control Milne, who screamed profanities at us as she threw underwear from her bag. Police and the center's security were on their way, so we maintained our distance and continued to follow behind a very irate Milne, who would stop every 15 feet, turn and punch the air and scream at us, threatening to punch our faces in.

As we passed by a hedge, Milne made a futile attempt to dump the remaining underwear, and a bunch of flash drives (that we hadn't even seen her take) by deliberately falling into the bushes and disposing of them. Alexis leaned into the bushes and picked up a little clear bag that contained the remnants of what appeared to be Marijuana.

"I wonder if this belongs to her?" Alexis laughed.

"It might explain her bizarre behavior, but it is highly unlikely," I giggled. □□We later found out that Milne had a long history of drug use, so it was actually possible that it had come from her handbag.

Security arrived and tried to speak with Milne who began hurling cans of tinned beans at the unsuspecting guard! Milne was not going down without a fight and even slapped the attending female officer in the face as she tried to resist being handcuffed.

As Milne was led away the abuse continued, and even when we were almost a block away we were sure we could still hear her screaming;

"I'm going to kill ya's ya sluts, watch your backs coz I'm coming for you's!!"

We collected the underwear and flash drives from the bushes, and as we walked back through the car park we saw a couple arguing beside a car.

"Well Carl, they aren't my fucking undies now are they?" The lady shouted, "so which whore put them on my antenna hmmm? Have you been shagging that bitch down the street again? Is she trying to mess with me Carl? Coz I'll fucking choke her with these and hang her with them from the fucking tree in her own fucking front yard!"

"Babe, I swear, I haven't been fucking anyone else, I don't know who's they are," Carl was edging away from the woman, waving his hands in the air in despair.

We hadn't noticed during our pursuit, but when Milne had thrown some of the underwear from her bag, a pair had strategically landed on this couples car antenna and was now the subject of a very heated argument.

"Umm, excuse me, but this underwear is actually evidence to a shoplifting incident, the offender threw them there on her way past," Alexis explained as she removed the underwear, she showed the irate woman the rest of the underwear in her hand and then quickly walked away.

"Jesus, there's crazy fuckers everywhere today," Alexis laughed as we walked back to the store.

I'd like to say that this is where the saga ends with Milne, but unfortunately, it does not. Milne pled not guilty, claiming she was set up and stated she wanted to have her day in court.

The big day arrived, and Alexis assured me that in all her years as an LPO she had never once had to speak directly to a judge, that *usually* once the offender and their lawyer see you are present, they immediately change their plea to guilty.

But Milne was not only the exception to the rule, she was clearly crazy because she had fired her legal team after they suggested she plead guilty and decided to represent herself. Her line of questioning made absolutely no sense, as she spat question after question at me, not even waiting for me to reply. I glanced at the police prosecutor who looked slightly amused at the scene playing out before him. The judge, however, was quickly losing his patience. Her attempts to get me to look directly at her, gave me flashbacks to the Kath and Kim DVD Alexis had subjected me to when I first arrived in Australia.

"Look at moi look at moi!" she screamed angrily.

I shook my head in absolute disbelief as she cursed like a sailor when the footage of her stealing was shown in court. Milne claimed the footage was fake, and that it wasn't her and that we had no solid proof. The gavel banged more times than a hammer on a construction site! The judge too had clearly had enough of this circus and found Milne guilty.

22

She was almost arrested again as we exited the courtroom for threatening to push me down the stairs.

"You sucked the judge off, didn't ya's ya dirty sluts?!" Milne screamed over and over.

"She's batshit fucken crazy!" Alexis said looking back over her shoulder as we left the courthouse.

"I almost feel sorry for her Alexis, it's like she's that nutty that she believes everything she is saying," I shook my head in disbelief.

"Awwww, but bless her cotton period undies she got her day in court," Alexis joked.

I had a feeling that it wouldn't be the last time I'd lay eyes on Milne, and that as crazy as she was, she wouldn't forget our faces either.

CHAPTER 3
PICKED UP

One of the perks to being a single lady is, you reserve the right to give a good looking guy more than a 'once over', don't you think?

I wasn't in the habit of chatting up customers, but Lucas Meadow was kind of cute. Blonde shaggy hair, blue eyes, nicely toned arms, and his one size too small black BONDS shirt left little to the imagination of what was going on underneath, he was ripped! He seemed to be struggling to decide between which shoes to buy. There was nothing else going on in the store, so I thought I'd go over and help him out. I pretended to browse beside him for a few minutes, watching him in my peripheral vision before making my move.

"Hmmm, I don't think those shoes will match those shorts or much else for that matter, you're about a size ten right?" I asked casually handing him another pair of shoes.

"Yeah, I am thanks," he replied, grinning like a little kid and deliberately flexing his arm muscles as he headed toward the chair in the next aisle.

On closer inspection, I realized he was probably around 20, 21 tops, and I actually felt like a bit of a pervert. I walked away…, thinking that maybe I needed to get laid, or at the very least go buy a vibrator…, which seemed like the safer option. I took one last look over my shoulder and was a little surprised to see him remove and discard the tags and string from the shoes.

He put the new shoes on and stuffed his old pair under the shelf. It was definitely time to make my retreat. I moved back into a hidden location and saw the disappointed look on his face as he came back to the now empty aisle. I watched as he wandered around the footwear department as if looking for me, and followed him as he left the area when he'd given up. Lucas went to various sections of the store, where his five finger discount continued. Eventually, he made his way to the registers and paid for one bag of candy. I called the mobile police unit, fortunately, they were just across the mall and said they would make their way over. Lucas exited the store and was walking down the mall, as I stepped in front of him I noticed the police had come up from behind.

"Hi, I'm the…" I attempted to introduce myself, but Lucas cut me off.

"I knew you were into me, you want my number huh?" Lucas said puffing his chest out.

"Oh, I don't *just* want your number; I want your full name, date of birth and address!" I replied boldly.

"Geez that's a bit full on, I thought we could just hook-up," Lucas said looking puzzled.

"I'm actually the store's Loss Prevention Officer, and the police that are standing behind you will want all of that information too," I replied, pointing behind Lucas to the two officers who were trying to suppress their smirks.

Lucas turned and groaned, and was promptly escorted to the back office. Once the formalities were over, Lucas Meadow was escorted out by Constable Michael Steer.

"So, do you make a habit of flirting with offenders before apprehending them then?" smirked Senior Constable Roman Beach, cocky now that we were alone.

I looked up from my laptop and it was then I truly noticed him. His intense dark chocolate brown eyes, and cheeky smile that was accentuated by the deepest dimples I had ever seen. His black hair carefully groomed into that messy just got out of bed look. At 6ft 2 he towered over me. I guessed he was around my age (I'd later find out he was three years my senior).

Wow, he was hot! I laughed at the comment trying furiously not to blush!

What was wrong with me today? Were my pheromones running wild? This police officer who I had just met was gorgeous, sex on legs I would later joke to Alexis. No wedding ring?? But that didn't necessarily mean anything though, did it?

The attraction was instant, his eyes danced with mischief as he looked me over, his stare momentarily resting on my cleavage before moving his gaze upward to meet my eyes. He obviously enjoyed what he saw, and the feeling was very mutual. I was glad I'd gone against the dress code and worn my favorite figure-hugging red dress.

The eye fucking continued, and I'm sure he was having the same erogenous thoughts as I was. We both looked away at the same time, and as he sat down beside me I shifted a little in my chair, my stomach fluttered uncontrollably and I was sure my face was slowly turning as red as my dress.

"Now, I'm also going to need a few details from you.., let's start with your name. Is it Miss, Ms or Mrs?" Roman teased winking at me.

"*Miss* Eliza Raine Fox," I said emphasizing the Miss.

Roman looked up from his notebook,

"WOW! That is a really cool name, I like it," he said. His lips were pursed as he casually nodded his head.

"Thank you," I replied and flashed him a smile.

I loved my name, people often said it sounded like I should be a Hollywood celebrity. Alexis joked that when she received my first email, she thought she was being sent something from a porn site when she saw my name. I continued giving my particulars but was in total awe of this Adonis that sat beside me. Forget a knight in shining armor, I'd settle for this Officer in uniform with handcuffs any day! I smiled at the thought. Pull yourself together Eliza! I scolded myself as I caught my brain wandering off yet again.

As I tapped away on the keyboard finishing my statement, Roman relaxed in the chair beside me, slowly flipping through his notebook, taking down notes and occasionally giving me the once-over. He inched a little closer…, damn, he smelt good.

"How long have you been in Australia?" Roman asked casually as he put his notebook in his pocket.

"About six months," I replied.

"Are you planning on sticking around?" Roman asked as he pulled a business card from his pocket.

***

"Yes I think so, I mean..., I definitely like what I see," I replied as I made eye contact with Roman.

SHIT! I hadn't meant for it to come out like that, it was as though the words had just leapt out of my mouth before my brain even processed what I was saying. I was still staring at Roman, as a huge grin spread across his face. I sighed, caught my breath, and attempted very poorly to compose myself. I couldn't stop staring at his dimples. They were so deep I wondered if I could do tequila shots from them? The thought made me smirk.

FUCK! FOCUS ELIZA!! I told myself, yet again my mind had wandered off.

"Me too," he laughed, "me too."

He stood up and as he left he handed me his card, nothing to get excited about I reminded myself, I had a business card holder full of police contact details it was all part and parcel of the job.

"So, *Miss* Eliza Raine Fox, you call me if you need anything. I'm going to be running the unit here for a while so we may as well get acquainted," he winked, turned, and just like that he was gone!

I sighed loudly as I sat back on the chair and tried to still my thumping heart. I started turning the business card between my fingers (a trick I'd picked up in Vegas). It was then I noticed a cell phone number written on the back of the card. It couldn't be, could it? Roman's personal cell phone number? It appeared I may have been 'picked up' after all!

CHAPTER 4
I DIDN'T SEE THAT COMING

Every Loss Prevention Officer has made the error of losing an offender (or even a potential one). Making sure to follow all of the rules, setting up the perfect apprehension only to have the person you're following slip away. Alexis often joked that there must be a giant crack or black hole that opens up on the shop floor and swallows them up because no amount of circling around or looking ever finds them. It's more annoying when you've seen absolutely everything, remained completely unseen, and the offender leaves with their loot, never knowing they were being tailed in the first place.

Usually, it's human error, you lose them within the store and kick yourself for the rest of the day that you took a wrong turn, or looked down when you should have looked up. I would like to say that is how it happened for me on this particular occasion, but unfortunately for me and my back, it's not! I had a call from Madison, who was by far my favorite customer greeter, she had an eye for thieves, and I often remarked that she should join the Loss Prevention team.

Madison's main job was to stand at the door greeting customers, check receipts and give assistance when needed. But she went above and beyond in her role and was a very valuable asset, an extra pair of eyes to us floor walkers.

She had noticed a regular customer (who she was always suspicious of) enter the store and make a big deal out of needing to purchase a birthday card for the gift she had in her enviro bag.

Those fabric bags that customers brought from home might be great for saving the environment, but they were also a great tool for thieves to remove large quantities of stock from the store without being questioned.

It didn't take me long to find Lara Best, with her outlandish hippy like clothing, huge red lips and big floppy hat she obviously didn't get the concept of blending in. I was a little confused when I first saw her remove what appeared to be a perfectly wrapped gift box from the bag until she took the lid off and I could see the box was empty. Well, it wasn't empty for long because Lara began selecting children's DVD's and clothing and filling the box to the brim.

She removed tape from her bag, sealed the lid shut and placed the box back into the enviro bag. As Lara walked down the card aisle she haphazardly grabbed a birthday card from the $2 stand and headed toward the registers. The whole idea of what she had just done was genius really, but not when you have the store's security tailing your ass!

and chill out. I'm certain he told me that rum and raisin was his favorite just to appease me. Either way, he was a sweet kid with a good head on his shoulders and his compassion and handling of my bullshit plight would definitely serve him well with the ladies when he started dating.

I'd gone back inside, picked up my cell and began typing a message to Roman when I caught my reflection in the mirror. I saw the birds nest of hair piled up on my head, and dark circles under my eyes. I knew I needed to sort my shit out before I even thought about starting something with him, I was a hot mess! And just because the bed hair look suited Roman, it definitely wasn't working for me. He'd just have to wait, and if it were meant to be something would happen.

CHAPTER 5
MORE BANG FOR YOUR BUCK

It was 9 am and I was walking into the store with my first cappuccino of the day, prepared for hours of paperwork and reviewing endless CCTV footage.

Light duties sucked!!

But the day I had planned in my head, changed quickly when I spotted Mike Lee strutting his way toward the home entertainment section. It wasn't his overall look, more his demeanor and the pace in which he was walking that grabbed my attention. I cursed, knowing that yet again I was going to end up with a cold coffee. It seemed to be an occupational hazard.

Mike didn't disappoint me, he grabbed a very expensive iPod dock from the shelf and made his way to the registers. Now…, most would *assume* that would be the end of it, and that I had misjudged Mike. But I wasn't ready to give up just yet, and rightfully so, as Mike just pushed his way through customers and walked out of the store without even paying. The gate alarm sounded, and his pace quickened as he headed toward the main exit. The stunned staff just stood there as I thrust my coffee at them.

"Get a manager, and tell them to call the police," I instructed as I chased Mike to the car park where he was unlocking a late model silver Nissan patrol.

As I heard the familiar thumping of running feet behind me, coupled with jingling store keys, I knew back up was only a few feet behind me, so I attempted to approach Mike and asked him to return to the store with me.

"In your dreams lady!" He said laughing as he casually put the iPod dock into the back seat of the car.

He jumped in the car and started to reverse out when I heard an angry voice behind me; "Mike you fucken dog are you going to just leave me here?" The large lady with badly bleached hair screamed loudly as she ran toward the car.

Mike, in a panic, pulled the car out too sharply, smashing into the car beside him. The woman continued screaming like a banshee and Mike unlocked the car doors. As the woman was getting into the passenger seat, I seized my chance and opened the back door and grabbed the iPod dock, handing it behind me to Cole Warner, who had run out after me. Mike drove forward quickly and then began to reverse again. Somehow I'd ended up with half of my upper body in the car. Fearing I would be run over, I scrambled up onto the running board on the side of the vehicle, (and was hanging on for dear life to the handrail inside) as Mike continued to move forward and then backward, this time hitting a car driving by.

The impact flung me from the vehicle, and Mike drove off with the passenger door still open almost sideswiping other cars on his way out of the car park. Cole looked at me in shock and we both burst out laughing realizing the enormity of what had just happened.

"Bloody hell girl are you completely crazy?" Cole said with wide eyes, he offered me a hand and pulled me up off the ground.

"Wow, let's keep this on the down low, I already have enough paperwork to finish from the disability scooter incident," I mumbled as I brushed off my jeans and t-shirt.

"Don't I know it!" Cole said laughing "I had to do a presentation at a regional safety meeting about the dangers of disability scooters in the stores. Try keeping a straight face while watching that footage of you being thrown in the air like a bloody rag doll and then run over. Sorry Eliza but it looks fucken hilarious!" Cole was laughing harder now.

I ended up seeing the footage so many times it was permanently burnt into my brain. The remix that Alexis had put together to the song Tubthumping, (better known as "I get Knocked Down") by Chumbawamba was something I'd never forget.

I was actually surprised at how well my back had held up with being thrown from the side of the car, my elbow, on the other hand, was missing a bit of skin. Bending over and holding my knees I stretched my back, oh that felt good. I sat on the ground and leaned forward putting my head into my lap giving my lower back a good stretch also. Even my ribs felt ok, thank God because cracked ribs are no joke. The jangle of police belts could be heard and I looked up to see Senior Constable Roman Beach and Constable Michael Steer running toward me. SHIT, it would have to be him, wouldn't it? I thought.

"What on earth are you doing down there?" Roman asked looking baffled at me sitting on the ground.

He put a hand out and I took it, and he pulled me up off the ground.

"Oh you know, just sitting around waiting for you guys to turn up, but you're too late," I teased.

I realized we still had each other's hands, and after giving his a bit of a squeeze I pulled my hand away. I gave them the registration plate details and a brief (and very watered down) version of events. Unfortunately for me, there was no chance of keeping my stunt act a secret as at least a dozen witnesses had come forward claiming it looked like a scene from a movie and were offering their details if it went to court.

Constable Michael Steer moved to the side and put a BOLO (Be On the Look Out for) over the radio for all car crews in the area and then started taking witness details in his book.

It was beginning to sound a lot like the game Chinese whispers and getting exaggerated to stories of me on the roof of the car, being run over, backflipping from the vehicle and even pushed from the car by the alleged offender. If some of the witness's accounts were to be believed I had as many moves as Jackie Chan!

Senior Constable Roman Beach had finished taking details and strode over to where I stood looking slightly amused.

"There's never going to be a dull moment with you around is there Fox? Now..., I know that everything I've just heard couldn't be possible, but please tell me you weren't thrown from the alleged offender's vehicle?" He asked pursing his lips together to contain a smirk. As he did so, his dimples were accentuated.

Oh boy..., I could get lost in those things, I thought to myself. I attempted to paste a look of innocence on my face but failed miserably.

"Ummm I wasn't *thrown* from the vehicle," I said biting my bottom lip.

"Jesus Christ, Eliza what were you thinking?" Roman paused before continuing with his lecture. "You could've been seriously injured or worse, why didn't you just get his rego details and put a report on, do you know how dangerous some of these grubs are that you are dealing with?"

The lecture was lost on me..., because all I could think was how sexy he looked when he was serious. His eyebrows were scrunched up and a cute wrinkle had appeared on his forehead.

Damn..., I could have some fun with him I thought.

Attempting to hide what was clearly written all over my face I looked down at the ground. Roman, thank goodness, completely misread my look of lust and thought I was upset at the scolding. He reached out and gently squeezed my shoulder.

"I'm sorry, I just don't want to see anything bad happen to you, promise me you won't pull a stunt like that again? Hey, look at me will you?" He said as he brushed a strand of hair from my face, using his index finger to raise my chin upwards to look at him.

As our eyes met I saw the same look of lust I was trying to hide, only mixed with concern. I was unusually quiet.., drinking in his chocolate brown eyes..., I wanted nothing more than to kiss his full lips. Well, if I'm honest I wanted to do a lot more than that.

What was it about this man that made me lose my head? I was always so professional when dealing with police, never even stepping close to that blurred line. But with Roman..., it was like I couldn't help where my brain went. Caught in the moment he ran his fingertip along my lower lip, I knew this was going to be the beginning of something. What exactly, I hadn't quite figured out but the chemistry between us was electric!

Constable Michael Steer had joined us and cleared his throat in an attempt to get Roman's attention. We both took a step backward.

"The offender was just picked up by a car crew at a Sandgate Servo and has been taken into custody. He had warrants and was also displaying stolen plates on the vehicle. The Sarge wants us to go to the watch-house to process him now," Constable Steer finished, he turned and walked away quickly to Cole to collect the iPod dock, and no doubt to remove himself from the awkward situation that was unfolding before him.

"Are you sure you're ok?" Roman looked down at me and asked quietly.

"I'm fine, I think my ego is more bruised than my ass is. You better get going, I'll have a statement and footage ready for you later," I replied.

As he walked away he stopped, turned and looked back at me…,

"And for Christ sake, Eliza…, would you just call me already?" He grinned.

A smile spread across my face, but before I could answer him he was gone.

"Flirt!" Cole accused as we walked back to the store.

I laughed, unable to wipe the smile from my face. As I entered the store and collected my now lukewarm coffee, paperwork was the furthest thing from my mind. I was determined to turn over a new leaf when I moved to Australia. I wanted to make a life for myself and, for once, not be caught up in the drama and bullshit of relationships and men.

I'd made a decision to forgo men for an entire year and I was *almost* at the year mark. I enjoyed this single, solitary, celibate life, or did I? The fact I even questioned this, it meant I already knew deep inside what I wanted to do, and I was annoyed with myself for allowing these feelings to creep back in. There was no denying the attraction, it was obvious to everyone in our orbit, but I wasn't sure if I was ready to jump back in.

My marriage to Michael and subsequent divorce had been long and painful and the string of men that followed was nothing to be proud of. I'd used sex as a band-aid trying to soothe my broken soul, but it didn't make any of the feelings of failure and betrayal any easier no matter how good the sex had been!

I had some serious soul searching to do, and fast by the looks of it. Roman was getting impatient, and he'd made it clear what he wanted. Now I had to decide if that was what I wanted, too?

As the saying goes, life is what happens to you while you're busy making other plans and it appeared, life had snuck up on me and bitten me on the proverbial ass (hard may I add!). This was in the form of one very irresistible Senior Constable Roman Beach.

CHAPTER 6
CRAZY FOR YOU

I should have known when I saw Mai Fung put the glass saucepan lid down the front of her pants that she wasn't the full ticket. I mean, who the fuck steals a saucepan lid?

Or perhaps when she ripped the tags off of a jacket in front of staff and other customers and then put it on, should have been a light bulb moment for me that she was a few sandwiches short of a picnic. She certainly looked harmless enough…, but as I was about to find out, looks can be very deceiving.

The center was having a police operation focusing on shoplifters so I didn't hesitate to call to have them involved immediately. Senior Constable Roman Beach answered and I felt a stab of guilt as I still hadn't contacted him outside of work. I wanted to, I'd even started several messages and stared at his number so much I already knew it by heart. But I just hadn't followed through.

I wasn't sure if I was going to stay in Australia, and even if I did I wasn't certain that I was completely ready to jump into something new. All I knew for sure was that Roman was the last thing I thought about before I closed my eyes for the night, and the very first thing on my mind in the morning…, and that scared me.

I'd decided to see where it went, but lacked the courage to take the first step. I knew I shouldn't procrastinate but I was so conflicted about the whole situation. I also worried about the implications if it didn't work out and I needed him in a professional capacity. Would he be able to separate his personal feelings and still do his job? I'd heard of a few horror stories about LPO's dating Cops. Simon strongly discouraged (almost frowned upon) any form of 'relationship' outside of work with staff, security, AND police.

Roman arrived quickly, and this time was all business, barely glancing at me at all, I'd obviously bruised his ego. I knew as soon as I saw him that I did want him, that I needed to at least explain how I was feeling. I hoped it wasn't too late. But now was not the time to be focused on that I needed to keep my head in the game right now.

As Mai Fung exited the store I approached her and asked her to return to the store with me, initially she complied. Well…, that was until she saw Senior Constable Roman Beach walking toward her and then all hell broke loose!

Mai began screaming at the top of her lungs and threw the saucepan lid at Roman, she then removed the jacket and hurled that across the mall. Our attempts to calm her fell on deaf ears as the screeching continued. Roman restrained Mai against the wall but this made her behavior worse and she kicked out wildly.

***

The decision was made to take her down to the ground, so following Roman's instructions, I swiped her legs out from underneath her and we lowered a screaming Mai to the floor. Roman attempted to put Mai's arms up behind her back, but for a little lady, she certainly had some strength.

"Eliza get my cuffs for me and hold her legs down," Roman ordered, whilst struggling to restrain Mai.

I sat on Mai's legs and in a panic started feeling..., well..., truth be told it looked more like groping around Roman's waist and utility belt, hopelessly trying to find the handcuffs. Eventually, I found them and pulling them out, I attempted to pass them to Roman.

"You're going to have to get underneath me and cuff her for me," he directed.

I felt my face flush, partly from the struggle of the situation but also because I felt aroused being this close to him. I climbed underneath Roman's arm and put the cuffs on a screaming Mai. Once the handcuffs were on I attempted again (more successfully this time) to soothe Mai and assure her she was going to be ok.

Roman radioed for backup, they soon arrived and escorted Mai to the watch-house, Roman told them he would follow them soon. I looked at a flustered Roman who had beads of sweat running down his face.

"I think we could both use some air?" I suggested.

We walked silently outside to the car park and stood in the cool night breeze. As I leaned against the wall I closed my eyes for a minute trying to make sense of what had just happened.

"Jesus Christ Eliza, all that over a fucking glass lid and a jacket…, FUCK!!" Roman's angry voice pierced the night air.

"I'm sorry, I didn't know she was a nutcase," I said apologetically as I reached out and touched his arm, running my fingers up and down his forearm in an attempt to calm him down.

Caught in the moment Roman turned toward me, pushing me hard against the wall pinning me with his arms. His mouth found mine, his kiss a mixture of anger, sexual tension and lust as his tongue probed my mouth. The urgency of the kiss so ferocious in the beginning then slowing to one of tenderness and pure passion as his body relaxed against mine.

Oh wow! He kissed better than I imagined he would I thought.

He pulled away and leaned beside me on the wall, the gravity of what we had just done lingered silently between us. We both knew we should not be fooling around like this while we were both on duty, we could be disciplined, I wondered if we could even be sacked? But the attraction and sexual tension had been building since that first meeting.

We stood silently, both of us savoring the moment, enjoying the lack of distance between us, and also hoping that no one had passed by and witnessed the encounter.

"Sorry Eliza, I'm just so fucking…" He began.

"Roman," I cut in, I knew I owed him an explanation, and wanted to tell him everything I was feeling…, but my thoughts were interrupted by the shrill of his cell phone.

"She was a mental health patient out on day release," Roman said when he hung up.

"Shit, no wonder she was going off." I said wringing my hands together.

"We better head back, can you bring the footage and statement down ASAP. I will need to do a full brief on this one for sure," Roman sounded a little bothered, as he rubbed his head.

"Ok, I'll see you in a bit, do you want anything?" I asked. Thinking maybe I could bring him a coffee or donut, (as cliché as it was) as a peace offering.

"Jesus Eliza, you know what I want, do I really have to spell it out?" Romans response gave me the final push I needed.

"Ok…," I paused "I want that too," I grabbed his hand as he went to walk away, I pulled him back toward me and we kissed again. This time I didn't give a shit if Simon himself were to walk by. Well…, maybe that's a bit of a stretch, but when you're caught in the moment, consequences are the furthest thing on your mind.

"See you soon," I said as I pulled back.

We parted ways, and as I casually strolled back to the store I made myself a promise, it was time to let some walls down and see where this went.

After what had just happened, it was clear that there was no turning back now and truth be told I really didn't want to. An hour later I handed my typed statement and CCTV footage to Roman at the police beat on my way home.

"I think I owe you a drink," I said cheekily.

"Indeed you do! There's a bar near my place, I can meet you tonight if you're free? Let's say 10-ish" Roman grinned, writing down the address on a sticky note and handing it to me.

"I guess it's a date?" I winked.

I headed home, showered and spent the next hour trying on different outfits. By the time I'd settled on a sapphire blue strapless dress and evening shawl, my bedroom looked like my wardrobe had exploded!

Somewhere underneath a pile of clothing, I could faintly hear Iris by the Goo Goo dolls playing on my iPod dock. I sat at my dressing table in my lingerie humming along as I applied my makeup and fixed my hair into a messy updo, leaving a few strands down to frame my face. I chose a pair of silver filigree leaf earrings, they were my favorite, three leaves hung down one after the other. I loved the way each individual leaf caught the light shimmering subtly as I moved my head. I was a little obsessed with leaf earrings and had quite a collection still packed in a jewelry box in the storage unit back home in Vegas. I was glad now that I'd at least bought this pair with me.

It had been a long time since I'd been on a date or even dressed up for a night out. And although I knew my attire was perhaps a little over the top, I wanted to make a lasting impression on Roman. I slipped the dress on and draped the shawl over my shoulders, I chose a pair of black heels with small diamante gems sprinkled across the bridge of the toes. As I stood up I caught my reflection in the mirror and eyed myself carefully. Not bad I thought, certainly a big change from the usual jeans and t-shirts I was used to wearing most days.

I heard a car horn beep outside, so I grabbed my evening bag and headed out. Climbing into the taxi I gave the driver the address. 30 minutes later I pulled up in front of a bar; *'Brisvegas'* the sign blinked. How ironic I smiled…, of course I had the American accent, but to my knowledge Roman didn't know exactly where in the US I was from.

I found a comfy lounge with a coffee table in the corner of the rooftop bar, I was sipping a Jack Daniels and coke when I saw Roman enter. My stomach flip-flopped as he walked toward me. I guess this was the butterfly feeling my Daddy had told me about?

Wearing faded jeans and a short-sleeved black collared shirt, he was dressed far more casually than me but he looked just as yummy in civvies as he did in his uniform. I stood up to greet him, Roman pulled me close into a hug and bent to kiss my cheek. I inhaled deeply, oh boy he smelt so damn good!

"Sorry I'm late I got held up with that case," he said stepping back, he looked me over.

"Wow Eliza, you are gorgeous!" he said grinning and pulled me into him again. This time kissing my lips softly and caressing my jawline with his fingertips.

"I don't want to ruin your perfect lipstick," Roman said pulling away.

His eyes looked devilishly mischievous as he looked me up and down, he sat down on the couch, pulling me down next to him. I looked at Romans handsome face, his dimples on display, looking deeper than ever as he smiled at me.

"You aren't too bad yourself officer," I said shyly.

We were silent as we drank each other in. Well.., if I'm honest we were eye-fucking the shit out of each other again!

"This place is nice," I gestured around breaking eye contact.

"Yeah it's quiet here, and they have the best barista who makes the most sensational coffee too," Roman boasted.

It seemed we both shared the same addiction to a good cup of coffee. A waiter came over and took our order, returning moments later with our drinks and then we were alone. Feeling a little homesick as I looked around the bar with all its Vegas Paraphernalia I could feel the first sting of tears welling in my eyes.

Christ Eliza, get your shit together I willed myself furiously.

"Hey what's wrong?" Roman asked as he moved closer.

"Nothing, I'm ok," I replied trying to brush off the melancholy mood that was threatening to take over. "This place kind of makes me miss home though. I was born and raised in Las Vegas and it's the first time since I arrived that I've actually missed it, or been reminded of home.., well except tonight when I was thinking about my earring collection," I laughed trying to lighten the mood.

Humor was always my defense mechanism against the emotional crap I didn't want to feel.

"Shit Eliza, I'm sorry.., we can go if you want? I had no idea," Roman said apologetically as he put his hand on my leg.

"No it's fine, it's actually quite cool here," I smiled as I looked around. "If you don't mind, I might claim this place as my new home away from home."

"As long as you can put up with me living here with you too," Roman winked.

"Hmmm, I'm sure I can handle that," I smiled again and raised my glass.

"Cheers," I said cheekily as I clinked his glass and gulped at my drink.

Roman pulled me close and kissed the top of my head. His scent..., his warm embrace..., oh I could certainly get used to this. The ice was completely broken and now it was time to come clean!

"I hope you don't think I've been playing hard to get?" I began, "but I have had a lot going on and to be honest, I wasn't looking to hook-up or.."

"Hook-up?" Roman interjected, "do you think that's what this is? That it's what I want with you?" He looked genuinely offended, perhaps even a little irritated.

"I didn't mean it like that, I just..., I don't know? Look, I'm just going to be completely honest with you. I have recently come out the other side of a very bad marriage and nasty divorce, and I didn't know if I were ready for anything just yet," I explained while looking down at my hands.

"Let's just see where it goes. I know we just met, but I'm kinda crazy about you already. There's no need to rush this.., no pressure. Let's just enjoy each other's company for now ok?" Roman finished. He tilted my head toward him and gently kissed my lips.

"Sounds good to me," I grinned, this time I kissed him.., enjoying his lips against mine and allowing his hands to roam over my body, momentarily forgetting we were in a bar and not somewhere more private.

Pulling away I picked up my glass, finished my drink and ordered another.

"This has to be said though, your ex-husband must be a complete D-bag to have had you and let you go," he stated as he moved a stray lock of hair from my eyes, caressing my face as he tucked it behind my ear.

"You're too sweet," I smiled back weakly, but I didn't want to think about Michael tonight. I really didn't want to think about that piece of shit ever again!

We talked for hours and had swapped Jack Daniels for coffee. Roman was right, it was fantastic! Checking my cell I saw it was almost 3:30 am and I had to start work at nine.

"Ugh…, I really have to get home, I have to work in the morning…, well, actually this morning, I have a 9 am start," I said, sad that the evening was over already.

"You could always have a sleepover at my place? I promise to be a total gentleman and we could *just* sleep?" Roman suggested casually while stroking my leg with his index finger.

It was certainly tempting, but I didn't trust myself that much yet. I knew if I went back to Roman's there was no way either of us would be content with just sleeping, and I didn't want to sleep with him right on the first date. Roman was someone I could see myself getting serious with, and this time around.., I wanted to do things right.

"I would love to do that, but I really can't. I don't have a change of clothes for work or my toothbrush," I grinned.

"You could wear one of my shirts to work, you're that bloody tiny it would be like a dress," he teased.

But we both knew by that point I was going home alone. After several goodnight kisses I got a taxi home, stripped off and kicking all of the clothes to the end of my bed I climbed in.

*'**Home safe, thanks for tonight Xx**'* I texted Roman as promised.

*'**Sleep with angels beautiful x**'* he sent back as I fell asleep.

CHAPTER 7
THE BLUE BADGER

"79480, that was going to be my badge number," declared Charmaine Porter. 49 years old, morbidly obese, with dandruff soaked scraggly black hair and tuck shop arms, I was far from impressed with our newest recruit! Now don't get me wrong I am not a bitch by any stretch of the imagination, I don't care about appearance, color, religion or race, as long as you are a decent human being I can get along with just about anyone. But everything about Ms. Charmaine Porter rubbed me.., well, actually scratch that she rubbed EVERYONE up the wrong way!!

In her late 20's Charmaine had attempted to join the Tasmanian police force but failed to pass the physical requirements and was also reprimanded for stalking several married police officers. She was kicked out of the Police Academy, her file stamped "UNSUITABLE" they probably should've had a stamp that read "UNSTABLE" because that was far more fitting!

She was a classic case of "it's not what you know it's *who* you know," her Uncle was a Loss Prevention Manager in another state, and he'd made the call to Simon about giving her a trial and against his better judgment Simon had.

The first day I had the displeasure of working with her I heard her entire fabricated life story. Her vehement hatred for police was obvious to anyone she came across, which is why I was so surprised that she would even want to work in a role that dealt with police on a daily basis. All police officers were crooked cheaters, drunks and liars who cared more about getting their dicks wet than doing their job she would often ramble.

"What about the ones with no penis?" I mocked one day.

"They are all sluts on a power trip," She grunted.

"So, were you a slut on a power trip too? I mean you were almost a cop right?" I retorted.

She mumbled something incoherently and was silent for at least a good hour, thank God!

It annoyed her immensely that I flirted up a storm with the very cheeky and far too good looking Senior Constable Roman Beach.

Roman and I had decided it was best if we kept our new relationship a secret, but we couldn't resist being a little playful with each other at work. After all we were only human. His detest for her was apparent in their first meeting when she had attempted to tell him how to do his job, he also knew that she hated it when we fooled around, so we put on quite an Oscar-winning performance *mostly* for her benefit.

"He only wants to get into your pants you know," Charmaine snarled one day after Senior Constable Roman Beach left the room.

"Who says I'm wearing any?" I smirked sarcastically.

You'd think after a month of working with me that she would have learned that I always have a come-back. But I'm sure by that point it was already well established that there were 'a few Kangaroos loose in the top paddock' a saying I found highly amusing when Alex's husband Thomas and son Tyson schooled me on some Aussie slang.

***

A few snags short of a barbie (BBQ), was another description thrown around whenever Charmaine Porter came up in conversation. If ever there was someone who could use a lesson or two on how to blend in, it was Charmaine.

"Never in my years of being a Loss Prevention Officer have I heard someone abused so often for sticking out like dogs balls for fuck's sake!" Alexis moaned at me one night after working a shift with her. "It's fucken embarrassing" she went on.

Before Cole Warner met her, he thought Alexis and I were being extremely harsh in our opinions of her, that was until she nit-picked the shit out of him on a store audit (that she wasn't even supposed to be doing) and gave him a result of 98%. Anything over 5% had to be reported to head office, and it resulted in him being formally spoken to by a regional manager about a lack of security compliance. She believed that Loss Prevention Officers were far more superior to all of the other staff and would talk down to them or scold them for not doing exactly as she asked. We argued a lot because I firmly believe you treat everyone with respect. I don't care if you are the cleaner or the CEO if you are respectful and polite to me I will give you the same courtesy. I think the saying 'treat others as you would like to be treated' was completely lost on Porter. Her big mouth and 'in your face' approach to offenders landed her on her well-cushioned ass on many occasions. In fact, she was *the most* assaulted Loss Prevention Officer in history!

Her wardrobe choice left very little to the imagination, with her t-shirts and short shorts that were several sizes too small. Alexis concluded that she must have a magic mirror at home because she cannot be seeing what we all see!?

She was all about statistics and numbers and overly competitive, bragging about how many pickups she had each week to anyone who would listen. Mind you, most of her statistics were complete bullshit. she would write someone up for selecting items and then changing their mind. Stating that they had "seen her and dumped", why the hell would you even want to admit on paper that you are that shit at your job is beyond me, but it sure gave for some funny reading!

Alexis had only worked a week with her. They had immediately clashed, and Alexis had called Simon threatening to quit if she had to work even another minute with that "insufferable dickhead!" So, Simon had palmed her off to me, hoping that I'd be able to train her.

After a few too many drinks with Alexis one night we somehow decided that Charmaine would now be referred to as The Blue badger. We couldn't recall the next morning how we'd come up with the name, but just like the nicknames we'd given to others..., slut guts across the street who we were sure was a prostitute, Pirate Pete on the corner and Grandpa Simpson next door, the name had stuck!

Thank God I didn't have to tolerate her for long, because Charmaine's lack of self-control and inability to follow the basic rules, or even simple instructions earned her more than one title. For not only did she hold the record for the most assaulted LPO she also carried the title for the one with the most false apprehensions ever! It was certainly not something to be proud of, and definitely the reason she was given the boot before her trial even ended!

When you're costing the company more money in lawsuits than you're saving in loss of stock, it's a no-brainer that you'll be sacked, regardless of WHO you know. And so ends the tale of The Blue Badger.

CHAPTER 8
WHEELIE DEDICATED

Some might call me a bit of a gym junkie, I mean what other reason would you have to be running on a treadmill at the 24hr gym at two in the morning. I was really in the zone when out the corner of my eye I saw a male standing behind me. In a panic, I slipped and went flying off the end of the treadmill, quicker than a bowling ball being thrown down the bowling lane…, and crash landed into a stack of protein powder tubs.

It was then I realized that this was the culprit, there was no man behind me. In my drowsy state entering the gym, I had failed to notice the six-foot stack of protein powder tubs. Why they were left unsecured, I don't know? But the LP side of me kicked in, and I began moving them to an empty storage cupboard under the stairs. As I walked back and forth, I realized something was terribly wrong with my foot. A searing pain shot through my right heel and up the back of my leg. I hobbled home feeling very foolish, and after a few hours of sleep I had Alexis drop me at the emergency room where an ultrasound confirmed I had torn my Achilles tendon.

Fitted with a moon boot I left the hospital with strict instructions to put my foot up for at least two weeks. But instead of heading the doctor's advice, I got a taxi and headed to work. Simon was taking a few days off and had asked us to only contact him in a dire emergency. I figured this wasn't one, and it would take more than a moon boot to stop me from working.

After all, I was in the final stages of training a new recruit. Georgia was a mid 40's average built woman with mousy light brown hair, she looked just like a regular housewife and fitted into the role perfectly. In fact, I'd go as far as saying she had what it took to be one of the best. With her ability to spot a grub from a mile away, stern "Mom" voice and steely blue eyes she would have frightened me if I didn't know her!

I guess when you're the Mother of seven boys you have to be able to command a room with only a few words and rule with an iron fist. Georgia's husband Mark, knew she wore the pants in the house, what she lacked in height she made up for in mouth, and he and their boys knew her sharp tongue and quick wit were no match for any of them. The boys all toed the line, and Mark's motto of 'happy wife happy life' kept him in good stead.

Knowing all of that, you would think I'd have known better than to hobble in with the moon boot (which went almost up to my knee) and tell Georgia that I was going to attempt to work against the Doctor's orders.

Georgia insisted that I needed a wheelchair, and had one organized in less than ten minutes via the concierge in the center. She joked that she would be 'pushing me around' today. After a half hour of her pushing the chair, I insisted that I could wheel myself, so, we split up to cover more of the shop floor. Minutes later I wheeled past Bryan Cole, he was pushing a stroller covered in a blanket, and looking up at the ceiling as he went along.

A dead giveaway that he was up to no good. A regular shopper shows little.., actually they show *no* interest in ceilings, a grub however, wants to see where all the cameras are.

Bryan went into the DVD section and selected 25 DVD's, as he walked quickly to the other end of the store (all the while still looking at the ceiling) I attempted to keep up, madly pushing the wheels on the chair round and round. I was not used to this new contraption, so I got caught on a metal safety rail attached to the bottom of an aisle.

SHIT I WAS STUCK!

Usually, we have this rule of thumb…, If the person you are following sees you at least three times you may as well stamp SECURITY, in bold writing on your head because you've been made. Most times they will dump the stock, hurl abuse at you and leave quite pissed off because now they have to go to another shop to steal. It's such an inconvenience to them.

I think in this case though, Bryan was not expecting the store security to be wearing a moon boot Michael Jackson would've been proud of, and confined to a wheelchair. Because bless him, Bryan came to my rescue and unhooked me from the railing I was stuck to.

I thanked him kindly and doubled back around just in time to see him conceal all of the DVD's in the stroller chair, (which did not even have a baby in it). He covered the entire stroller with a blanket and headed toward the registers. Georgia, who had been following a dead lead, was walking by and I informed her we were about to make Loss Prevention history with the first ever wheelchair apprehension.

As Bryan went through the registers buying just a bottle of coke, I contemplated my approach. I decided to ditch the wheelchair and approach on foot. When I introduced myself, the look on Bryan's face was one of utter disbelief! He was a good sport though, and said that his mates at the pub would find it hilarious that he'd been busted by a cripple.

Constable Mark Sands, and newly promoted Senior Constable Matilda Berry arrived and initially thought I was pulling a prank, or trying out a new approach after my recent dry spell. I'd had a few 'runners' lately, and didn't seem to be able to get any apprehensions to 'stick.' The day before they had been in another stores back office with me collecting footage from what Simon referred to as 'a trolley walk out' that I'd missed while I was on a coffee break.

They couldn't wait to file the report and tell their fellow officers about the 'shoppy' that got caught by the wheelchair-bound LPO!' They were sure such an apprehension had never taken place. Constable Mark Sands couldn't resist snapping a selfie with me in the chair, and even poked fun at the offender telling him he must feel like a right dickhead being caught like this.

Word traveled fast, and whilst Georgia and I were finalizing paperwork, Loss Prevention Officers Jessica Kroger and Adam Walker from another retailer had come down to see if what they'd just heard was true.

"Knock knock," I heard someone say.

I looked up from my paperwork into a pair of eyes as green as my own, with his sandy brown hair and boyish grin, Adam Walker, who was just 22 years old could easily have been passed off as my younger brother.

"Can we come in?" Adam asked. But without waiting for a response he entered the room and introduced himself to Georgia and me, shaking our hands.

He also introduced a very reserved and steely looking Jessica Kroger, she was technically Adam's supervisor. I'd later find out she had been with the company for ten years and was a well-seasoned floor walker and investigator who thankfully hadn't lost touch with the little people.

"So, I'm having a dry spell..., I might have to get myself a wheelchair for work. What do you think Jess?" Adam laughed.

"I don't think our safety manager would approve," Jessica replied trying to keep a straight face.

As I told the story of the wheelchair apprehension we all laughed at how ridiculously easy the pick-up was. After swapping details we agreed to keep in touch and work more closely together in the future. Adam and Jessica said their goodbyes, and Georgia and I quickly finished up the paperwork.

"Do you want me to take the chair back Eliza?" Georgia asked.

"Yes please if you don't mind, I'm going to burn this footage real quick and head home," I replied.

"Do you want a ride? It's on my way," Georgia offered.

"No..., you have the twin's basketball game to go to, I will catch a taxi its fine..., honestly. Tell the boys good luck," I said as Georgia was leaving the room with the wheelchair.

A half hour later I'd burnt the footage and pulled my cell out to call a taxi, I noticed a message from Roman;

Are you ok? I just heard you are in a wheelchair with some contraption on your leg?? What have you done now?

Smiling I replied immediately;

News travels fast! *I'm fine.. I had an accident at the gym and tore my Achilles tendon. I will have to rain check drinks at BrisVegas tonight sorry xxx*

I had been looking forward to seeing Roman again too, damn it! Obviously, he felt the same.

His response was quick,

How about dinner instead? Are you still at work? I'm coming your way soon I can pick you up??? Early night I promise x

Sounds good, I'll meet you out the front☺ I replied.

Putting my cell in my bag, I slowly packed up and headed toward the car park.

Ten minutes later Roman pulled up, he got out of the car and came around to the passenger side shaking his head and laughing.

"I honestly can't keep up with you. In the time I've known you, you've been run over by a disability scooter, thrown from a moving vehicle, and I'm almost certain you have a crazy magnet on your head, and now this!" Roman teased, pulling me into a hug and then kissing me softly on the lips before continuing.

"Are you in much pain babes? We could just go to your place or even mine and eat in? He asked sounding concerned.

"I'm ok. I've taken my pain killers, but I am kinda tired though, wheelchairs are hard work! Let's just go somewhere local to eat. Let me buy us dinner and then you can drop me home after," I insisted as I climbed into the car.

Two hours later we had eaten dinner and were pulled up in the little driveway at the side of my place.

"You can come in if you like?" I suggested seductively as I unbuckled my seat belt.

Roman pulled me toward him and kissed me deeply, his hands roamed up the inside of my

t-shirt and into my bra, caressing my nipple. I gasped, and as my head tilted back Roman moved his mouth to my neck kissing me as his hands pulled my top up. I pulled back, worried that Tyson might be home and catch us behaving like a pair of horny teenagers in the car.

"Sorry, I can't help myself, I get so carried away with you," Roman smiled sheepishly before continuing. "As much as this kills me to say..., I won't come in tonight, I can see you are tired and we both have an early start, so go get some rest ok, goodnight babes," Roman pulled me to him and kissed my head.

***

"Thanks for picking me up, and thank you for understanding. I will see you soon ok?" I replied, kissing Roman goodnight I got out of the car and several minutes later I was climbing into bed.

The next day the news of my wheelchair apprehension had gone viral, I must admit I enjoyed the notoriety; although it was very short lived. Because once Simon was back at work, and even though he found the entire situation highly amusing, he decided it was safer if I spent the next two months off the floor doing paperwork, and also fraud investigations.

CHAPTER 9
CATCH ME IF YOU CAN

Confined to a desk with boxes of paperwork in front of me, I felt like I was being punished in the worst possible way.., REFUNDS!

My job, while on light duties was to sort them all alphabetically and try to find customers who frequently refunded stock with no receipt. With no electronic system, it had to be done manually which was a long and arduous task. I often quipped that even a monkey in a zoo could do the job, but in reality, it took determination, good recollection of names and dedication to perform the task. A week into sorting refunds, I came across a group of four people who had refunded thousands of dollars' worth of stock, so I called Roman to ask for his advice.

"Call Detective Charlie Rowe," he said giving me his details, "fraud is his thing. Oh, and Eliza, before you go..., can I take you to dinner tonight?" Roman finished.

"Sure you can, pick me up at 7 pm from my place," I answered. We exchanged goodbyes, and I hung up grinning like a giddy school girl.

I called and spoke with Detective Rowe, who said I would need as much evidence as possible, original signed receipts, CCTV and possibly the stock to make a case.

After informing Simon of my findings, he assigned me to complete the entire investigation. He told me not to hold my breath, as often fraud is the hardest of all thefts to prove and even harder to get a conviction, he finished by telling me "well done, but you're probably wasting your time," clearly he was still underestimating my ability to achieve results, I hadn't let him down so far in any role he'd given me, and I had no intention of wasting my time sorting mountains of refunds for nothing.

A few hours later I headed home and got ready for my date with Roman.

Over the next few weeks, and with the help of Alexis and Georgia we were able to get quite a lot of CCTV footage showing several offenses. The four targets were still conducting suspicious refunds during this time, and it appeared we were missing them by only hours on some days. I decided to put together a timeline, to thoroughly profile them..., and was not the least surprised to find that they were habitual thieves.

I was able to determine the stores they frequented down to the days and even windows of time. I'd been working on the case now for a little over a month, piecing it all together and preparing all the evidence. It got me to thinking..., if they were getting away with this at our store, where else were they doing it?

Out of curiosity, I called Jessica Kroger. We'd spoken briefly on the phone a few times since we first met after my wheelchair apprehension, but were yet to actually catch up outside of work. I'd had lunch with Adam a few times when we'd been working in the same center, and he'd told me that Jessica handled most of their internal investigations for QLD, and sometimes traveled to other states to assist in training new LPO'S. He said that she had also set up their company data base for frequent refunders.

"Hey Jessica, it's Eliza the wheelie dedicated LPO," I joked.

Jessica laughed loudly.

"Hi, how are going? Are you out of the chair yet?" She asked.

"Yes, but I still have the moon boot on for a while. So for now I'm confined to desk duties, refunds actually..., and I thought I might ask if a few names sound familiar to you?" I went on, "Ramsay Black, Mackenzie Black, Tyrone Barr, and Nikita Miles. They use the same home address and have been hitting us pretty hard."

"Hmm, the names do sound familiar, I'll check our database and if they are on there, I'll call you back," Jessica promised.

I was envious that Jessica's company handled all of their refunds electronically, everything was entered into a computer at the refund counter, and then automatically cross-matched with the frequent refunder list. There was no sorting mountains of paper receipts, it was far more efficient. Although they weren't actually doing anything with the information, other than refusing refunds to those customers on the list. There were no proper investigations, or police reports being filed, which seemed ludicrous to me. I couldn't see the point.

A few minutes later Jessica called and confirmed that they were indeed on her frequent refunder list. I explained that I had profiled them, and could pretty much guarantee where they would hit next. So we organized to set up LPO's in the stores for the following week.

Alexis and Georgia were going to be in place in our store, as were Jessica and Adam in theirs. Unfortunately, because of the moon boot I was not allowed to be a part of the apprehension, but it didn't mean I couldn't watch it all unfold from the safety of the coffee shop located just outside of the store. I called Detective Charlie Rowe and told him our plans, he was keen on making an arrest, and agreed to be there and have an undercover team on standby. I informed him that they were also conducting fraudulent refunds at another retailer and he said he'd be interested in speaking with Jessica about those too.

Finally, the day arrived, at 1 pm (as I predicted) I saw the four alleged offenders walk past the coffee shop and into the store. I called Alexis and Georgia to make sure they were in place and ready to follow them.

"Are you sure you don't wanna come to the dark side and join my team?" Detective Rowe asked. He seemed impressed that my profiling of the four targets was so on point.

"Hmmm..., not really..., to be honest I'm not sure if I'm going to stay in Australia permanently yet," I replied.

"Well if you change your mind, let me know..., I'll help you out through the process, you have a good eye," Detective Rowe grinned.

My cell rang, and looking down I saw it was Jessica.

"Hey Eliza, did they turn up?" Jessica asked sounding anxious.

"Yes, I was just about to message you and Adam. I'm sitting at the coffee shop with Charlie, come down," I said excitedly.

Jessica and Adam didn't need to be told twice and were already on their way before I could hang up. Detective Rowe excused himself and made his way over to his team who were strategically placed at other tables around the coffee shop. As Jessica and Adam approached, I could see how people often mistook Adam and I as siblings, the resemblance was striking!

"Heyyy it's my brother from another mother," I joked hugging Adam.

"How are you sis?" Adam laughed as he hugged me back.

"I'm alright, just a bit pissed off that I can't be in the thick of the action, but hey, it could very well be dinner and a show," I said picking up my turkey sandwich and laughing.

Several minutes later the four offenders strolled smugly out of the shop. Their bags bulging as they exited paying for nothing, Tyrone began abusing the customer greeter who asked to check their bags as they exited. Alexis and Georgia exited behind them, and the six undercover officers got up from their tables and walked toward the offenders.

"You're all under arrest!" declared Detective Charlie Rowe pointing his finger at the four.

"What for?" Snorted Ramsay Black, he immediately began flailing his arms around wildly, it was obvious he was on something.

Tyrone Barr attempted to escape, and was taken down by two male officers and quickly handcuffed.

"They made me do it, it was their idea, I told them to stop," Nikita Miles yelled loudly, she began pulling stolen goods from her bag and started to cry.

"Shut the fuck up you stupid bitch or I'll smash you in your dumb dog head," yelled Mackenzie Black.

But Nikita was too far gone to listen, and continued to ramble on.

"You've fucked my whole life up Tyrone, I still love you, but you have really fucked my life up, I can't go back to jail again for this shit. Officer, officer, the drugs in my bag aren't mine ok. I'll tell you everything, just please don't send me to lock up again," Nikita was sobbing uncontrollably as she was handcuffed and led away.

Mackenzie Black, who was also now in handcuffs, kicked out wildly at Nikita as she went by, the kick sent Nikita sprawling to the ground.

"That will be enough of that!" Shouted a female officer as she pulled Mackenzie backward by the handcuffs.

Nikita was helped up by the escorting officer, and as she was led down the mall Mackenzie continued to scream at her.

"Bitch, you shut the fuck up, don't tell em nuffin or you're done for! You hear me Kita? You shut the fuck up and say nuffin, they don't know shit!" Mackenzie's verbal assault continued even after Nikita was out of sight.

Georgia and Alexis made their way over to where I sat with Jessica and Adam. We began discussing the pickup. Deciding who was going to take care of what paperwork and who would collect today's footage. Everything seemed to be under control, Mackenzie had finally shut up and was about to be escorted to the watch-house. We were almost ready to leave when we heard more shouting.

Ramsay Black (who had been until this point compliant) pulled a knife from his pocket and started waving it around at the police, threatening to stab anyone who came near him. I was actually shocked that he hadn't already been handcuffed like the other three.

Detective Charlie Rowe immediately drew his gun, and the other remaining police officer pulled his taser, yelling at Ramsay to drop the knife.

"Fucken PIIIIIIIG!" Ramsay screamed running toward the officer.

He was subsequently hit with the taser and dropped to the ground writhing about screaming, once subdued he was handcuffed and escorted away.

"Well shit, that was entertaining. See Adam, I told you we might get dinner and a show," I joked, laughing as I ate the last corner of my sandwich.

Jessica's attempts to suppress a smirk failed and she laughed loudly along with Adam, Georgia, and Alexis.

"You're too much Fox," Jessica said trying to compose herself.

I sat back and relaxed in the chair, pleased that it was finally over, and confident that all four would now be charged and found guilty. It was one of the biggest customer fraud cases within our company, and the only one of its kind via refunds so I was quite proud of my achievements.

Kudos also had to be given to Georgia and Alexis who had dedicated their time to the investigation. I was also pleased that a solid relationship had been built between the other retailers Loss Prevention teams, something that up until now hadn't been encouraged but some rules were meant to be broken.., right?

I called Simon and informed him of the capture, he was impressed with my work and asked if I would be interested in a more investigative role. He'd dangled that carrot a few times recently but snatched it away just as quickly so I was not convinced that anything would eventuate.

The moon boot was due to come off permanently and I was keen to get back into my covert duties anyway, so I guess I'd just have to wait and see what would happen? A few hours later I met with Alexis, Georgia, Jessica and Adam at a nearby bar. We had decided that a drink was in order to celebrate the success of our teamwork and successful capture.

"Cheers!" we all toasted.

Talk quickly turned to work, and we shared stories of our funniest apprehensions, comparing notes about the lamest excuses we'd heard from offenders about why they had stolen. We all agreed that if we got paid a dollar for every time we were told "this was my first time" we'd *all* be rich!

"Eliza, if I got paid a dollar for every time your reply was, 'MORE LIKE THE FIRST TIME

YOU'VE BEEN CAUGHT' I'd be even richer!"
Georgia exclaimed.

We all laughed, it was no secret I had zero
tolerance for liars.

Alexis told us about a boy who had tried to
convince the police that he wasn't responsible for
stealing because his hands made him do it, he said
that he had no control over his hands and they got
him into trouble all the time, she said he tried to
pinch her ass when he was escorted out and blamed
his uncontrollable hands for that too, apparently he
went on and on until the attending officer hand
cuffed him, telling him now his hands had no choice
in behaving.

"At least he spoke to you," Adam chimed in "I
had a lady yesterday that didn't appreciate my sense
of humor, there was a trolley full of marked down
stock ready to be wheeled out, and as we passed by
she pointed to it and asked "what's all that?" I
jokingly told her it was all the stuff I'd caught
people stealing today, then laughed. After that, she
was all like "you're a sneaky little bastard, a
sneaky, sneaky little bastard and I'm not talking to
you anymore. I know my rights, I'm remaining
silent," I had to get Jessica to come in and finish the
interview, because she refused to give me any
details, she wouldn't even speak with me in the
room so I had to leave completely," Adam finished,
sounding perplexed.

We were all laughing, then I remembered an
apprehension I'd had when I first started.

"I caught a foreign male Doctor who refused to cooperate with me or the police because we were women, he spoke over the top of us saying that we should respect him because he is a Doctor and he is a man and we are just mere women. He didn't want to tell me anything because I'm American, I'm not sure what that had to do with anything because he wasn't Australian either.

S/C Matilda Berry was furious with him and threatened to lock him up, so he faked a heart attack for fuck's sake! We had to call an ambulance and instead of the watch-house he was taken to the ER first," I shook my head.

We had all encountered some form of bodily fluid during an apprehension, Georgia had apprehended a lady who wet herself thinking that if she did that, they would let her go and not call the police. After she had been dealt with and released, Georgia went to find the store manager to ask him what to do with the chair that had been urinated on.

She failed to find him, so went back to the office only to discover the manager sitting on the wet chair. The entire management team was in the room for a meeting, and she had asked the manager to step outside, but he said he was too busy. So, Georgia had no choice but to tell him that the chair he was sitting on had been urinated on. The room erupted with laughter, but the store manager did not find the situation as funny as everyone else. The poor guy was called pissy pants for months after.

Jessica had caught a man who threw up when he was nervous, she said she had been tempted to let him go after an hour of him dry heaving into the office bin.

I'd apprehended a young lady who had diarrhea, instead of waiting in the back office for the police to arrive, we spent 40 minutes in the women's rest rooms. Unfortunately for me she had a nasty gastro virus, so not only did I catch her, I caught her tummy bug and was violently ill for days afterward.

"I've caught a few girls who were on their period," Adam said apprehensively, looking a little embarrassed..., and unsure whether he was crossing into forbidden territory.

"You realize none of them were probably on their period at all, I'm sure we have all caught a female who has tried to use that excuse, actually I'm certain it's a line right up there with it's my first time!" Jessica pitched in.

"Damn it..., really? Well played females well played," Adam laughed feeling foolish.

As we laughed about our experiences I heard the familiar ringtone 'Iris by the Goo-Goo dolls' assigned to Roman coming from my bag, the song reminded me of my first date with Roman. We didn't really share the same taste in music but he admitted it was a very solid tune.

I excused myself and answered his call,

"Hey babes are you still coming to see me?" Roman asked.

"I sure am, I'm just having a few drinks with the team at The Kookaburra Inn, I will order a taxi now though," I replied.

"I could come and get you? I'm leaving work now it should only take me about 10-15 minutes," he suggested.

"Yes that would be good, I'll meet you outside," I replied ending the call.

As I walked back toward the table, Alexis eyed me suspiciously.

"You have a look of mischief on your face, and a sparkle in your eyes who's the guy?" Alexis whispered.

I'd been seeing Roman very casually for a few months now, but with our hectic work schedules and my injury, we were yet to actually spend the night together. The sexual tension between us was ridiculous and I didn't know how much longer either of us would be satisfied with just texts, calls and the occasional grope in car parks (or the bar) so I'd agreed to spend the night with Roman at his place.

"Its Senior Constable Roman Beach but shhh..., I don't want everyone to know just yet, I don't want to jinx it," I said quietly.

"Ten-four," Alexis smirked, raising her eyebrows up and down wildly and grinning like a maniac.

"I did wonder if anything were happening with you two. You realize the chemistry between you both is so obvious even a blind man would pick up on it, but your secret is safe with me" Alexis finished.

"I really like him Alexis.., a lot, but I'm kind of scared," I said almost in a whisper.

"You can't live in a bubble forever Eliza, sooner or later you have to let some walls down, and Roman seems like a good guy," Alexis said wisely before adding, "plus he's hot as fuck and you should get some of that!"

"What are you two whispering about?" Adam asked nudging my arm.

"Girl stuff," Alexis replied trying to look serious.

"Oh yeah? Well, I'm kinda like one of the girls aren't I?" Adam suggested teasingly.

"We're talking about cravings, cramps, PMS, periods and tampon brands," Alexis lied.

"Oh..., umm..., ok, well fuck that, I don't really want to know," Adam laughed, his cheeks looked a little flushed as he turned back to his drink.

"Thank you," I mouthed at Alexis. I finished my drink, said my goodbyes and headed outside to wait for Roman.

CHAPTER 10
TIED UP

I heard the familiar rumble of Roman's car in the distance. It was usually that way, that I could hear it before I could see it. The car was Roman's pride and joy, a black Holden HSV GTS. It got a lot of attention from the young lads, and I'd even caught some ladies admiring it too. Or..., maybe they were actually looking at Roman?

He pulled up, jumped out of the car and ran around to open my door. It was something that caught me by surprise when we first began dating, I'd never had anyone open doors for me before. It just added to his sweetness and charm.

We kissed briefly, and I climbed into the car. Roman shut my door and ran back around to the driver's side. Before I could even put my seatbelt on he pulled me toward him and kissed me. His hands wandered across my chest and into my top where he momentarily fondled my breast.

"Down boy," I laughed pulling back, "let's get out of here and go someplace more comfortable..., like your bed."

Roman didn't need to be told twice. He fastened his seat belt, then put his foot down hard on the accelerator. I relaxed back in the seat, placing my hand on Romans leg. Less than thirty minutes later we pulled up in his driveway.

"Wait here for a minute, I have to do something," Roman ordered as we entered the corridor, he led me by the hand to the main living area.

His apartment was cozy, with its open plan modern kitchen and living space, that had a huge leather lounge positioned so it was overlooking the city lights. It was a fairly impressive bachelor pad I had to admit. I walked to the huge windows and admired the view of the colorful lights dotted across the skyline. I knew it wasn't my business, but I wondered how many other women had had the pleasure of being up here.

"Many times I wondered if I'd ever get lucky enough to share this amazing view with anyone," Romans words caught me by surprise, it was as though he had read my mind.

Standing behind me, he kissed my neck and ran his fingers down my arms.

"I thought you would have shared more than just the view with a few ladies here Roman, it's quite impressive," I replied, not really sure whether I wanted an honest answer or not.

It was a conversation we had never had, the whole "what's your number?" had never come up.., thank God!

"My life until recently has been all about my career, I've worked really hard to get to Senior Constable. I didn't want or need the distraction, and then I met you," Roman responded as he turned me toward him.

"Come on, I don't know how much longer I can control myself, I want to just rip your clothes off and fuck you right here," He said as he pulled me toward his bedroom.

I sat on the end of the enormous king size bed and removed my light jacket, scarf, one sock, and one shoe.

"You don't sleep with that thing on do you?" Roman laughed pointing at my moon boot."

***

"Hell no! It's coming off permanently in a few days, I can't wait," I sighed as I removed the boot and stretched my foot out. Man, it felt good to be able to flex and move my foot freely.

"Come with me, I have a surprise for you," Roman said flashing me one of his famous dimply smiles.

I walked toward him.

"Do you trust me?" he asked.

I nodded.

"Close your eyes then, and stay right there," he ordered.

I shut my eyes, and as he moved away it sounded like he opened and then closed a drawer. Roman returned and slipped something over my head, as the padding covered my eyes and the elastic band snapped at the back of my head I put my hands up to my face.

"Is this one of those eye masks they give you on flights?" I giggled touching the flimsy padding that covered my eyes.

"Yes, now shush," Roman said sounding a little sheepish.

"What are you..," I started to question but Roman interrupted and shushed me again.

"Shhh, just trust me, I told you I have a surprise," he said bossily whilst taking my hands and leading me slowly from the room.

I knew by the coolness under my feet that I was in his bathroom.

Roman stood in front of me and undid my top and slid it off my shoulders, while kissing my neck his hands worked their way behind my back as he expertly undid my bra, he removed it quickly. I felt his hot mouth again on my neck, slowly he moved to my left breast, cupping it with his hand I felt his hot tongue on my nipple. I gasped and could feel myself becoming excited. I touched Roman's head and ran my fingers through his hair.

His lips were gone; he undid my jeans and slid them to the floor, laughing as he realized I wasn't wearing any underwear. Oops! I had forgotten that myself! I shifted position a little, wondering what was coming next, wondering if he were pleased with what he saw. I couldn't believe I was completely naked in front of Roman..., well..., other than the eye mask! I moved my hands up to remove it, but Roman stopped me.

"You're so sexy," Roman murmured as he nibbled at my naked skin.

He was now kneeling in front of me and licking and kissing my stomach. I could feel myself becoming aroused. He kissed his way up my stomach and stood up, moving behind me. I could feel his erection through his pants pressing into my naked body, his fingertips traced from my stomach, over my breasts and up to my neck and as he removed the blindfold, I saw a huge tub full of steamy water and bubbles. Lit candles lined the window ledge and edge of the bath. Behind the flames I could see the city lights twinkling, this view was just as gorgeous as the one from the main living area.

"Oh wow Roman...," I said lost for words, it was the most romantic thing anyone had ever done for me.

"I hope it's not too hot?" he said as he moved away and dipped a hand into the water.

"The hotter the better," I replied winking.

As he turned back to me I moved forward and began unbuttoning his uniform, he was wearing a white undershirt, (singlet as they are called in Australia).

YUM! I thought.

***

I don't know why, but a tight white undershirt on a man always turned me on. I never really understood what it was about them, but it almost has the same effect as a man in uniform. There's just something sexy about it. As I removed the undershirt I pulled it to my face, inhaling the aroma, it smelt of Roman's cologne, with just a hint of sweat, my stomach tingled and I felt a pull in my groin area.

"Ok, get in and I will be back in a minute," Roman ordered as he slapped my ass. He took the undershirt and helped me into the hot bath. As I lay back into the bubbles the water covered me completely as I sunk down into the tub. This was heaven! I closed my eyes, immediately I felt completely relaxed, so much so that I wondered if I were dreaming, this stuff usually only happens in the movies.., doesn't it? I must have been completely zoned out, because I didn't even hear Roman enter the room, as he climbed into the tub his feet touched mine and I jumped a little and opened my eyes.

"Sorry babes, I didn't mean to startle you," Roman said gently as he handed me a glass of Moscato.

"It's ok, it's probably a good thing you did or I might have fallen asleep in here," I grinned.

I moved around and laid back against Roman's chest, his hands wandered over my naked body as we chatted about our week, our childhoods, and our dreams for the future. All too soon the water was cold, so we climbed out of the tub, wrapped in big soft fluffy towels we made our way to Roman's bedroom. After drying off, I pulled back the covers and sunk down into the mattress. Roman lay beside me, his fingers tracing my breasts and circling each areola before gently pinching my nipples.

"You know you have the most amazing breasts?" Roman said eagerly taking a nipple into his mouth.

He moved on top of me and kissed me deeply, his hand made its way down my stomach and he gently spread my legs apart. His fingers pushed eagerly inside of me, making me groan with excitement. Roman wasted no time moving down the bed and positioning himself between my legs, he spread them wide and pushed his face into my pussy, kissing, licking and sucking my clitoris like his life depended on it.

"FUCK, I'm going to cum already!" I gasped, grabbing the headboard behind me with one hand and pushing Roman's face harder onto my pussy with the other. As I climaxed noisily on Roman's mouth he moaned, obviously enjoying what he tasted. He moved up the bed looking impressed with himself, I kissed his mouth, I could feel his hard cock against my inner thigh. I wanted him so bad.

"Sorry to ruin the moment baby, but I need to get a jacket or three from my drawer," Roman winked as he leaned across me toward the nightstand.

"I do have one of those IUDs in, and umm, there's no proper way to say it but I'm clean, If you know you are too then we are good to go," I said shyly, thinking it was probably a conversation we should've had previously.

"Yeah.., babes I'm good.., I promise," Roman answered. He spread my legs open and entered me; fucking me slowly, pushing in and out as I moved my body against his. I could feel another orgasm building, and began clawing at Roman's back and sucking on his shoulder as he pounded away on top of me. I came again, this time far more intense than the last.

"Fuck me harder," I muttered into his ear.

Roman pulled himself from me and roughly turned me on to my stomach, he entered me from behind fucking me harder and harder, until he exploded inside of me.

His hot body slumped on top of mine momentarily, as he removed himself from me he lay beside me panting to catch his breath. Once Roman's breathing had slowed I moved beside him and pulling his arm around me lay my head on him.

We spoke for a few minutes while I caressed the soft hair on his chest, soon we fell asleep in each other's arms. I woke at 3 am, slipping out of bed I made my way to the bathroom, on the way back to bed I noticed my scarf had fallen on the floor. Hmmm I wonder if he is into bondage? I thought as I picked it up and climbed back into bed. As I snuggled next to Roman he stirred from his sleep, feeling brave in the darkness, I whispered,

"Have you ever been dominated.., can I tie you up?" I brushed my lips over his nipple.

"You're a little live wire aren't you Fox?" He laughed pulling me closer and kissing me, "go nuts," he whispered into my ear and placed his arms above his head.

Using the scarf I bound Roman to the headboard and straddled him, I lowered myself on to his cock and fucked him slowly at first, enjoying the rhythm as his hips lifted off the bed and we moved together, then fucking him harder and harder until I climaxed and he came inside of me again. I untied him, and as we lay back against the pillows I thought to myself; I could certainly get used to this, and maybe..., just maybe one day I could love this man, in and out of his uniform!

CHAPTER 11
HE OR SHE?

I'd recently educated Alexis and Georgia about the "people of Walmart" having shown them a series of emails with random people dressed..., or usually underdressed in the popular US chain. Lately I'd noticed quite a few questionable outfits on shoppers in the stores I worked in, (and even on offenders) and began snapping a pic here and there and sharing it with Georgia and Alexis.

The ladies began to reciprocate and over dinner one night we decided to have a weekly competition. The rules were, if by the end of the week you didn't share a picture, or it was voted the lamest, you had to buy a round of drinks, be it coffee or cocktails.

So far we were all having a fairly good run, and had each had to buy drinks a few times. One particular shift I'd snapped a picture of a young man dressed in black leather pants, a black leather studded jacket and high black lace-up boots. He really didn't look that bad from behind, but as he turned I was a little shocked to see that his face was painted with an excessive amount of white makeup, thick black eyeliner and painted black lips. His mop of black hair stood on end as though he'd stuck a fork in a power outlet! It came to me immediately that he looked like Edward Scissorhands. I snapped a front profile picture and sent it to Alexis and Georgia. As I walked away my cell beeped, looking down I saw Alexis had sent a message.

I dare you to get a selfie with him, breakfast is on me if he agrees to pose with you :p

Several minutes later, I not only sent her a pic of me posing with him, but I'd also convinced him to accompany me to the garden section, to do a mini photo shoot of him pretending to prune some bushes, with large gardening shears in each hand. Billy, aka Edward Scissorhands, had in fact never even heard of the movie, he told me he was going through an experimental phase and the makeup was to piss his stepfather off. I said goodbye to Billy and continued to wander the store.

My cell was blowing up with messages from both Georgia and Alexis.

LOL!!!!! Bitch!!! Flying nun, Sunday at 11 am for brunch... Are you going to join us too Georg? Alexis messaged.

Hahahahahaa only you could pull that off Eliza, I think I may have pee'd my pants a little.. Yes I'll be there! Georgia responded.

Alexis attempted to redeem herself immediately, sending a picture of a lady dressed in monkey pajama bottoms and a pink flamingo Hawaiian shirt, her hair was a mass of long dreadlocks, that even Bob Marley would've admired.

100

Over the next month the pictures flew back and forth, Georgia was certain that her picture of a lady who wore the tiniest pink mini skirt, black tassel bolero jacket and blue cowboy hat, and whose legs looked like someone had melted down a thousand Barbie dolls and pasted them onto her legs, would guarantee her an easy win that week. It was certainly a tough competition.

So, you can imagine Alexis' delight when she saw a man dressed very poorly as a woman, in a bright orange mini skirt, knee-high red boots and a purple sequin top! The fascinator on his head was like the proverbial icing on the cake and Alexis was certain she wouldn't be buying the drinks that week!

She was right.

As she pulled out her camera phone she was unaware that she would soon be capturing more than just a winning photo, for Bob Hart (as he was known on his driver's license) put five DVD players into his shopping cart and walked right out of the store!

I had just arrived to pick up CCTV footage, and the stores refund receipts, and was walking into the center when I passed Bob on his way to the car park. Doing a double take, I was about to take my phone out and snap a picture when Alexis appeared from out of nowhere;

"Hands off Fox, this one is mine!" Alexis said as she followed Bob.

I turned and began walking beside Alexis as she quickly explained that everything in his shopping cart was stolen. So, without waiting for backup we approached Bob.

"Ummm, excuse me, sir, um Ma'am errrrr sir?" Alexis stammered, she was unsure how she should be addressing the offender in front of her.

I very unprofessionally burst out laughing, but I couldn't help it because I wasn't entirely sure how I would have handled the conversation either. Alexis bless her, held it together and finished the usual spiel and we escorted the offender back to the store.

When the police arrived, they too attempted to keep a straight face whilst interviewing Bob, who couldn't believe that his plan of dressing as a woman had failed so terribly.

"What was it? Was it the hat or the skirt?" Bob asked.

His serious, deep baritone voice made the situation even more ridiculous, and I struggled to keep it together. He wasn't even a cross-dresser, and had apparently gone to the thrift shop only hours before to buy his disguise.

"Pretty much everything," Alexis replied dryly, biting her lips together to contain a grin.

I didn't know whether to be more offended as a woman, or for my friends in the cross-dressing community who would not have been caught dead in such a garish getup! Bob looked like an entire 70's wardrobe had thrown up on him, and I wondered whether he had bothered to look in the mirror before leaving the house! We couldn't decide whether to photograph him as a male or female, so we took both, it would certainly be an interesting report. The funniest thing was, as a male, Bob probably wouldn't have even caught Alexis' eye, and maybe.., just maybe he would have gotten away with it.

It was certainly a week for things out of the ordinary, because Georgia caught a male dressed as a chicken, accompanied by a female in a cow costume. They were stealing music CD's for the Old McDonalds farm fancy dress party they were on their way to. The same day she also apprehended a woman who looked like a living Monster High doll. Georgia had asked her if she were on her way to a fancy dress party too? The female looked at her with a blank expression and had apparently replied with;

"Ummm, no? It's casual Friday.., der!"

Chapter 12
Twat's the Time?

It was almost Christmas, and police operations focusing on shoplifting were happening in all of the centers I worked in. I was working with Alexis and Georgia, and the day was turning into quite a successful blitz. The grubs were coming in, in droves, and we were struggling to keep up with the paperwork and apprehensions.

When I saw Mary Burger and Jane Thomas in cosmetics, I knew they were up to no good. Their beady eyes darted around as they filled Jane's bag with lipsticks, eyeshadows, and foundations. Mary grabbed a watch and they went to the underwear section, I watched through the racks of clothing as she pulled the watch from the packaging and concealed it in her pocket. Jane, still not satisfied that she had enough in her overstuffed bag, selected multiple pairs of BONDS underwear and hid them in her bag.

We had been briefed at the beginning of the shift to call the police mobile unit once we'd seen concealment. So, I put the call through requesting back up, and then followed the women around the store to the registers. Jane grabbed two bottles of coke and scanned them at the self-serve registers, they then exited the store looking cocky, sure that they had gotten away with it.

Senior Constable Matilda Berry and Constable Rachel Perris approached them with me and they were led to the back office.

"Right-O ladies put everything out onto the table," S/C Berry barked.

Jane Thomas emptied the contents of her bag onto the table but Mary Burger just shrugged.

"I don't got nothin," Mary mumbled.

S/C Berry looked at me, raising an eyebrow she pointed at Mary as if asking me to confirm if she had stolen merchandise.

"What about the watch in your right pants pocket?" I said knowingly.

Mary remained silent as she removed the watch from her pocket and put it on the table. Due to the large quantity of stock, I left to go get a symbol gun so I could scan, and compile a printed list for the police and for my report.

As I walked back to the office, I was advised by the store manager that Jane Thomas and Constable Rachel Perris had been moved to another room due to an altercation between the two offenders. As I walked through the large plastic door to the back office, I saw S/C Berry had also left the room and was on her cell. I entered the office, and a very smug looking Mary Burger was slouched back comfortably on a chair, her beady eyes darted back and forth from the table to the door.

"Miss, can I go to the toilet?" Mary asked.

"I believe you're under arrest, so you'll need to speak to the officer about that," I replied dryly.

As I scanned the stock on the table, I noticed the watch was nowhere to be seen.

"Ummm, where's the watch?" I asked S/C Berry as she returned to the room.

"Should be on the table," She said casually whilst still writing in her notebook.

I began sifting through the pile of underwear on the table, but could not locate the watch. S/C Berry put her notebook away and began looking under the table and shaking the underwear, looking puzzled when she realized the watch was gone.

"Righto, where's the watch?" S/C Berry asked accusingly while pointing at Mary.|

"Dunno what you're talkin bout, what watch?" Mary sniffed indignantly.

"Look, put the watch back on the table or you're going to the watch-house after I strip search you," S/C Berry declared becoming more annoyed by the second.

The banter continued back and forth until S/C Berry insisted that she would find the watch one way or another.

"Get up and remove your pants and underwear," S/C Berry said sternly to Mary.

"See, nothin here," Mary declared as she pulled her t-shirt up, exposing her tiny tits.

Before we even had a chance to react, Mary pulled the front of her pants down exposing her bald vagina.

"Or here, see. I dunno what happened to the watch," Mary said as she pulled her pants back up and sat back down on the chair.

She's right about that, I thought as I grimaced.

"That's enough of that. I didn't ask you to expose yourself, you're going to be searched properly," S/C Berry barked at Mary, sounding more irritated than I'd ever heard her before.

I exited the room, but the words "Squat and cough!" could be heard clearly through the door and will forever be etched into my brain. I'm certain that I even heard the 'plop' sound of the watch hitting the floor after being coughed out of Mary's snatch.

"You can come back in now," S/C Berry said loudly a few minutes later.

I entered the room where a very red-faced Mary Burger was now sitting quietly, her arms crossed, she kept her head down looking contrite. I couldn't believe the stupidity of her. Did she really think she could have pulled that off? I wondered.

True to her word, S/C Berry had Mary Burger taken directly to the watch-house, she no longer looked confident and cocky as she was escorted out in handcuffs. I filled Alexis and Georgia in on what had taken place, they stood wide-eyed in disbelief shaking their heads.

"Yeah, poor Matilda Berry had a cunt of a time with her!" I remarked laughing.

"Actually twat is the time?" Alexis asked, sending us all into a fit of giggles.

"Tits time for a little break," Georgia added as we all burst into hysterical laughter. It was several minutes before we had composed ourselves.

"Can you grab me a tuna sub when you go on your break?" The store manager Brian Page asked as he entered the room.

Alexis, Georgia and I burst out laughing at the irony of his request. Brian had not yet heard about the pickup that we were now referring to as a 'fishy apprehension.' As we filled him in, he grimaced, and quickly changed his order to chicken.

"I'm going to go get a price for the watch she stole, the police took the other one. I said we definitely do not want it back," (I shuddered at the thought.) "Do you two want to wait for me, or meet me in the food court?" I asked.

"I have to catch up on this paperwork, and Georgia needs to burn some footage for the last apprehension too. So we can wait, it looks quiet out there now anyway," Alexis replied.

"Ok, back in a few," I said leaving the office.

I couldn't believe it when I walked into cosmetics and saw Jeremy Gray select a watch and immediately start trying to pull it from the box.

What on earth is it with watches today? I thought as I followed him to stationary where he selected scissors. He ripped them out of the packet and used them to cut the watch out of the box. I was 99% sure he put the scissors in his pocket but a customer had obstructed my view. Stuffing the watch in his pocket he headed off toward the front of the store.

"SECURITY TO SECTION B," someone yelled over the loudspeaker.

I wasn't sure what was going on, because the staff were not supposed to do that when we were in the store, well.., unless we'd requested it or they had asked. I was annoyed because the overly loud call, had spooked Jeremy into diverting into an aisle, where he removed the watch from his pocket and dumped it on the shelf.

Game over! I thought to myself.

I'd decided I would still apprehend him for wilful damage, because the box was completely wrecked and we wouldn't be able to sell the watch at the full price. He moved to another aisle, and walked around for a few minutes, attempting to look like a regular shopper. But the temptation and allure of the watch must've gotten to him because he returned to the aisle where he'd dumped the watch, picking it up he bent down and stuffed it into his sock.

110

Game on! I thought, feeling elated that today was turning out to be quite a successful day for pickups.

Jeremy had what we floor walkers refer to as the typical 'grub strut' going on as he left the store. I knew the police were busy with other apprehensions, they'd already warned us they possibly wouldn't be available for at least another hour, so I called Alexis for back up, and followed him into the mall. I attempted to approach and apprehend Jeremy, who instantly became abusive, he began yelling that he had dumped the watch back in the store after hearing the security call.

"Well, if that is true, I will be the first to apologize to you sir, but right now you are going to follow these guys back to the store and we will discuss it further there," I said calmly as I pointed to Alexis, Georgia, and manager Brian Page.

I gave Georgia the signal to call the police, she stepped to the side, waited for us to walk by and then fell back while making the call.

"I'm going to sue you ya stupid fucken bitch, I'm going to call my lawyer right now and sue your fucken arse!" Jeremy spat.

His futile attempts at intimidating me on the way back to the store were as pathetic and appalling as the language that was now spewing from his mouth. As we reached the office, he pulled his pants down exposing himself.

"See, you dirty fucken slag, I have nothin, nothin down here at all!" He screamed, showing off a mass of unkempt pubic hair.

"Well..., you said it, so who am I to disagree. There *is* nothing down there, nothing I have any interest in. Now, pull up your pants, take the watch out of your sock and sit down," I snapped becoming increasingly annoyed.

Jeremy pulled his pants up, and removed the scissors from his pocket, and began waving them about in a threatening manner.

"What about these then you smart cunt, do you want to have a closer look?" Jeremy yelled angrily.

"No..., I'm good, however..., you can put them on the table too, seeing as they belong to the store also, AND, I will have the watch that is *still* in your right sock," I said flicking my hair.

I was hangry, (hungry/angry) I hadn't eaten yet today, and now this asshole wanted to drag this shit out longer than he needed to.

"How bout I come over there and cut all your fucking blonde hair off, you fucken stupid bitch!" Jeremy yelled.

"Why don't you put the scissors to good use, and cut through the jungle in your fucking underpants, maybe you might actually be able to find what little penis you do have down there, fucken Moron!" I yelled back angrily.

Alexis looked at me shocked, but it was too late, my mouth had reacted before my brain.

***

SHIT! What was I thinking? We were supposed to de-escalate situations not throw gas on the fire.

Right on queue S/C Dan Simpson walked in, and couldn't help but laugh at what he'd just heard me say to Jeremy Gray.

"Put those scissors down right now, or you are going to find yourself in a world of pain," S/C Simpson instructed while pulling out his Taser.

Jeremy quickly dropped the scissors onto the floor, and placed his hands on the table.

"He also has a watch in his right sock, hopefully he will be more compliant with you and not show you what he doesn't have down his pants like he did to us. I need a few minutes if that's ok?" I spoke quietly, gulping back tears as I left the room to head outside for some much needed fresh air. I knew I shouldn't have reacted to Jeremy when he threatened me with the scissors, but I'd had a temporary brain snap. Without realizing it, he had hit a nerve.

"Are you ok Eliza?" Alexis asked, concerned as she sat down beside me.

"Yeah, sorry about that," I paused "he just dug up an old wound.., I should know by now not to take it personally but sometimes you just can't help it," I shrugged.

"You want to talk about it?" Alexis asked.

Taking a deep breath I started.

"A few weeks after I got married, my husband and I were at one of his work functions, I had had a little too much wine, and a little too much fun, and Michael didn't like the way people.., well.., the way men were looking at me so when I fell asleep that night he cut all my hair off, it was the start of his attempts to control me," I whimpered, and wiped away the few stray tears that had crept out the side of my eyes and were sliding down my cheeks.

"What the hell? What a bastard!" Alexis said sounding shocked.

"Just when I think I'm over it, that I've dealt with my demons, something happens like that and it all just comes back. The anger, frustration, and humiliation that I could've been so foolish to stay. That someone could get another human being to such a low point.., that you would gladly welcome death, because they have taken away your will and reason to live anyway. I knew it was bad.., I knew I shouldn't have stayed as long as I did, but these fuckers have a way of making YOU feel like the crazy one, that somehow YOU need them, and that YOU are the one that makes them behave how they do. One day, it was like a light bulb went off and I knew that I was done being his plaything.., passed around like a fucking Xbox game to his friends when he was drinking and snorting cocaine. It was bad Alexis, he made me do things.., I swear, actually I'm almost 100% sure he drugged me several times. I liked to drink and party but I never would have agreed to the things he was making me do. In the morning when I couldn't recall exactly what had happened he would taunt me, and tell me how much I'd enjoyed it," My voice cracked and I cried.

My sobs became louder, and I wasn't even sure if Alexis could understand what was coming out of my mouth. I looked at her, and saw from the look of horror on her face that she was absorbing exactly what I was saying. I knew I should've stopped but it was as though someone had opened the floodgates and it was all gushing out.

"He took pictures and videos of me, and threatened to put them online if I ever left him.., he'd smack me around a bit and call me a dirty whore. He looked like the good guy, and I looked *and* felt like nothing more than a slut! It literally makes no sense Alexis, the guy was a jealous fuck, always accusing me of screwing around behind his back, it was some sort of sick game to him. He didn't want men showing me any type of attention in a normal setting but then he'd do all that, I'll never understand it. The day I finally kicked him out.., I didn't care about living or dying, I didn't care if he took out the front fucking page of the paper with the photos. I had no one left in the world that I cared about anyway.

***

So I had people come in when he went to work and pack up his shit, I had the locks changed, and I met with my lawyer and filed for divorce. He lost his temper at first when he came home and couldn't get in. Had I known he would run back to LA at the first sign of the police, I would have left him in the first month," I finished, feeling lighter for having shared such a dark and disgusting part of my past with my best friend.

It was a different feeling than having shared it with a therapist, and somehow I felt like this confession would be far more healing than any type of therapy.

"Fuck Eliza, I never knew.., never would've even guessed…, you are one hell of a woman to go through that and come out so positive and so, so strong," Alexis lamented tears rolled down her cheeks as she hugged me.

"Look at us pair of saps..., sooky la la's as you always say," I laughed weakly, wiping my eyes and attempting to restore some light-heartedness to the situation. Humor and bravado as always, my coping mechanism.

"Come on, let's get back in there. Oh, and I'm staying away from the watch section for the rest of the shift too, if I see any more boobs or pubes today I'm going to puke," I joked, still trying to lighten the mood.

"If you ever wanna hunt that mother fucker down Eliza, say the word and I'll help hide the body," Alexis said half-jokingly.

Alexis headed back to the office, I told her I needed to go straighten myself out, so went to the bathroom to splash my face. Looking in the mirror, I knew I looked like shit, my eyes were puffy and red and I knew it would be hard to hide that I'd been crying. FUCK!! Why did I have to have a bloody break down at work for Christ's sake?

Several minutes later I was feeling composed enough to go back to work. I entered the office and kept myself busy with paperwork, trying my hardest to avoid any and all eye contact. Senior Constable Dan Simpson asked if I would like to have Jeremy charged with indecent exposure, as well as the theft of the scissors and watch.

"Honestly Dan, as Mr. Gray said, there is *nothing* down there. So, it wouldn't be right to charge him with indecent exposure of his pubic hair now would it?" I quipped sarcastically.

"We just want restitution for the property and we will call it a day," Alexis cut in, giving me a stern look.

Sometimes I needed reminding of when to shut up, and now was definitely one of those times. I was angry that I'd let this grub get to me, that I had lost my shit and allowed old wounds to resurface. Jeremy was escorted from the building, and I locked myself away completing paperwork until the end of my shift. I'd lost my appetite but Georgia and Alexis insisted I eat something and brought me sushi rolls.

Pulling out my cell I typed a message to Roman,

Hey babe are you busy tonight? I had a rough day and need a hug.

Before I even had time to put my cell down, Roman called me.

"Me to babes.., me too," Roman sounded as drained as I did. "Are you ok? Do you want to come over to my place and have dinner, and a long hot soak in the bath?" Roman asked.

"Throw in a ton of cuddles and maybe some loving, and that sounds like a perfect night in," I responded seductively.

"Hmmm, I like where this is heading, go home first and pack an overnight bag babes, and I'll see you when you get here. I'm going to take good care of you hun," Roman promised.

***

I hung up, feeling better already for having heard his voice. No matter how bad my day was, no matter what demons resurfaced, he had this way of reaching into the darkest places of my heart, and filling me with light and hope. No amount of time could ever truly erase the horrors of my past. But the nightmares *had* become less frequent, and I knew that had every bit to do with Roman.

CHAPTER 13
HOME SWEET HOME

It took a while, but I eventually confessed to the rest of my friends that I was seeing the very insatiable Senior Constable Roman Beach.

I had also made an offer on a property I'd found near Dayboro. With Alexis' son Tyson turning 18 and wanting a bit more independence, I knew it was time to hand over the little granny flat and lay some more permanent roots.

The following month was hectic, I'd insisted on a quick settlement and spent almost all my spare time shopping with Roman for furniture for my new home.

Situated on five acres, the ranch style home, complete with American barn (that badly needed renovating) backed onto the mountains and was picturesque, especially as the sun set over the range. Ironically, "The Ranch" as it was named, was owned by a Texan couple who'd built the home in the early 80's, and were now moving back to Waco Texas to retire. I wasn't quite sure what I would do with four bedrooms, but it was the first time since Roman had introduced me to the BrisVegas bar that I felt like I was home. The newly redecorated kitchen with double baker's ovens, butler's pantry with custom made wine fridge and granite work surfaces was every chef's dream. Unfortunately, everything except the wine fridge was completely wasted on me because I couldn't cook!

The little odd shaped almost round room with floor to ceiling shelves off of the kitchen, and its quaint wood fireplace was what had finally sold me on buying the house. I knew now that I'd unpacked my library of books, that Roman and I would spend hours in there reading by the fire in the cooler winter months. It was as though the room was made just for me, the shelves were almost bursting with my collection of books. It had cost me a small fortune to have them sent from Vegas but now they were unpacked I was glad that I hadn't sold them.

Roman was impressed with the broad array of literature, I had complete collections of horror, classic romance novels, thrillers, science fiction, true crime, history, the list went on.

Freshly showered and wrapped in a luxurious nightgown, I unpacked the final kitchen box. Leaning back against the counter, I sighed loudly.

"Here babes," Roman said passing me a cup.

The aroma of chocolate macadamia invaded all my senses. As I sipped my drink, I was reminded of the previous weekend we had spent up the coast in a little beach shack, relaxing by the water and then exploring the Eumundi markets, where we'd found this aptly named 'Gourmet Coffee.' We finished our drinks and I rinsed the cups and placed them in the dishwasher, as I turned around Roman scooped me up and placed me on the black granite Island bench top.

"You know I plan on fucking you all over this house, starting with here," he declared.

I seductively lay back onto the bench spreading my legs wide and opened my gown. My exposed nipples jumped to attention at Roman's touch.

"Hmmm a little regrowth huh, this is different," Roman murmured, kissing my thigh as his fingertips grazed across the bit of pubic hair that I usually had waxed. His hot mouth moved to my labia, sucking, kissing and nibbling he parted my lips with his fingers as his tongue darted in and out of my pussy. As he pushed two fingers inside me, he licked his way up to give my clitoris some attention. His mouth clamping around me as he flicked away at my clit with his tongue at expert speed. I could feel the orgasm building already, it never took me long to cum with him like this, especially when he started moaning into my pussy, the humming vibration of his groans tipped me over the edge every single time. I climaxed loudly on Roman's mouth as he continued to lick me up and down. The sensation quickly became too intense and I pushed his head away. He removed his shorts, pulling me to the edge of the bench he entered me, I wrapped my legs around him as he thrust harder and harder into me.

Roman lifted me up from the bench and carried me to the library, he sat on the overstuffed suede lounge and positioned me on top of him. I lowered myself onto him and rode him hard climaxing again. Roman grabbed a handful of my hair and pulled it back, he moved his mouth to my neck and sucked and kissed me as I fucked him harder until he said he was going to cum. I quickly climbed off leaving him a little stunned, kneeling between his legs I took as much of his cock as I could into my mouth and sucked him, running my tongue along the back of his shaft.

Knowing I like it a little rough, Roman pulled at my hair as he fucked my mouth with his cock, his cum shot down my throat and I swallowed and slurped on him noisily.

"My god woman is there anything you won't do?" He sounded genuinely surprised.

Laughing, I moved away and lay down on the soft shag pile rug we had chosen together, as Roman recovered he joined me beside the fire. Pulling me toward him, my head rested on his chest with his arm around me, it was possibly my most favorite place in the entire world. As I ran my fingers through the soft hair on his chest he stroked my back gently;

"I hope you don't freak out, but I love you Eliza," Roman said quietly hugging me tighter.

"I Love you too, you're my everything," I whispered.

Oh my.., I'd said it.., the words I'd never been able to bring myself to say when I was married.

My ex-husband Michael had often screamed at me, and lashed out in frustration that I wasn't capable of love. I knew now that it wasn't because I *couldn't* love.., but until now I had never loved before. I'd made the mistake (like many women) and married a man who could have easily passed as my father, he was certainly old enough to be. I'd lost my father to a heart attack only a few months before I met Michael. Initially, he had been very charming, and had wooed me with flowers, jewelry and the finest wining and dining in the most elite restaurants.

I was not at all attracted to him physically, or even mentally, but his interest in me had been a welcome distraction to the grief and depression I felt from losing my daddy. My life had become a blur of prescription medication, uppers, and downers, and copious amounts of alcohol when I felt like nothing else could numb the pain I felt in my heart. I'd agreed to the wedding only weeks after we met. It had happened far too quickly, and all too soon I'd learn that he was nothing like daddy, in fact, the only thing they had in common was their age, because Michael was cruel and manipulative with a vicious temper. By the time his true colors had emerged, it was too late, it had taken me two minutes to get into the relationship and two years to get out.

The only smart move I'd made, was having a prenuptial agreement drawn up to protect my fortune and assets. We had purchased four investment properties during our marriage, they were all sold during the divorce and the little profit we made was divided between us.

The profit I made was promptly spent in therapy, trying to talk out and undo the abuse I'd suffered at Michael and his friend's hands. My therapist Anthony reassured me that in time I'd be able to move forward, trust and even enjoy a meaningful intimate relationship. We now had regular appointments via Skype. He'd helped me work through the mixed feelings I had about wanting something solid.., maybe even permanent with Roman. I'd spoken candidly about how I couldn't help but still like it a little rough in bed, even after all I'd been put through.

He had encouraged me to be open with Roman about exactly what had happened during my marriage, especially because Roman enjoyed being a little rough with me too. Anthony had been concerned that if I didn't divulge my past, that Roman would unknowingly and unintentionally trigger a painful memory. Those conversations were hard.., Roman had had feelings of immense anger and then sadness, and had cried with me when I told him about my past. He had raged that he was going to find Michael and snap his fucking neck for what he'd done.

Roman was also pissed at me for not pursuing charges against Michael, but I couldn't, I was so ashamed of what had happened and ultimately I had no proof, I also knew that any evidence Michael had would have long been destroyed. It would've become a case of my word against his, and while I knew it was fucked up, and that he could possibly do this to someone else, I needed to put it all behind me now, and with the help of Anthony, I was slowly getting there.

I wished with all my heart that Roman had met daddy. My father had been the center of my universe. I did not remember my mom at all, she was killed in a car accident when I was a baby, so daddy had been everything to me. "You and me against the world kiddo" he would always say. He'd never remarried, I remember the occasional girlfriend here and there but nothing serious.

"Lize, are you awake?" Romans soft voice pulled me back to reality.

"Mmm hmmm, just," I replied groggily.

"Would you like to meet my family this weekend?" Roman asked almost in a whisper.

"Yes, of course I would," I answered smiling.

"We should go to bed soon babes," he said stroking my back.

The warmth of the fire coupled with Roman's body heat was soothing and sedating. Half an hour later we were curled up naked together in my bed. Could life get any more perfect than this? I wondered as I drifted off to sleep in Roman's arms.

CHAPTER 14
THE PRANK

I felt like an addict who hadn't had a fix in quite a while. It had been at least six weeks since my last pinch, I was in a drought and needed something or someone to take the edge off the boredom. As I walked about aimlessly, I saw a familiar face walking toward me, it was Alexis. Conveniently for us both, she had mixed her roster up, and Simon had just told her to work the shift with me to see if she could help me out of my dry spell.

Relieved to have each other's company we paced the floor around and around but there was 'not so much as a sniff!' (A saying often quoted by LPO's in our communication logs).

"Let's get coffee?" suggested Alexis, so we headed off to our usual place and grabbed cappuccinos to go.

Once back in the store we ambled about, burning a circle into the shop floor, contemplating our sometimes boring existence in the job, exchanging ideas on how to keep from going insane. It was then we heard it loud and clear over the PA;

"Step right up ladies and gentlemen and get your hands on one of these little beauties," the voice waffled on and on, and Alexis swore he sounded more and more like Alf Stewart (from the Aussie TV soap Home and Away) as he went on.

"Come on folks, head on doooooooown to the yellow-covered table and get yourself a free gift!" The demonstrator finished excitedly.

Alexis and I burst out laughing and couldn't resist taking a look. We headed to the area, mostly curious to see what the man demonstrating looked like. He did slightly resemble Alf Stewart which just made the scenario even funnier. *Apparently,* there is this little device that can extract an entire glass of juice from a single orange. Could this be true? I knew first hand it was bullshit, because daddy had been sucked into buying me one of these gadgets in a US theme park, and I knew firsthand you could get no more than a few teaspoons of juice, but all the same, it would kill at least ten minutes of our day.

I looked on a little puzzled, as Alfie (well, we didn't know his real name so Alexis had dubbed him Alfie) got an entire glass of orange juice from the orange. The audience gasped, and OoOOOoooooOOO's could be heard amongst the crowd. I knew something suspicious was going on, and suggested that we should watch Alfie to investigate.

We joined the queue and collected our free gift, not as easily as we would have liked, because Alfie was quite rude and insisted that everyone buy his products or they couldn't claim the "free gift," I certainly got a bit of a 'grub vibe' from old Alfie and automatically went into covert mode, moving back and observing him from an obscure position. Alexis and I looked at each other in mock surprise as we saw him pour the juice from the glass back into the orange, he even topped it up with a bottle of orange juice, and then placed them back under the counter. I gave Alexis a knowing nod, and could barely contain my excitement at what was running through my head.

The minute Alfie left his post, I lunged forward pulling Alexis with me.

"Let's teach this scammer a lesson," I said boldly, "I'm going to pour the juice into my empty coffee cup and leave only a few teaspoons in there, which is what you really get from those bullshit juicers, let's see how impressed the crowd is next time around." I laughed wickedly.

Alexis was laughing and shaking her head. I felt like a criminal, acting as a lookout as Alexis took the orange from underneath the tablecloth. We moved quickly to a vacant aisle, and I removed the lid from my cup. Alexis emptied the orange juice into my cup, leaving just a tablespoon of juice inside the orange. This time Alexis was supposed to be the lookout while I put the orange back. It didn't go as smoothly as planned, because Alfie returned from a different direction, and as I was making my retreat I almost bumped into him. I walked calmly over to where Alexis stood frozen in place.

"Sorry, he snuck up on me," Alexis whispered as we made our retreat.

Several minutes passed, and we heard the galah like call start over the PA, racing to our well-hidden positions we watched the demonstration. The look on Alfie's face was bloody priceless as he attempted to pour the juice into the glass, confusion, shock and annoyance flashed across his face. Flustered he tried to redeem himself by blaming the orange!

Alexis and I probably could have filled the glass for him with the tears that were rolling down our faces as we laughed and laughed at our antics. We couldn't help ourselves, and pulled the prank again later during the shift. After the second time, Alfie took the orange with him every time he had to leave the area.

I almost felt sorry for him, but the feeling was short-lived, because Alfie was not only a con artist, he was also a thief. At the end of his shift, Alexis happened to be walking by the tool department where Alfie was loading up his briefcase with tools, he was apprehended for stealing, and given a banning notice, which resulted in him also losing his job.

CHAPTER 15
A CLOSE SHAVE!

I was on cloud nine, I'd just apprehended Joel Berry, he'd been breaking into our home entertainment section in various stores, and stealing large quantities of stock. A grand total of $12,000 to be precise!

Alexis, who had called in to meet me for a quick coffee on her way home listened as I filled her in on the latest bust. As we walked past the health and beauty section, I had my head down flicking through a pile of paperwork and I failed to notice the two men filling their baskets with Razor blades.

We headed to the police beat so I could drop off the reports, statements, and footage and speak to the arresting officer. On my way back to the store I grabbed a coffee with Alexis, but took mine to go because I still had a lot of paperwork to complete for our own store reports. Upon my return, the duty manager Cole Warner thrust a basket full of empty 'safers' (store security devices) and several razor blade boxes at me.

"Shit Eliza, have a look at this, we're not sure when it happened but this lot was found down in gardening, and Margie the associate is sure it wasn't there when she went on her break," Cole said frowning.

"Has anyone touched these Cole?" I asked, rubbing my forehead in annoyance that I'd missed a big pick up.

"No not that I know of," he replied.

We went to the health and beauty section and realized the entire display of razor blades was missing!

"Oh my god!" We both exclaimed.

Taking the basket, I headed to the office and sat down to view the CCTV, within minutes I had found the two male offenders. The footage was perfect, upon entry they had left a large gym bag behind a rack by the door, they'd grabbed a shopping basket each, which they then filled to the brim with razor blades. I followed them on various cameras out to the garden shop where they used their own tools to break open the safers. Any multipack boxes that had electronic surveillance tags on them had been ripped open, the inner casing of razors had been taken out and the empty boxes were discarded.

I was actually surprised at how many packets of razor blades the men were able to stuff into their cargo pants pockets. They'd strolled back through the store separately, and the last male to exit the store had collected the large bag as he left.

I called the security manager in the center and alerted him to the theft, giving him the time that the two males had exited my store, hoping that perhaps they were still in the center, or at the very least praying that he'd be able to give the police details of a vehicle. □After burning the footage I headed to the center's security office, it seemed the two men had been extremely busy, and it looked like we had been their last stop. Prior to entering our store, they had been into four other retailers.

I called Jessica, because the two offenders had been into her store first.

"Hey Jess, I'm at Pinewood center and we've just had two grubs knock off our entire razor stand, I'm with center security now and it seems they were in your store here first. Are you close by or do you want me to go and check it out for you?" I asked.

"Bastards, they've been hitting our stand-alone stores hard in the razor section, I bet it's the same guys. Yeah if you wouldn't mind taking a look for me I'll try and get there in the next hour," Jess replied.

I hung up and called Simon, it went directly to voicemail so I left a message with the details of the time of offense so he could put out an alert to the other stores and covert teams.

I went to the health and beauty aisle in Jessica's store and was not at all surprised to see the entire razor blade stand had been emptied. Within minutes I'd found two shopping baskets full of empty boxes. I sent a message to Jessica letting her know I'd given the baskets to the store manager and was heading back to my office to begin a report.

Further investigations throughout the center revealed the men had stolen almost $15,000 worth of razor blades and two expensive designer briefcases.

I immediately called Detective Charlie Rowe, he had specifically asked that I work directly with him on large cases of theft or fraud, and I knew he had a dedicated team at his disposal. Pleased that most of the legwork was done for him, he organized his forensics team to come and fingerprint the evidence. I was thankful that detective Rowe liked to jump on these cases the minute they came up, and I was confident they'd be caught.

I was still annoyed at myself though, for not having seen them when they were in the store. I knew Alexis would be kicking herself over it too when I told her, because while viewing the footage, I noticed she had looked in their direction (albeit briefly) but then put her head back down into her phone. After all, she wasn't on the clock, I was.

Even though we knew it was physically impossible to see everyone and to catch every offender it still made you sick to your stomach when shit like this happened and you were in the store. Some staff were especially critical of an LPO who'd missed such a big pickup, believing that we were too busy socializing or walking around doing nothing, they often commented on how easy our job must be.

I couldn't help but wonder, what were they going to do with so much stock? How on earth were they going to offload it all? As I pondered their options, I had a light bulb moment..., eBay!

The next day, forensics came and fingerprinted the packaging, it could be up to a week before we would have a result (if we got one at all.) As predicted, Alexis didn't take it very well when she saw the footage of us walking past, me with my head buried in paperwork, and her giving them the once-over before replying to a text message from Thomas.

"Fuck me, I was going to point them out to you, because their likeness to those comedians 'the scared weird little guys' is uncanny. But I didn't want to interrupt you because I knew you were busy with that other bust," Alexis scowled.

"We will get them, if not at the markets then on eBay for sure" I attempted to reassure her.

While we waited for forensics to come back to us, I was scouring eBay several times a day, hoping that something would come up. Simon was convinced that they would be selling at the markets, and had rostered the entire team, including those on days off to attend their local markets to look for the stock.

***

Four days later I got my big break!

Ten pages of razor blades and two briefcases appeared from a new seller. I felt like I'd won the Loss Prevention lottery! I couldn't help but feel a little smug when I called Simon to tell him what I'd found. I emailed the listings to detective Rowe, feeling like an enormous weight had been lifted off my shoulders.

I hadn't been able to shake the feeling of failure, and as ridiculous and unreasonable as I knew I was being, I'd taken it personally that this had happened while I was rostered on in the store. I'd overheard a few floor staff gossiping about how hopeless I was and that they wished they had my job, being paid to walk around all day and do nothing. I had wanted to say something to them, to put them in their place, but it was pointless. The only way they would ever get it would be to walk a week in my shoes. It was something that Alexis often remarked they should all have to do, so they'd truly appreciate just how hard the job is, and how much pressure you're under to perform.

A little over two weeks later, detective Rowe called to tell me that the two men had been arrested in an undercover sting. Two officers had posed as customers, and lured them to a meeting spot to do a deal. He didn't elaborate too much, but with the footage, fingerprints, eBay listings and then the sale, there would be no close shave for these two, they'd be getting prison issue razors in jail for a long time.

CHAPTER 16
SETTLED

After a nightcap and coffee with Roman at BrisVegas (something we tried to do at least once a month), we headed back to his apartment to grab a change of clothes and his uniform. It was hard to believe a whole year had gone by, he was spending more and more time at my house these days, enjoying the peace and quiet away from the hustle and bustle of his city life.

"You should just rent this place out and move in with me," I suggested casually while he packed a bag.

"I guess it would make sense, seeing as I'm always staying over anyway," he replied as he strolled over dropping the bag to the floor.

Standing in front of me, we kissed as he removed my dress and underwear, he picked me up and threw me onto the bed, wasting no time in tying my wrists and legs up above my head, it was one of our favorite positions. Removing his clothing, he climbed on to the bed and entered me slowly, as his thrusts became quicker and harder, I realized this would be the last time we would ever fuck.., or make love in this bed, in this room or in this house.

It was the perfect end to this chapter in our story, and I couldn't wait to see what would come next.

By the end of the next week Roman had completely moved into The Ranch, he rented his fully furnished apartment to a young constable, Evan Steer who was quite the Casanova, he would enjoy the benefits of the close city proximity, and amazing views that came with this bachelor pad.

We were in the process of planning a trip to my hometown, I felt it was time to sell my father's penthouse apartment. I'd let it out after his passing, but it was time to let it go. I also wanted to show Roman where I'd grown up, he'd never been to the states, and I was excited to see him experience the craziness of Vegas.

As much as I craved home at times, I knew I would never return there permanently. I didn't miss the insane summer heat with temperatures so scorching you felt like your throat and lungs would burn if you inhaled too deeply.

But I did miss the atmosphere of Fremont Street, and the Bellagio water show would always have that special something that thrilled me and ignited a passion and love of the place deep in my belly. Mostly, I loved to just sit and watch people going about their lives, seeing the look of wonder on the faces of tourists who'd traveled from all over the world to experience all that is Las Vegas!

I couldn't wait for Roman to see and feel that too, and I knew already that of all the people I'd ever watched I would enjoy watching him the most.

I loved this man, more than life itself, we brought out the best in each other and as corny as it sounded sexually we were each other's match. We were both highly sexed and our encounters were becoming more and more risqué and far more frequent. Nothing was off limits, bondage, toys, and forbidden pleasures, mixed with bouts of pain. I loved that he enjoyed my naughtier darker side, we'd just discovered purely by accident that I loved hot candle wax. I'd spilled the contents of a lit candle down my arm when I was carrying it from the kitchen to the dining room, and instead of feeling discomfort, I'd felt an odd sensation of pleasure. I'd begged Roman to drip it slowly onto my naked body, especially on my nipples, it drove me crazy. We'd had the craziest longest sex session that night, we'd gone 7 rounds almost back to back, then slept until lunch time the following day. I was so sore, I knew I'd been fucked six ways from Sunday as the saying goes.

Roman later admitted he wasn't comfortable with using proper candles, insisting that the wax was too hot and that he felt it was a little too sadistic and fucked up, so we'd compromised with soy wax massage candles purchased from an adult store, they weren't anywhere near as hot a regular candle, but they did the job.

We were insatiable in the bedroom, something that was very new to both of us. 'Try everything in life once, and the fun stuff twice' was my new motto with Roman, so far there was a lot we were doing more than twice. I was not submissive by any means; actually, I was quite bossy..., I knew what I liked, what turned me on. I enjoyed being spanked and even bitten lightly whilst gagged and bound, but I also liked to tie or cuff and dominate Roman too.

At first Roman was shy, and a little shocked at how far I would go to please him. But quite quickly he embraced his wilder side, and we took great delight in exploring each other and engaging in new sexual trysts.

It was very clear to both of us, I would never tire of this man or him of me. Apart from work we were completely inseparable, and had kept ourselves so busy with each other that our friends and even Roman's parents had complained that they barely saw us anymore. We had agreed to go to his parents for dinner, they didn't yet know that he'd moved in, or that we were planning the trip back to Las Vegas. So dinner was the perfect opportunity to fill them in on all the news.

His Parents, Philip and Jill were very good people, they were high school sweethearts and still very much in love. His Mom had remarked after meeting me a few times that she was pleased Roman was finally seeing someone steady, telling me she had feared he would not settle down and would focus solely on his career.

When we broke the news that Roman had moved in, Jill clapped her hands excitedly, and said how happy she was. She was very forward in asking how serious we were, and if marriage and grand kids were now in the near future. We were saved from answering by the beeping of the oven timer.

Roman was catching up on all the family news, his younger brother Liam had just come home from university for a few weeks, he looked exactly like a younger version of Roman. He was studying law, and not entirely sure whether he was going to follow in his brothers footsteps and join QPOL or if he'd go on to be a lawyer like his father. He was very outgoing, and from what Roman had told me he was a bit of a ladies man.

We ate dinner, and I shared a bottle of Moscato with Jill, she chattered away asking about the ranch, and fussing over Philip, filling his plate with food and pouring his drinks. I loved seeing Roman with his family like this, I was envious that he had grown up in such a wholesome loving family, with two parents and a sibling.

When it was time to go, I invited them to visit our home when we returned from Vegas. We promised that once we were back we'd make more of an effort to get together. We drove home, showered and climbed into bed, and for the first time in my adult life, I finally felt completely settled.

CHAPTER 17
TO MARKET TO MARKET

I'd recently had the pleasure of meeting another Loss Prevention Officer from a small clothing boutique. Madeline Moore had worked across Australia as an LPO for the same company for a little over 20 years, and had just transferred to Brisbane.

I came across her in my store purely by accident, I was walking the floor when I noticed her staring intently at a group of women. My instincts told me she was an LPO, but I still watched her for a good 15 minutes before finally having a manager approach her, and ask her if she needed help with anything.

Once she had shown her ID and confirmed she too was a Floor Walker, I approached her and introduced myself. Madeline informed me that the group of women she was watching, had stolen from her store on several occasions but were only detected via CCTV, she had never caught them in the act.

This particular day she had arrived as they were leaving the store, she'd followed them down the mall and had overheard one of them bragging about how they had just "acquired a load of underwear, that had fallen off the back of a truck," The female was asking one of the other women if they would come to the Hill top markets to help her sell it that Sunday.

Half an hour later the women left empty-handed, we followed them to their vehicle, (a white transit van). We snapped a few photos of the van and license plate, which we later found out had stolen plates.

Madeline and I exchanged numbers and agreed to meet at the market that weekend, we weren't sure which retailer the property they had referred to had been stolen from, but thought it was worth taking a look. Plus the markets were always fun to frequent, occasionally I'd stumbled across some cool antiques.

Sunday morning arrived, I felt like shit, but couldn't let Madeline down, so still bleary-eyed from a bad night's sleep I met Madeline at the market gates.

"I found footage from the other day of them stealing stock. Quite a bit too, If I recognize any of this as mine, I'm going to buy some of it and have the store run a mini stock take," Madeline informed me.

"I'm still half asleep, I need a good strong coffee before we go any further," I yawned.

As we strolled around the market, we soon came across the women who were unpacking boxes from the back of a blue van. I noticed the registration plates were the same ones that had been on the white van, so discreetly took a few photos on my phone.

As we looked at the underwear and bras on the table, Madeline noticed that there were boxes and boxes of stock in the back of the van, the boxes were stamped with her store's logo. Three of the women left to buy breakfast, so while Madeline kept the fourth woman busy asking her prices and checking for sizes, I moved to the back of the van and started snapping photos of the boxes.

Due to my short stature, I couldn't reach the camera far enough back to capture pictures of the boxes. I bravely climbed into the van and put my cell on video record. I climbed up onto the corner of two boxes to see what was up the back of the truck. As I suspected, there were more boxes of stock. I put my cell on record and was leaning toward the back of the truck when the box I was standing on gave way, I was flung forward and fell quite hard onto a pile of smaller boxes in the middle.

"SHIT!" I scowled after I caught my breath.

The wind had been knocked out of me, struggling to catch my breath I got up and quickly waved the phone around capturing footage of the stock and the bar codes, and was just climbing back out when the female came to the back of the van.

I sat on the tailgate and pretended to be tying my shoelace.

"I have heaps more in here if you want to have a look?" She told Madeline whilst eyeing me suspiciously.

"Oh, so can we get in and have a look through the boxes then?" Madeline asked.

"Yeah go for your life, we just need it gone" She replied.

The woman walked away to speak to another customer at the tables. The left side of my ribs and hip were now aching from the fall so I told Madeline to climb in while I stayed outside.

Madeline was satisfied that she had enough pictures and information from the boxes, so we went and sat at a stall and had breakfast. I showed Madeline the footage, which had also captured me falling and we both couldn't stop laughing. My ribs were still a bit sore where I'd caught the corner of a box and I knew I'd have a nice bruise later on. I also had the beginnings of a headache, and my stomach felt a little crampy too. I popped a couple ibuprofen with my second coffee. I knew we could be here a while, and with a busy evening ahead I didn't want to be struck down with one of my infamous migraines.

Madeline made several phone calls, and it was confirmed that a warehouse had been broken in to, and all of the property in the back of the van was likely the stolen merchandise. She knew she had enough evidence now to call the local police, she spoke with one of her contacts who said they'd send a car. A short time later they arrived, and after conducting a brief investigation they arrested the four women and seized the van and property. I didn't need to stay any longer so said my goodbyes.

"I'm having a barbecue tonight with some other LP teams, you should come along," I invited as I picked up my bag to leave.

"Sure thing, text me your address and a time and I will be there," Madeline replied before turning back to the police.

I headed home, and went right back to bed.

"You ok babes?" Roman asked looking concerned as he shook me awake several hours later.

"Honestly hun, I feel fucken rough..., I'll take a shower and maybe I'll feel a little better. I keep getting these sharp pains in my shoulder, and my neck hurts, I either slept funny or I'm coming down with something," I complained.

"You want me to call everyone and cancel tonight?" Roman asked. "Seriously Lize, you look terrible, and you never complain so something is definitely up."

"No..., we've all been looking forward to tonight, I'll tough it out," I climbed out of bed and headed to the bathroom. As I sat on the toilet I realized I had the beginnings of a period.

For fucks sake! I thought feeling irritated, as if I didn't feel shitty enough..., now this!! I showered, took some stronger pain relief that I had found in the medicine cabinet in the bathroom, and a few hours later I was feeling slightly better.

CHAPTER 18
BROKEN

By 6:30 pm everyone had arrived at The Ranch, after the formalities and introductions were done, Adam asked if they could all get a tour of the barn. Both Roman and I were very proud of how it had turned out, we had done some of the work ourselves but left the bigger stuff to the professionals.

As I fixed a round of drinks, Roman showed everyone around. The lower level was perfect for entertaining, with four big wooden wine barrel tables and tractor seats made into stools, positioned right beside a fully stocked bar (complete with a mini light up Las Vegas sign that Roman had purchased as a surprise online). There was a full-size billiard table off to the left of the bar, and on the right 3 comfy lounges with a chunky coffee table made from old railroad sleepers in the center. The barn had two wall mounted flat screen TV's, one near the bar and the other by the built-in BBQ kitchen in the patio area outside of the barn. We'd even included his and hers 'rest rooms' to fit with the ranch style American theme.

Upstairs was breathtaking, an open plan bedroom with a custom-made round bed. The sitting area had an overstuffed corduroy long chaise lounge, it resembled a double bed and Roman could stretch out quite comfortably on it without his feet hanging over the edge.

In the other corner stood two giant black and white striped high heel shoes that were actually chairs. In between them was a coffee table shaped like a ladies hand with a round beveled edge sheet of glass on top. Roman had initially protested against me buying the chairs and table, complaining that they were too feminine, we'd compromised (or so Roman thought) and had bought the chaise lounge instead. But I later returned to the store and ordered them anyway.

Roman came home one day to find me draped over one of the chairs wearing only heels..., and he was sold!

The hot tub was sunken into a wooden platform by huge windows that overlooked the mountains. A large dormer window on the other side of the room housed a wooden desk and large leather office chair and my MacBook air, it was my writing space. I loved the view from there, it was tranquil and inspirational to overlook nothing but rolling mountains while I typed away, creating new characters and stories and becoming lost in my own imagination.

I'd told Roman about my passion for writing, it was something that I hadn't shared with anyone except my father, often people scoffed at writers and felt it was their God-given right to critique every single word and sentence written, and I didn't know if I could handle the judgment or bad reviews if I were ever game enough to actually publish my writing.

When I said this to Roman, his sentiments were "Fuck the haters! Wouldn't you rather be someone's shot of whiskey than everyone's cup of tea?" He had a good point! He thought that someone should have a job writing reviews about the people who wrote the reviews because some of them were shit! I had laughed at how serious he had sounded. He always knew how to pick me up, and for the most part, he always found the silver lining in any situation.

He began work on the barn the very next day, insisting that I needed somewhere exquisite and peaceful to write. He had certainly pulled it off. The barn was quickly transformed, and soon became our favorite place to unwind. When it was completed we joked that we should just live in the barn, and let out the house. In the first month after it was completed, we barely slept in our own bed in the house, preferring to lie in the enormous round bed and gaze through the huge open windows at the stars.

The only thing that stopped us from moving in there permanently was our deluxe coffee machine back at the house and the love of my little library.

But it was nice to have the space to mix things up a little.

"This place is fucken impressive!" Adam marveled, patting Roman on the back as they returned from the tour.

"It really is huh," Roman said proudly.

After dinner and drinks we all sat on the lounges, I snuggled up close to Roman as we each shared stories about our lives, and of course our jobs. I looked around at everyone, feeling very content with my life. I had the most amazing man, outstanding friends, and a beautiful home, the only thing that didn't feel right at the moment, was the constant stabbing pain in my stomach that wasn't easing. If I took any more pain medication today I'd rattle when I walked. I must be coming down with the flu, my body was aching, and my ribs were still tender, and I wondered whether the pain I was feeling in my stomach was associated with the fall I'd had in the back of the van at the market, or just because of the period I was getting.

As thankful as I was for the company of my friends, I was wishing the night away so I could curl up in bed. I excused myself and headed to the restroom, the pain in my stomach suddenly intensified. I sat on the toilet, and as I looked down I was not at all prepared to see the amount of blood that I did.

I got up feeling dizzy now, and felt like I was going to throw up. As I attempted to make my way back to the others I saw Roman walking toward me then I passed out.

Flashes of white, blue, red, fuzzy images, mumbled words, in and out of consciousness, nothing made sense, except sleep..., Yes sleep.

"What's going on, where am I?" I asked feeling scared at the sea of strange faces hovering over me.

"You're in an ambulance babe, just relax ok?" Roman attempted to reassure me.

I closed my eyes tightly, tears crept out from the corners and slid down my cheeks, the ripping pain in my stomach was so unbearable.

I woke again, and saw Roman's worried face above mine.

"What happened where am I?" I was fuzzy and confused, I couldn't remember a thing.

"Babes you're in the hospital now, everything's ok just sleep hun," Roman whispered gently, he brushed the hair from my face and kissed my face.

Closing my eyes I fell back against the pillow and slept.

A few hours later I woke again, Roman was asleep in the chair beside me. Pressing the buzzer, I attempted to get up, I was still feeling dizzy, so I lay back and waited. What the hell had happened? I wondered as a nurse appeared.

"What is going on, why am I in here?" I asked, my mouth felt so dry.

With that Roman woke up and was immediately by my side.

"It's ok, I will explain," Roman told the nurse, taking my hand he continued, "babes I don't know if you knew or not..., but you were pregnant, something happened and there were complications, you had to have surgery, the baby..., our baby..., it's gone."

He allowed the words to sink in. I was now in total shock.

***

"A baby? What? No..., I couldn't be? This must be a mistake, I have an IUD," I started crying, quietly at first and then painful wracking sobs that could be heard down the hallway in the visitor's lounge where Alexis, Georgia, and Jill, were waiting.

Roman pulled me into his arms, "It's ok Lize, don't cry..., babes..., it will be ok," Roman's voice cracked, he was trying to hold back his own tears and be strong for me.

But I couldn't stop sobbing. How could this happen? How could I have not known? So many questions were running through my foggy head and I couldn't make sense of any of it.

A Doctor appeared briefly, and explained that I'd had an ectopic pregnancy that required surgery to remove one of my fallopian tubes as it had ruptured. As he carried on explaining that it was still possible to get pregnant again, I spaced out. I could hear him talking but I was not listening or absorbing the information at all.

With tears filling my eyes again, I wondered..., had my foolish actions earlier in the day at the market caused me to lose a baby I never even knew existed? Between sobs, I incoherently asked the Doctor if it was something I'd done that made me lose my baby. He reassured me it was nothing I did, or didn't do and went on to explain what an ectopic pregnancy was, and how serious the situation had been.

I continued zoning in and out, and heard him tell Roman that he would check on me later, and with that, he left.., leaving Roman to pick up the broken pieces of my heart.

We had never even talked about starting a family, we were so consumed with each other that it just hadn't come up. I looked at Roman, and could see this had shaken him as much as it had me. I suddenly felt so irrevocably sad, I could feel the hot sting of tears pooling again in my eyes and as I looked at Roman I saw his pain mirrored mine.

Holding each other we cried, for a baby we never even knew I was carrying, for a life that would now never be.

The next morning I woke up to the sound of a wailing baby, a new mom was shushing her new born as it cried incessantly. The crying stopped almost as quickly as it had started, and I could faintly hear her complaining to the nurse that her nipples were sore from feeding all night long. I realized when I heard another baby begin to cry, that I must be on the maternity ward, and it felt like someone was playing a cruel joke on me. Even though I hadn't known about the pregnancy I was now feeling an overwhelming sense of grief, and guilt. Wondering if I'd done something to contribute to losing our baby. Wishing we'd at least known what it felt like to get those two pink lines on a pregnancy test, to be excited even if the feeling was fleeting.

"Boy or girl?" The lady in the doorway rocking her swaddled baby asked.

"Ummm..., I don't know..., I had a...," I couldn't finish the words and began to cry.

A nurse appeared and ushered the woman away. She returned shortly after, pulling the curtain around shielding me from well-meaning prying eyes.

"Sorry about that love, how's your pain?" The nurse asked.

"I'm ok, I just want to go home.., when will the Doctor be seeing me?" I asked my bottom lip quivering.

"He's on the ward now, so it shouldn't be long," the nurse responded.

"I don't mean to be a bitch, but do you have any ear plugs? Actually I think I have headphones in my bag..., the sound of all these babies crying is really quite upsetting," I blinked back the sea of tears I could feel stinging beneath my eyes.

The nurse looked at me sympathetically, she passed me my bag and left to continue her rounds. I lay back against the pillows, the headphones pushed firmly into my ears, with the music blaring I attempted to drown out the noise of new moms, babies, and happy families. I let myself cry, I couldn't believe how close to death I'd been, the Doctor had told Roman that if I'd come in too much later I probably would've died..., that was shocking enough on its own.

Several hours later I was discharged from hospital and home in bed with Roman. He fussed over me making me tea, and insisting that I eat something. I just wanted to sleep, to wake up and for all of this to have been a nightmare. As I lay in Roman's arms and drifted off to sleep I wondered how long it would take for me to feel normal again?

CHAPTER 19
VEGAS BABY

As we touched down at the McCarran airport in Las Vegas the excitement emanated from Roman, his eyes danced with the same mischievousness as the day we'd met. God I loved him!

I'd hired a black ford mustang convertible similar to the one I'd owned when I lived here, and only minutes into driving I made a decision that I would have to buy an old classic when we got home, for as much as I now loved Australia, I missed the American cars.

The heat was already a scorching 95 degrees and it was only mid-morning. We'd escaped the Aussie winter, well..., not that it was particularly cold in Brisbane, but this winter was apparently the coldest in more than 100 years and I'd even had to buy a coat and scarf, so I more than welcomed the Vegas heat.

We approached the strip, and for the first time, I felt like a tourist as we stopped to have our photo taken at the 'WELCOME TO LAS VEGAS' sign. The familiar buildings were stirring up warm feelings inside of me.

Driving past New York New York with lady liberty proudly on top, M&M and coke world, The Venetian and of course my favorite landmark The Bellagio water show. I could hardly believe it, I'd come home! I drank in the marvelous view beside me..., Roman. He looked as excited as a kid on Christmas morning. I knew I'd enjoy watching him here. We were both relaxed, completely in vacation mode with not a care in the world. A far cry from where we'd been a few months ago. Losing our baby had been hard on us emotionally, but it had brought us even closer together, and opened the door to discussions of children and even marriage. Something we both agreed we would like eventually, but not right now. We pulled up in the valet of the Stratosphere, and Roman pulled me toward him and kissed me.

"Can you believe we're in Vegas baby!" He said excitedly.

"Welcome home Miss Fox," Roland the valet attendant said smiling as I climbed out of the car.

I hugged him warmly. I'd given up asking him to call me Eliza.

"Thank you Roland, it feels good to be back. How are Maria and the girls?" I asked.

"Very well thanks," he answered.

"Roland, I'd like you to meet someone special. This is Roman, Roman this is Roland, he was daddy's driver for 15 years," I introduced the two men.

The two men shook hands.

"Babes, I need to use the toilet. I'll let you two catch up for a bit," Roman said, he kissed my head and disappeared into the casino.

I was about to go look for him because he'd been gone almost 20 minutes before he reappeared.

"It's been great seeing you Roland, we are here for a few weeks, I'd love to take you and Maria to dinner one night to catch up properly," I said.

"That would be good Miss Fox, enjoy your stay. Roman, sir it was a pleasure to meet you," Roland cordially tipped his head at Roman, and squeezed my hand affectionately as I slipped a tip into his hand.

"Likewise." Roman replied as we walked hand in hand into the casino.

As we entered our suite I gasped when I saw the bathroom, tea light battery powered candles lined the edge of the freshly filled tub, and I was instantly pulled back to the first night I'd spent with Roman.

"You always manage to surprise me," I grinned pulling him toward me.

"It took some organizing I can tell you," Roman laughed. "I figured after the long flights we might be tired and could make the most of our room, well..., at least for the next few hours."

Wasting no time we tore our clothes off and climbed into the huge tub, soaking away the jet lag. We slept for a few hours and then made love in bed before showering and heading downstairs to Roxy's diner for dinner. The 1950's inspired restaurant with its singing staff and retro booths was a unique twist to a regular American diner. It wasn't anywhere near as fancy as other Vegas restaurants, but the atmosphere was always fantastic and the staff are friendly and, well, who doesn't enjoy dinner and a show? We ate burgers and fries and were serenaded by our server, who very fittingly sang Stand by me.

Over the following weeks, I showed Roman the sights of Las Vegas, we spent hours reliving our youth in the pinball museum (one of Vegas' hidden treasures) we jumped from the Stratosphere, took a gondola ride at The Venetian, and saw the animals in Siegfried and Roy's secret garden. Seeing Vegas with Roman was almost like experiencing it for the first time, his enthusiasm and infectious laugh were contagious. Almost every day we enjoyed my favorite place, sitting by the Bellagio and watching the tourists and the water show. We learned that in addition to our coffee addiction, we also shared the same love of chocolate, we sampled many flavors of m&m's from the wide selection at m&m world, peanut butter being our favorite.

We ate at IHOP most mornings, Roman couldn't get over all the different flavors of pancakes and omelettes. In the evenings we made our way down to Fremont Street, enjoying the live entertainment and posing for photos with some of the entertainers in the street. (Something I'd never done when I lived there, it was something that daddy had frowned upon).

During our last week I had a surprise for Roman, a limo arrived and we were taken to the airport where we took a helicopter to the Grand Canyon, landing in the bottom we had breakfast and toasted with champagne, after a flight over hoover dam and then the entire Vegas strip we were back in the limo and on our way back to our room.

"Hands down the most amazing thing I've ever done," Roman beamed as he looked through the photos of the Canyon on the camera.

"I knew you'd like it," I smiled while sifting through a pile of paperwork.

I'd organized the sale of my father's penthouse apartment on our arrival, and given its prime location, and view of the strip it was under contract after the first viewing.

"Is there anyone else besides Roland you wanted to catch up with before we go home babes?" Roman asked.

"No..., the only person other than daddy that I really cared for here was my childhood Nanny Elva, and she passed away before I moved to Australia. I was going to take William out for dinner, he's the man to thank for putting my name forward for the position in Australia, but he's in New York on business. To be honest Roman, I have hundreds of acquaintances here but no real friends. I went off the rails after daddy died and then again after my marriage ended, there are people I'd sooner avoid than see here. I told you I was no angel, and if I am honest I'm quite ashamed of some of the things I did," I finished the last sentence quietly, looking down at my hands.

"You're perfect now though babes, I wouldn't have you any other way," Roman said taking my left hand and kissing it.

All too soon it was time to leave Sin City and head home to Australia. I couldn't help but wonder when, or even if I'd ever come back. Stopping at the cemetery on our way to the airport, I laid flowers on my Nanny Elva's grave.

"She was the closest thing to a mother I ever had," I said sadly to Roman "she took daddy's death hard, and I don't think my actions after his passing helped her either, I'm certain she died of a broken heart, I think she was in love with my father, but just never told him. She tried to be there for me but I was just too fucked up to see it or accept her support. I only wish she could see how happy I am now. She would've really liked you Roman."

"I believe she's looking down right now, along with your parents and can see how far you've come Lize," Roman said kissing the top of my head.

The thought was comforting, we walked hand in hand to my Parent's grave.

"Goodbye mom, goodbye daddy," I whispered as I kissed my fingers and gently placed a hand on their headstone.

Looking at my mother's name in bold silver writing 'Elizabeth Mary Fox' I felt a pang of sadness that I never knew her. All I had were some picture albums and a box of unopened documents that had recently been sent to me by our family lawyer. I hadn't looked over them yet, I had a feeling it would be like opening Pandora's box. Daddy had told me in my teenage years that there were things he would one day tell me about my mother, that there were things that I could only understand as an adult. Mostly though, he didn't speak about mommy much at all, the pain was clearly etched in his eyes whenever I had asked about her, and it killed me to see him hurting like that, so I learned not to speak about her at all.

It was as if Roman sensed the depth of my sorrow, and perhaps some would even call it a sign, but with his arms around my waist, he said a phrase that my father would use whenever I felt down, or when he was having a tough time.

"It's you and me against the world Eliza," Roman squeezed me tightly against him, then taking my hand we headed back to the car. It was time to go home.

CHAPTER 20
HIT THE ROAD JACK

It had been a crazy day and I was drowning in a sea of paperwork. I'd just finished dealing with two very feral looking women, who'd claimed they were strippers from a nightclub on the Sunshine Coast. Roxie Horn and Fantasia Whip were their stage names, and what I'd had to write in my report, as neither would comply with giving me their correct information.

After hurling vibrators, cock rings, and a few dirty thongs at us from her bag, Roxie had eventually been cuffed and taken directly to the police van. Fantasia was a little more submissive, but her offers of free lap dances, if we'd let her go, fell on deaf ears.

The general consensus on the pair, was that there must be some very dingy, low lit places, because beaten with the ugly stick didn't even begin to describe these two.

"Beaten with the ugly stick? Shit, they looked like they'd been whacked by every branch on the way down the tree, or, were gang banged by the entire fucken forest!" Cole had inappropriately quipped.

It was shocking to later find out both females were only 23 years old, years of drug abuse and neglect had aged them, for I'd put them down in my report as at least being in their late 30's. I was sipping on a coffee while finishing a report, when I thought I heard my name being called over the PA. I paid more attention now, but didn't hear it again so I put my head back down and carried on with my work.

"Eliza, we've been paging you, some guy has just stolen a push bike and rode it straight out of the store," Cole burst in the office sounding shocked.

"Are you serious? Jesus Christ, I thought I'd heard it all. Is anyone tailing him?" I replied.

Jumping up I grabbed my bag and headed towards the door.

"Yeah, hang on my phones ringing," Cole said pulling his cell from his pocket. "Yep..., yep..., we're coming now," he hung up and followed me out.

"Michael one of the night managers is on him, he's following him in his car," Cole told me.

"Fuck..., Cole this better not get messy," I worried

I'd promised Roman and Simon that I wouldn't do anything crazy anymore, but jumping in my car with Cole we headed off in the direction of the male who was being tailed by Michael the night manager.

"Mad wheels!" Cole exclaimed as he climbed into the passenger seat of my newly purchased 1967 mustang convertible.

"Yeah I like it," I grinned, "Here, use my cell and call the police and see if we can get a car to come, coz I don't want to approach this guy too far from the store on our own," I ordered.

As we pulled up in the train station car park we saw the offender getting off the bike, he leaned on the wall waiting for a train.

"Put this on," I said as I threw Roman's sweater from the back seat at Cole.

The last thing we needed was the grub being spooked by seeing Cole's uniform. We casually headed to the platform to wait for the police, or the train, whichever would come first. Unfortunately for us, it was the train. I purchased two tickets and we got on, moving to the other end of the carriage we sat down facing the offender who was waiting by the door with the stolen bike. As we pulled away from the station we saw the police walking on to the platform. They called my cell, and I told them we were already on the train, heading towards the city and that the offender was right by the carriage doors.

A few stops later, the police had caught up and the offender was arrested. He was well known to police and was extremely violent. I was told that it was a good thing we hadn't tried to apprehend him without them, as he had a history of violence toward women and had just recently been released from jail for grievous bodily harm to his ex-partner and her young daughter. After giving our details to the arresting police, Cole and I changed trains and headed back to the car with the bike.

"Hey Eliza, how about you ride back to the store and I'll drive your car," Cole joked as we got off the train.

"In your dreams buddy, and there's no way that's going in the back of my car so on your bike son," I laughed.

The offender, Jack Jones was at least a responsible thief, because he'd also stolen a helmet. I couldn't help but laugh at Cole as he hesitantly put the helmet on and rode off. Ironically when I turned the radio on in my car, Hit the road Jack was playing and I laughed to myself at the irony of it. I turned the radio up loud and tapped away on the steering wheel in time with the music as I drove back to the store. At a red light, I saw Cole approaching the side of the car, so I put the top down;

"Hey Cole, I hope he doesn't have nits," I joked.

Cole looked mortified, he ripped the helmet off, and threw it into the back seat of the car. Still laughing, I pulled away as the light changed. I saw him in my rear view mirror walking with the bike back to the store.

"I can't stop itching my damn head Eliza," Cole grunted as he entered the office with the bike.

"Sorry mate, it was just a joke. I'm sure you don't have head lice..., yet," I teased.

"I'm going to get nit stuff and go home," Cole complained as he left the office.

Grinning to myself, I turned back to my paperwork and gave my own head a little scratch.., damn it! What is it about the word 'nits' or 'lice' that instantly made your head crawl I wondered? An hour later I'd finished my reports and faxed my statements to the necessary police.

With my head down, completely oblivious to my surroundings I was typing a text to Roman as I walked to my car. Just as I opened the car door to get in I heard someone yelling across the carpark;

"You fucken slut, who's cock did you suck to get that car?" Whipping my head around, I saw Patricia Milne (the silly old bag from court) running toward me, still screaming profanities as she hurled cans of what I'm sure were beans in my direction.

What the hell was her deal with throwing canned food? I wondered as I climbed into the driver's seat quickly. I started the engine and pulled out from my spot, hitting the accelerator. I pretended not to see the crazy old cow, who was shaking her fists wildly at me in my rear view mirror before she collected her cans from the ground.

"FUCK!" I cursed to myself.

Now she knew my car, it was usually second nature to scan the car park before approaching my vehicle, you just never knew who could be hanging about. There had been several attacks on LPO's over the past year, we'd all been warned to be cautious when leaving work, and especially when going to our vehicles. I'd been so distracted sending Roman a message that I'd completely disregarded my own safety.

Roman was sitting in the library sipping a cup of coffee when I walked in, I told him about Patricia, and to say he was pissed off would be a complete understatement. Picking up his cell he called the station, and several minutes later when he hung up, he told me that a car was on its way around to her house to give her a warning, either back off and don't approach me again, or she'd find herself back in court.

"By the way, did you have a nice train ride today?" Roman asked, still sounding pissed off.

Here we go, I thought.

"I'm not a child Roman, I was with Cole and the offender didn't even know we were following him. So just leave it ok.., actually why the fuck are you even checking up on me?" I spat sounding defensive and equally annoyed.

"I wasn't checking up, I heard it on the radio, you promised me no more crazy shit remember? So what the fuck was this? The guys fucking nuts Eliza, if he'd even gotten a sniff that you were a floor walker he could've really hurt you," Roman's voice now matched my angry tone.

"I'm sorry ok, I didn't intend on jumping on the train, I just got caught up in the moment, and again, he didn't know who I was. He didn't even look in our direction once. You're not the only one who worries Roman, look at what you deal with on a day to day basis. Some of the things you tell me scare the crap out of me Roman, but I don't wrap you in cotton wool or scold you like a damn five-year-old," I ranted.

"Yes that's true, but I have a fully trained partner, a Taser *and* a gun! You've got nothing but a notebook and a fucking pen," Roman scoffed.

I knew he was trying to be funny now and lighten the mood. I was still really annoyed, but I hated fighting with him, the only good thing was the angry make-up sex that followed.

"I could poke someone's fucking eye out with a pen, and don't underestimate the pain of a paper cut," I smirked at him, "and if you're that worried about my lack of equipment well, maybe I'll quit my job and come and join you then."

"Babes, I don't want to fight with you, I'm sorry but I can't help but feel overprotective. I love you so much..., come here hun," Roman's voice softened, he patted his lap and smiled.

Those damn dimples, they got me every single time. I was still fuming a little inside, but I knew just by looking at him the argument was over. I knew he had a point, I had a history of being a little reckless, but I never intentionally put myself or staff in danger. I was always careful, well..., except for the time I was thrown from the car that I probably shouldn't have been in, but mostly when I was injured it was just a case of shit happens!

As I made my way toward him I attempted to contain a smile, but it crept out the corners of my mouth. He was still grinning at me, his devilish eyes dancing with mischief. Pulling me onto his lap he kissed me.

"I hate it when we fight Lize," he murmured, then scooping me up he put me over his shoulder and spanked me on the bum, "but I think right now I need to teach you a lesson in keeping a promise young lady!"

I squealed as Roman carried me to our room and threw me on the bed. The scent of vanilla soy massage candle filled my nose, and I was immediately aroused at what I knew was going to happen.

"It looks like you've been busy," I laughed as I eyed the spider web-like contraption that was strapped to the bed.

"Yep, I have been. Right Miss Fox, strip naked then lay on your stomach over that pillow with your legs spread and your arms above your head," Roman ordered.

Once I was in position Roman used leather cuffs and straps to secure me to the web. He was always very specific about exactly how he wanted me positioned, so much so, that I often joked he should have been a porno director instead of a Police

Officer. As he pulled a leather heart-shaped paddle from his nightstand I laughed loudly.

"Are you serious?" I questioned, unsure whether he was actually going to whack me with it

"Very," Roman affirmed.

"Can you at least use the side with the fluffy bit in the middle?" I pouted.

"Nope," he said pursing his lips before disappearing behind me and smacking my bare ass playfully with the paddle.

He went to my nightstand and took out my clit massager and placed it on the bed next to me, he then went to our toy chest and removed a bunch of toys and other kinky implements and put them on the bed. Removing all his clothes, besides his white undershirt, he joined me on the bed. I'd confessed to him that I had a fetish for them and that as odd as it seemed, seeing him wearing just a white undershirt was a complete turn on.

I was thankful now our argument hadn't blown up any further than I anticipated. It had been a while since we'd had a huge row, the last time we'd argued, I'd stormed off and slept in the barn for two days, we'd barely spoken and had eventually had the wildest angriest makeup sex and had to agree to disagree and move on. We knew we were both hot-headed and stubborn, and both liked to be right, and whilst we agreed on most things, when we were on opposite corners of the page, or on completely different chapters about things, it made for some serious debates. Tonight, he just wanted to play..., and after the day I'd had I needed it too. Roman positioned himself between my spread legs, then strategically arranged the toys on the bed.

"Lift your knees up a little higher, keep your legs spread and put your head down onto the bed," Roman ordered me bossily.

He leaned over and picked up the scented candle as I positioned myself as he instructed. He slowly poured some of the warm wax onto my ass, as the wax ran down my back I inhaled deeply. Roman began massaging me, starting on my back he worked his way backward to my ass, down my butt cheeks, his thumbs grazing my outer labia as he massaged down my inner thighs to my knees and then back up again. Using one finger he traced a path from my spine, down the middle of my ass and around to my pussy.

WHACK! He smacked my ass hard with the paddle.

"Shit!" I yelled, I had forgotten about the paddle and was not expecting it!

"Too hard babe?" Roman asked sounding a little concerned.

"No, not at all..., I just forgot about the paddle and you just caught me off guard you cheeky fucker," I laughed.

"Good, that was the plan," he giggled.

He continued to massage me, and also introduced several new toys, pushing two vibrating beads deep into my pussy whilst using the clitoris massager, and occasionally when I least expected it, smacking me with the paddle. He was really going all out tonight! More hot wax, massaging, smacking and stimulation, I was right on the edge several times, but each time I neared climax he would take something away, adjust my position and try something else.

"I want to cum on your tits," he declared as he un-cuffed me from the web.

"Make me cum first, and then I want to do something new to you," I demanded.

He pushed me back down on the bed and ate me from behind, as his tongue furiously lashed at my pussy I came hard.

HOLY SHIT! He'd never done me that way before but I fucken loved every second of it. As he rolled on to his back I moved between his legs, I poured some warm wax onto my breasts and seductively massaged it in while Roman lay back playing with his cock. Pushing my tits together I placed his now rock hard cock between them and moved up and down tit fucking him. Roman groaned loudly as I engulfed his knob in my mouth, tasting his pre-cum minutes later, I knew it was only a matter of seconds before he'd blow.

"Ohhh Eliza, babe, I'm gonna cum," Roman grunted as he removed his cock from my mouth, he exploded all over my breasts and then sunk back against the pillows.

"Fuck that was hot..., YOU are awesome!" Roman said appreciatively when he recovered.

"Whatever you did back there with your tongue was pretty fucken impressive too my love," I reciprocated my appreciation as I wiped his sticky cum from my breasts with a hand towel.

We lay on the web facing each other, looking into each other's eyes, loving each other wholly, a tangle of arms and legs, and with all the sex toys still on the bed, we slept for an hour, before Roman woke me.

"You wanna come take a shower with me?" Roman asked quietly.

"Sure," I said yawning, I climbed out of the bed and followed him into the bathroom.

"Maybe I should misbehave a bit more often, that was so much fun, very erotic and a total stimulation overload," I winked at Roman as I squirted liquid body wash over my boobs and began to lather them up.

Pushing me up against the shower cubicle Roman kissed me, I could feel his dick springing to life again as it pressed into my stomach. God damn, this man could fuck. As I kissed him, and our hands roamed each other's bodies, I wondered (as I had done before) if we would ever tire of each other? If we'd lose that lust, and wanting of each other sexually. I doubted it.

The thought of us wrinkly and old, and still banging the hell out of each other played out in my head, and I burst out laughing, then cringed a little at the idea of us being horny and old and still getting it on.

"What's so funny Fox?" Roman asked looking a little confused.

I shared what was going on in my head, and Roman joined in on the scenario, making jokes about wrinkly old balls and saggy tits. We'd both now killed the mood for what should have been some steamy, hot shower sex.

Oh well, there was always tomorrow!

CHAPTER 21
RULES OF ENGAGEMENT

S itting in my usual spot at BrisVegas I waited for Roman to arrive. It was exactly two years to the day since I'd met Roman here on our first date, and I couldn't help but feel very nostalgic. He had been very preoccupied the past few weeks and I wondered whether we were finally settling into what others deemed as a 'normal couple?' Both Alexis and Georgia had said it would happen sooner or later, and were both quite surprised at how long our alleged 'honeymoon phase' had lasted.

Until this past month, I hadn't believed we would ever change, Roman and I were unique (so every couple in love likes to think). Instead of our sex life depleting as time wore on, it had become more intense, very adventurous and far more frequent, almost daily in fact, and when we both had the weekend off together we could easily spend the entire time in bed fucking and just being with each other. It wasn't just about the sex though, we thoroughly enjoyed each other's company and our similar interests kept us busy.

But something in this last month had changed, lately Roman was always busy, always out or on his phone, and I couldn't for the life of me put my finger on what was going on? He'd left before I'd even gotten up this morning, and messaged me asking me to meet him tonight at BrisVegas, I wondered did he even realize what today was?

I was so deep in my own thoughts that I didn't see Roman enter, nor did I notice his Parents Jill and Phillip and brother Liam sitting across at the next table. If I'd bothered to look up from the drink that I was drowning myself in, I'd have noticed that all of my friends, Alexis, Thomas, Georgia, Mark, Jessica, and her partner Rob along with Adam and his latest flame Gretchen were all there in the bar.

"Hey babes," Roman said kissing me on the lips as he sat down beside me, "I know I've been kinda preoccupied lately and I have an explanation, but before I say anything else there's something I need to do."

As he got up I looked at him a little confused, he knelt down on the floor in front of me, and in his hand, was a beautifully handcrafted miniature wooden heart-shaped box. I knew what was coming next but could hardly believe it was happening..., here..., tonight.

"Eliza Raine Fox, from the moment I saw you, I knew you were something extraordinary. No woman has ever driven me as crazy as you, never have I felt such passion or love or felt such a fierce need to protect someone as I do with you. I'm sure you know what is coming next but before I ask the most important question of my life, I have some demands and rules of engagement that I hope we can agree on," Roman bit his bottom lip, and grinned, his dimples looked deeper, and sexier than ever before.

"Go on then," I said laughing, my eyes glistened with tears.

"I want a Vegas wedding," he said, then lowering his voice to almost a whisper he continued, "I want you to promise that we will continue to make love as often, and as wildly as we do now..," he paused waiting for me to acknowledge his requests.

***

I nodded my head.

"I want you to have my baby, or maybe even babies, and lastly no more crazy shit at work," he added looking very serious now.

"With the exception of the work thing, anything for you babes," I replied wiping a single tear as it slid from the corner of my eye down my cheek.

"Eliza Raine Fox, will you marry me?" Roman asked as he opened the little wooden box revealing a gorgeous silver bridal set. The diamonds sparkled in the light, tears now slid freely down my cheeks as I nodded and said yes, over and over again.

Roman removed the engagement ring from the set, and slid it onto my finger as the room erupted into cheers and clapping. I looked up and saw a sea of familiar faces, OH MY GOD! Everyone was here!

Stunned; I looked at Roman and grinned like an idiot.

"I wondered when you were going to notice, some Loss Prevention Officer you are," Roman laughed.

I flung myself at him, how had I got so lucky? Hugging each of my friends in turn I finally got to a very proud Mr. and Mrs. Beach. Jill was crying, and Phillip was shaking Roman's hand, he then pulled both of us into a tight bear hug.

"Congrats big bro, welcome to the family Eliza," Liam said joining us.

The drinks flowed long into the night, and at 2 am Roman and I climbed into a taxi to head back to the ranch.

"You know..., I kinda thought you were fed up with me, or that we'd turned into a boring old couple," I said leaning back on Roman's chest.

"Oh God no, I've just been trying to organize everyone to be there tonight, and shopping to choose a ring, and I had to meet with the guy a few times about the proposal box, he engraved the wrong date in the first one, and I just wanted everything to be perfect. I have to confess, I did meet with Alexis and Georgia once to get their help with your ring size and some ideas on what type of bridal set to buy. So..., that over time I said I did two weeks ago, I didn't really I was out shopping," Roman said looking quite pleased with himself that he'd pulled all that off without me knowing.

"You're too much, tonight was perfect. Your anniversary gift is at home hun, I forgot to pick it up on the way out. So, when do you want to get married, and when should we start trying for a baby?" I asked sleepily as I lay against Roman's chest.

"We *could* just fly to Vegas and elope, and as far as a baby..., whenever you're ready, just stop taking the pill. In the meantime we can have some fun *practicing*, I know I've been a little neglectful in that department lately, so I think we should start as soon as we get home," Roman suggested seductively as he tweaked a nipple through my dress.

"Sounds like a plan," I replied yawning.

As I lay against Roman I thought about our future wedding, eloping did seem the easiest option, and we could always have a celebration with family and friends once we got home. I was excited at the thought of having a baby, after the ectopic pregnancy I'd had the IUD removed, and after one cycle I'd gone on the pill. But lately I'd been suffering regular migraines, and I was convinced it was because of the pill, so I was thankful that I could just stop taking them now.

"Babes, are you awake? We're home," Roman whispered, kissing my head.

"Mmmm hmmm," I answered sleepily.

We went into the house, and while Roman made us hot chocolate I went to the library to get his card and gift.

"Open this," I said excitedly as I handed Roman an envelope.

The rush of what he was about to receive dispelled any tiredness I'd felt on the taxi ride home. Roman opened the envelope, removed the card and unfolded the A4 piece of paper inside. He'd been looking at deep-sea cage diving with great white sharks in Pt Lincoln, a coastal town in South Australia, so I'd bought him a three-day adventure to go on with Liam. They'd spend three nights on board the Princess II, where they'd get to swim with seals at the Neptune Islands, and then in the safety of a cage, get up close and personal with great white sharks!

"Are you serious?" Roman exclaimed excitedly.

"Yep, but there's just one thing..., I'm not going with you. I feel like you and Liam could really use some brotherly bonding time. You've hardly seen much of each other since we began dating, and especially now that we are getting married and going to start our own family, this seems like the perfect opportunity for a boys trip. Plus, I could use the time you're away to focus on my writing," I surmised.

"You're fucken awesome!" Roman beamed as he hugged me, "now, let's go to bed."

Twelve days later I was sitting in the airport pick up area waiting for Roman and Liam's plane to land. I'd had very little contact with them since they'd set off on their 'great white adventure' and couldn't wait to hear all about it and see the pictures, but mostly..., I couldn't wait to see Roman, I'd missed him like crazy.

"The sharks were fucken incredible," Liam gushed as he put his suitcase in the trunk.

"Hands down, this is now the coolest thing I've ever experienced, thank you so much babes," Roman exclaimed appreciatively as he kissed me and held me close.

"You're welcome hun, I really missed you, I think we need a new rule, no more than one night apart..., the house, and our bed felt so lonely without you," I said getting emotional.

"Deal, now let's go home, I have so many cool pics and videos to show you," Roman boasted, before whispering in my ear, "plus my balls are so full I could've been charged with extra baggage."

He grinned mischievously at me as I laughed at his last comment. A few hours later, we'd showered, fucked like it was the first time, then looked through all of the photos and videos before falling asleep in each other's arms.

CHAPTER 22
NIKE, JUST DO IT

I groaned loudly as I noticed the new line of Nike clothing that had just hit the trading floor. Alongside the ever popular UFC clothing line, I knew the grubs would be in like droves once word hit the street. I didn't have to wait long.

Jim Jones fitted the 'lad' stereotype perfectly, striped polo shirt with the collar up, dark shorts, fanny pack slung around the front of his chest and the trademark Nike shoes. As he sauntered through the men's department, he did a double take and promptly stopped at the Nike stand.

Before he could even pull a tag off I called the police. I knew Jim was a bit of a face within the center, and was always wanted for questioning for one thing or another. As the shirt went down the front of his pants, my attention was momentarily diverted to another male who was pushing a shopping cart into the underwear aisle. The cart had what appeared to be a large opened box inside, and I knew immediately he was going to load it up.

I called a manager and asked them if they could come and watch the male while I dealt with Jim. Several minutes later Jim was arrested by police outside of the store, I explained to them that I possibly had a much larger offense occurring, and asked if one of them could wait around outside to assist with the apprehension. Constable Dan Simpson stayed behind, sitting at a nearby coffee shop to wait.

I went back to the men's department where the male, Gary Baker, was filling the box with entire racks of both UFC and Nike clothing.

How on earth does he expect to get that box out of the store? I initially wondered.

Gary moved to the far end of the store and found a quiet aisle, he removed tape from his pocket and used it to seal the box shut. He also glued a barcode on to the top of the box. As he headed to the registers I realized what he was about to do.

"Me backs stuffed love, I can't lift the box up, but the barcode is there," Gary stated, pointing to the bar code he'd glued on to the top of the box.

The young staff member leaned over the counter and scanned the barcode, it rang up as a printer, Gary paid the $98 in cash, and left the store with over 2k of stock in the box.

As he walked off with the 'trademark smug look' on his face, I couldn't help but smirk, because I too had a trademark face, one that said 'gotcha'. I knew in about ten seconds, his current expression would be replaced with an 'oh shit' one, and it always tickled me.

190

I was right, as soon as Gary saw Constable Simpson, his shoulders slouched, his face dropped to a scowl, and if looks could kill, I'd have dropped dead on the spot. Back to the office we went, and when Constable Simpson asked Gary what was the reason you stole today? Gary had responded with;

"I dunno I thought I'd just do it?"

Ironic really.

I called Alexis and added Georgia into the call,

"Hey have you two seen the new Nike line of clothing in the stores yet? I just had a guy try and take around 2k of stock using an empty printer box," I told them.

"We've got hard tags on all of ours over here," Georgia responded.

"Yeah all of ours is hard tagged here too, but some dickhead left the device to get the tags off on the counter in the fitting rooms, and apparently a customer took it..., and now an entire rack of men's BONDS underwear is missing, so I'm looking at footage to see if I can get them. Hey, guess who I saw knocking off women's underwear Eliza?" Alexis continued, answering her own question, "Patricia Milne, can you fucken believe that old bitch? It looks like I'm going to see her in court again once she's picked up."

"You're kidding!" I shook my head in disbelief.

We filled Georgia in on the crazy story of the Patricia and her period undies, it seemed that some people never learned.

CHAPTER 23
BEACH LIFE, BEACH WIFE

Any ideas that Roman had had about us eloping were quickly squashed by our friends and his family. In fact, his mother had been so upset at the thought of not seeing her eldest son marry that she'd cried. So it had been decided, we'd be having a destination wedding in Las Vegas.

Georgia had always wanted to see Vegas, and her husband Mark had dreamt of driving along route 66, so our wedding was the perfect opportunity for them to do both. They had decided it would be their very belated honeymoon, having had seven children in close succession, they hadn't had time (nor the money) to have one.

Alexis and Thomas flew out with Jessica and Rob, and Roman's Parents were due to arrive late evening. Liam and Adam, who had met the night Roman proposed were practically inseparable these days, the two very fine bachelors had taken over the lease on Roman's city apartment after Evan had moved out. They had arrived a few days prior to us, to make the most of the singles scene in Vegas.

I'd gifted everyone the cost of their flights and accommodation using some of the money from the sale of daddy's apartment. After all, I knew he'd have wanted me surrounded by the people I loved and cherished. We checked into the same suite that we'd previously stayed in at the Stratosphere. Slipping into a halter neck long black jumpsuit and pair of heels, I brushed my long hair and piled it high on my head, pinning it into a messy bun. I put on my favorite three-leaf filigree earrings that I'd worn on my first date with Roman. As I gave myself the once-over in the mirror, I saw the hot tub in the reflection behind me, sighing, I turned and looked longingly at the tub. I wanted nothing more than to just climb in with Roman, and forget about the plans we'd made to meet everyone downstairs. Roman had obviously sensed my thoughts, grabbing me from behind he kissed my bare shoulders,

"I'd love to be in there with you too babes, let's just get this stuff sorted out and we'll be back here in no time," Roman murmured, now kissing my neck.

As we walked into Starbucks hand in hand, I saw our friends were already seated, I waved and headed with Roman to the counter to place our order.

"Eliza, is that you?" My entire body stiffened as the familiar voice pierced through me.

I spun around quickly..

"Michael, what are you doing here?" I said coolly to my ex-husband.

Michael had moved permanently to LA after I left him, not even returning to collect the few things the movers had missed that belonged to him, or for the divorce proceedings, Instead I'd dealt with his lawyer. So I was more than a little shocked to see him here, *especially* in here, because he knew that this was 'my' place. I knew I was being ridiculous, but I felt like he had come here deliberately, and I hated that he still had that power to make me feel paranoid, like he was watching me, and knew my every move. I couldn't help buwonder if someone in reservations had told him that I would be here. Another ridiculous thought, it had to be a coincidence, didn't it?

***

Fuck him to hell, I hated him for making me feel so vulnerable, so exposed, so weak. Instantly I felt sick to my stomach, looking at him as he licked his disgusting lips, his beady eyes were piercing right through me as he looked me up and down.

"Wow, look at you, you look great," Michael drawled, ignoring my question and eyeing Roman suspiciously.

I glanced at Roman, he did not appear at all impressed with this unwelcome reunion.

"We have to go," I said grabbing Romans hand, and squeezing it reassuringly.

I turned around and pulled Roman with me, I wanted to leave, to get as far away from this fucker as I could.

"I'm here for a few days on business, why don't you ditch this latest conquest so I can take you to dinner, I'm also having a little party in my room later at The Luxor," Michael called out after me.

His reference to Roman was definitely his way of letting me know he knew of my debauchery after our separation, the fucking bastard! I stopped dead in my tracks, spinning back around it took all self-control not to lash out and slap his smug face. I was shaking with anger now.

"I don't think so Michael, I don't want to *SEE* you at all, let alone eat a meal with you, the very thought makes me feel like throwing up," I spat vehemently, then turned to walk away.

"You fucken dirty whore," Michael shouted losing his temper, he lunged forward and grabbed my arm and twisted it.

I knew he would have been angry at my rejection of him, but I was completely unprepared for this assault, he usually reserved such behavior for behind closed doors. I swiftly pulled my arm from his grip and stepped back, he lifted his hand preparing to slap my face, his face was contorted with rage. I flinched, and raised my arms covering my face instinctively, ready for the reign of blows that I knew would follow. In a moment of pure terror, I'd forgotten about one factor, Roman..., with a face like thunder he grabbed Michael by the throat, pushed him backward, and in one swift manoeuvre spun him around, pushing his arm up behind his back in a police hold, with one hand now on the back of his head, and the other holding the arm in place he shoved him hard against the glass display of cakes and pastries.

I stood completely frozen in shock!

Thomas, Mark, and Rob were instantly out of their chairs and rushed over to find out what was going on.

"Don't you ever lay a fucking hand on her you old cunt," Roman growled through gritted teeth. "I know all about what you did to her you twisted evil sick fuck. Eliza will be *my* wife tomorrow, and if you think I'm going to allow you or anyone to hurt her.., you better think again. I'm going to let you go now and you are going to leave, not just the hotel but Vegas entirely, because if I ever see you again I might just rip your fucking throat out"

With that, Roman pulled Michael away from the counter and none too gently pushed him toward the Starbucks exit. Michael had still clearly underestimated the situation, because as Roman turned toward me, Michael rushed at us with his fists up.

"Roman, look out!" Alexis yelled.

BAM! Roman's fist connected with Michael's nose and sent him sprawling backward onto the floor. Before he could get up Thomas and Mark dragged him from the ground, restraining him as casino security approached. Roman explained the situation to them and Michael was physically escorted from the premises.

"Babes, are you ok?" Roman asked sounding concerned.

Alexis and Georgia were now either side of me, I was in a trance, the memories of my horrific marriage flooded back in with as much force as Niagara Falls. The abuse that I'd kept locked away for so long, now very raw in my mind. Roman only knew the half of it. My therapist Anthony, had encouraged me to open up to Roman, and I had, but the pain in Roman's eyes, the look of absolute disgust on his face that a husband could do such abhorrent things to his wife, made me hold back all of the ugly truth. It was easier to leave things out, to shelter him from the horrors I'd been subjected to. I could barely believe some of it happened myself, let alone share these most painful memories with the man I now loved.

Mostly, I was ashamed, I didn't want his pity, and..., a deep-rooted part of me felt it was my own fault for staying as long as I did, for getting wiped out and leaving myself vulnerable to the abuse. I knew I was still a little fucked up in the head because of it, and I wondered if I'd ever be able to let it go?

Tears streamed down my face, this was supposed to be our time, the happiest moment of our lives, and in a matter of minutes that prick had unraveled me. I knew then and there that I had to make Michael pay for what he'd done. The fact that he even had the nerve to approach me, speak to me, and to lay his hands on me again I knew I had to make sure he never did that to anyone else. I couldn't move forward without taking care of my past, that fucker needed to see the inside of a prison cell and hopefully get even just a small taste of what he'd done to me.

As I stood sobbing into my future husband's shirt, with my friends trying to console me, I wondered if I'd ever truly heal from this? Or would the scars of my past always be present?

"Lize, baby don't cry," Roman held me tighter now.

I looked up at him, and an intense wave of affection rushed through my entire body, I knew then he would always look out for me, my lover, my best friend, my protector and soon to be my husband. I loved this amazing man more than ever, he was my everything.

"I want him arrested Roman, seeing him just now has made me realize you were right, I should've made him pay for what he put me through…, I don't care if I have no proof, I'll find it…, I can't live with the thought that he might do this to someone else," my voice broke, and I felt my knees giving out from beneath me as I sobbed. Roman held me as I wailed like a wounded animal.

I was all cried out…, eventually I pulled myself together, trying to focus on the reason why we were here in the first place, all this bullshit with Michael would have to wait. I wasn't going to let him ruin my happiness, my wedding.

"Let's go to the restroom ladies, panda eyes are not a good look on anyone," I laughed weakly, wiping my eyes that were swollen from crying.

I kissed Roman, and reassured him I would be ok. As Georgia, Alexis and I made our way to the restroom I noticed Jessica was missing.

"Where's Jess?" I asked.

"She's not feeling too well she will meet us for dinner later," Georgia blurted out all too quickly, giving Alexis a knowing look.

"Ok, out with it you two I'm not stupid, what's going on?" I demanded

"Jess didn't want to tell you right now Eliza, but she is pregnant," Alexis explained.

"She thought you'd try to talk her out of coming over, and well.., with what happened to you.." Georgia trailed off.

"It's only very early, she hasn't even had her first ultrasound yet so she's probably only a few weeks, but she's already having morning sickness, well actually all day sickness," Jessica added.

"I get it, and thank you all for wanting to protect my feelings, but I'm a big girl. Gosh, Jess is going to be a mom hey? Wow, this is great," I grinned. "Let's get back to our men, I want to sort this wedding stuff out and then there is a hot tub upstairs with my name on it."

"Are you sure you're ok?" Alexis asked as she squeezed my hand.

"I will be.., I have all of you," I hugged Alexis.

Two hours later everything was organized, so Roman and I made our way back to our room.

As I poured the vanilla and musk bubble bath into the water, Roman poured us a Jack Daniels honey on ice.

"Here babes drink this," Roman ordered. He didn't need to tell me twice and I gulped the drink down in two mouthfuls.

Roman took my glass and placed it onto the table, he stood in front of me and cupped my face, he kissed me tenderly, then picked me up. I wrapped my legs around him, his mouth wandered to my neck, nibbling and sucking it as he carried me to the bathroom.

He momentarily placed me onto the floor and untied my jumpsuit, as it slid to the floor he giggled when he saw I was wearing no panties or bra. He removed his clothes quickly, then lifted me again, a little higher this time and pulled a nipple into his mouth, sucking on it gently. His index finger traced down my back, down my ass and around to my pussy, as he stabbed two fingers inside me I groaned in delight and bit his shoulder.

"Righto' Fox, into the tub," he said as he lowered me to the floor and spanked my bottom playfully.

Not one to do as I'm told, I knelt quickly and took Roman's cock into my mouth and sucked him, he moaned loudly but pulled away after only a minute and climbed into the tub. Pouting I joined him, laying back against him I could feel his erection in the small of my back.

"I had a kinky surprise for us, but after what happened earlier..., I'm not sure if it's a good idea now?" Roman said quietly as he stroked my breasts.

I turned and straddled him, looking pleadingly into his eyes.

"Babe, we can't let my past stop us from doing what we want to do, we've gone over this a thousand times, you are NOT him..., and could NEVER be him, so please..., will you stop worrying. You know how much I enjoy making love to you, fucking you, being kinky with you," I pleaded, biting my lip I ran a hand down his stomach toward his cock.

"Ok wait here then," Roman grinned mischievously as he climbed from the tub.

I lay back in the bubbles and closed my eyes, a few minutes later Roman joined me, climbing in and laying back against me this time, I stroked the fine hair on his chest wondering what he was up to. Climbing out of the tub a half hour later, I laughed when I saw a contraption hanging from the closet door, it was a sex swing!

Roman grinned sheepishly, his dimples looking cuter than ever, he bit his bottom lip as I eyed the device wondering how on earth I would get into it. Before I had time to think about it further, Roman scooped me up and held me as I put my arms and legs through the stirrups hanging from the door.

Once I was in place he stood back admiring his work. I was in no position to object or react, as he used his iPhone to snap very intimate photos, nor could I protest as he set up a tripod with a video camera. Neither of us was into watching porn, it all just looked too fake. We did, however, like to keep things spicy and send each other naughty pics, and sometimes we'd record our sex sessions, Roman especially loved to watch videos of me giving him head.

He adjusted the camera and I couldn't help but laugh as he pulled up a chair in front of me and sat on it. He wasted no time getting down to business. Roman kissed the inside of my left thigh, biting, kissing then licking his way up. As he reached my labia he nibbled and licked and then pulled away and started the same thing on my right thigh.

This time as he reached my pussy he circled my clit furiously with his tongue, I closed my eyes and he stopped. I looked down at him, and he started to lick again, I closed my eyes and again he stopped.

What the hell? I thought.

I looked down at him again, and the pleasure continued. Ooh..., he really is in a kinky mood, he wants me to watch him. As I looked into Roman's eyes he continued to eat my pussy, the sensation was getting too much and I longed to close my eyes and lose myself completely in his mouth, I was almost on the edge ready to climax, my eyes fluttered closed, and he immediately pulled away.

"DAMN IT!" I cursed at him.

The sensation subsided immediately..., and as my eyes sprung open his mouth again enveloped my clitoris. I felt the familiar rush of an orgasm, and it took everything I had to keep my eyes firmly open. I was about to cum when I felt the invasion of a vibrator deep inside my pussy, the vibration was too much, and I let go and cum on Roman's mouth, he sucked furiously at my clit, I attempted to pull away.., writhing against the door, using the arm straps I pulled myself up higher trying to escape his mouth.

"Stop..., please..., no more!" I panted loudly.

Roman knew my limits, he knew if he continued, that frustration..., even aggression would replace the glorious sensation I was feeling right now. He removed the vibrator, and stopped his oral assault. He picked up the chair and moved it to the side, then went to the bed where he slipped on a vibrating cock ring. He stood in front of me and adjusted the straps, wasting no time he slammed his cock hard into my pussy. He pinched my right nipple as he sucked and bit my left, his thrusts were getting harder and harder, the vibration from the cock ring was pushing up against my already sensitive clitoris and we soon climaxed loudly together. Roman pulled himself from me and moved away, sitting on the edge of the bed trying to catch his breath.

"Baby, can you help me out here please," I laughed, trying to free myself. I was feeling a little uncomfortable now.

Grinning, Roman removed the stirrup from my left leg, I wrapped it around him as he freed my right. Pulling my arms free I placed them around his neck and kissed him passionately as he carried me to bed.

"Damn boy, you sure know how to fuck!" I purred.

"Ditto," Roman laughed, throwing me onto the bed.

Waking in the early hours of the morning we made love again, slowly, simply, sensually..., this would be the last time I'd make love as Eliza Raine Fox!

As I slipped into the elegant off-white Vera Wang strapless gown which flowed into a small train behind me, I felt as every girl should on their wedding day, like a Princess! My hair was in an up style with a few curled tendrils hanging to frame my face.

I had followed the tradition of something old, something new, something borrowed, something blue. The old, was my late mother's diamond earring and necklace set, it was the last gift she received from my daddy before she died in the car accident. The new, was of course, my beautiful dress. Roman's mother had lent me an antique bridal hair comb for my up-do, it was a family heirloom that she said she hoped would one day be passed down to a future granddaughter. As I slipped on the blue lace garter, I smiled to myself at the thought of Roman removing it later on. I heard a knock at the door, I turned around as Jessica entered the room.

"Oh my God Eliza, you look stunning," She gasped.

"Thanks Jess, I am really living the dream right now," I grinned.

"Here, Roman asked me to give you this," Jessica said handing me a large box.

I lifted the lid, and gasped as I removed the bouquet of rainbow roses, they were my absolute favorite. Amongst the arrangement were three small silver photo frames housing individual pictures of my daddy, mom and my Nanny Elva.

There was a card attached to the handle of the bouquet, it read;

You and me against the world!

Forever, Roman x

Tears sprung to my eyes, I blinked them back furiously, no wonder he had insisted on organizing my bouquet.

"You ready?" Jessica asked.

"More than ever," I concluded.

As I lowered my veil, ready to walk down the aisle to where Roman stood looking delicious in his tuxedo, I looked down at the photos in my bouquet and smiled. I wasn't going to be walking alone after all, I had three guardian angels on this journey with me. Words couldn't describe the overwhelming feeling of love and gratitude for Roman at that very moment, I just knew I loved him more than anything in this world.

The music began, and I walked towards Roman..., tears were shining in both of our eyes. I stood beside him, holding his hand as we exchanged vows, promising to always love, listen, and trust each other and be loyal. I looked at Roman, thinking for the millionth time..., how had I got so lucky?

"You may now kiss the bride," the Celebrant stated loudly.

Roman lifted my veil and kissed me softly on the lips. I was now formally Mrs. Eliza Raine Beach!

"You truly are the most beautiful woman in the world Eliza," Roman gushed as he kissed me again. I sure felt like it.

We walked hand in hand past our friends and Roman's family and climbed into the limo outside. The reception whizzed by quickly, we danced to 'Train's - Marry me,' and cut our chocolate fudge wedding cake. We skipped the traditions of throwing the bouquet and garter and after saying our goodbyes, we left our guests at the open bar and headed back to our hotel room. Roman picked me up and carried me as we entered our suite, and helped me out of my wedding dress. He actually looked a little surprised to see that I was wearing lingerie underneath, and stood back admiringly. I would have to thank the girls later for insisting that I make the extra effort! We pleasured each other orally and made love long into the night, before falling asleep in each other's arms.

Three days later we checked out of The Stratosphere and met everyone for breakfast at IHOP. The Cinna-Stack was now Romans firm favorite. I had assumed we were heading home that afternoon, but yet again Roman had a surprise.

"We're actually not going home today babes, we're flying to New York for a week first," he grinned.

Throwing my arms around his neck I kissed him. Roman knew of my love for the city that never sleeps, I'd spent a few summers and even the occasional Christmas there growing up, and often gushed to him about it, saying that if I hadn't taken the job in Australia, I probably would have ended up in New York.

Saying goodbye to everyone after breakfast, we headed to the airport and landed in JFK a few hours later. Roman had organized a town car, and we were whisked away to our hotel. Over the following week, we went to the Empire state building, saw the statue of liberty, and spent hours and hours wandering through Central Park, or enjoying the views from the famous horse and carriage rides on offer. We saw The Lion King on Broadway and ate way too many hot dogs and far too much pizza! :L: :SEP:

I didn't get to show Roman as much as I would have liked, because we couldn't seem to tear ourselves away from our room for any great length of time. We fucked with as much passion as new lovers, at every opportunity. After an incredible week, the honeymoon was over and it was time to go home to our ranch. We made a pact that we'd return here for our anniversary. I felt a pang of disappointment that we would soon be back to our normal, busy lives.

CHAPTER 24
ONE OF OUR OWN

O ver coffee, Georgia and Alexis filled me in on the latest gossip, and gave me the details of our newest recruit Melanie Brown.

Melanie 42, was originally from England, she was married to a corporal in the army and they had three children. She didn't really need to work, but enjoyed the extra money and an excuse to get out of the house and have some adult conversation. After a quick catch up with the ladies, it was time to hit the floor.

"Happy hunting," Georgia called out as I left the coffee shop.

I hadn't even completed a full lap of the store, when I saw Marnie Brown leaving cosmetics with an eyeliner and foundation. Her eyes darted around left and right and up and down, I knew right away she had no intention on paying for the makeup in her hand. Geez, they are getting younger and younger I thought to myself, shaking my head. I followed her as she walked to the motoring section.

Sometimes you can literally look at a person, and know they are going to steal something, sometimes you even just *know* what it is they are going to steal, before they even get to the section or select the item! It was an LPO instinct.

I watched as Marnie ripped the packaging from the two items, she hid the evidence behind a car battery and concealed the makeup in her bra. Usually, once someone (especially teenagers) steal something they want to get out of the store right away. So I was a little puzzled as I followed her past the exit and around and around the store. I realized after the second lap, that she wasn't trying to get the courage up to leave, she was looking for someone..., that someone was her mom.

I groaned to myself, I hated when this happened..., I hated having to deal with the parents. In my experience, there were two types of parents, compliant, or absolute cockheads! Compliant parents are always embarrassed, and or angry that their child has had the nerve to steal in the first place, they want us to call the police, to have their child taught a valuable lesson about being on the wrong side of the law. These Parents are usually fantastic to deal with, but unfortunately, in my experiences, they were few and far between.

Then there are the cockhead parents, they will scream and curse, and behave far worse than their child, shouting at you to get a real job, some even refuse to give the property back, and will just leave with their child. Even in police presence, these type of parents have a terrible attitude, and will rant and rave that they pay the officers wages with their taxes, and they sure as shit don't want *their* hard-earned dollars being used for shoplifting bullshit! They will scream that police officers should be focusing on finding the murderers, or rapists and that this isn't real police work.

***

Marnie and her mom exited the store via the registers and I approached them with a manager.

"Hi, I'm the Loss Prevention Officer in this store, I need to have a word with your daughter, if you could follow the manager we can discuss this somewhere more private," I said addressing Marnie's mom.

"Is this some kind of joke, or an initiation or something?" Her mom asked looking confused.

I was equally confused by her bizarre statement.

"I have no idea what you are talking about, but your daughter has stolen some items today, and I'm going to need you both to come back so we can sort this out," I stated firmly.

Once we were in the office, I asked Marnie to place all unpaid for items on to the table. She shrugged her shoulders, claiming she didn't know what I was talking about, and denied having stolen anything.

"We can do this the easy way, or the hard way, you either take the items out of your bra or I'll get the police to come down and strip search you," I said calmly.

Marnie knew she had been caught out, and removed the items from her bra and put them onto the table.

"What the fuck Marnie!" Her Mom yelled slamming her hand down on the table, "you've probably just cost me my job you stupid little mare!"

"Ma'am, please calm down, I don't see how her stealing would cost you your job?" I questioned.

"We haven't met yet, I'm Melanie Brown, the new LPO," she said as she extended her hand out to shake mine.

I felt instantly sick, OH.., MY.., GOD!

"Oh no, I'm so sorry..., Ummm I'm Eliza," I said shaking her hand in disbelief.

Melanie burst into tears, I pulled her into a hug.

"Honestly.., it's ok, you can't be held responsible for your daughter's actions, it isn't your fault," I tried to reassure her.

I left Marnie in the room with a manager while I stepped outside with Melanie to explain I'd still have to call the police. We had a zero tolerance to stealing policy, heck I'd had a staff member sacked for stealing chocolate bars!

Melanie explained that Marnie had been out of control lately, and thought this might be the wakeup call she needed. She'd been playing hooky from school, staying out late and just acting rebellious in general, and with her husband deployed in

Afghanistan she was having a hard time disciplining her child on her own. I assured her she had our full support, with the police on their way I sent Melanie to go freshen up while I went back in to speak to Marnie. I entered the room, Marnie was slouched back, laying in the chair, she sniffed indignantly, chewing her fingernails, not comprehending the trouble she was in.

"Firstly, get that bloody smug look off your face, and sit up straight in the chair. Not only have you completely embarrassed your mother, but you've gotten off on the wrong foot with me. I don't know what is going on with you little girl, but you better sort yourself out and stop behaving like such a brat. The police are on their way, you're going to be arrested, handcuffed and taken to the watch-house until the child services team comes to deal with you. I suggest you lose your attitude in the next ten seconds because the attending officers do not tolerate any type of crap, do you hear me?" I berated her.

"I'm really going to get handcuffed and sent to jail just for stealing some makeup?" Marnie asked wide-eyed, the reality of the situation was finally hitting her.

"That's what happens to criminals Marnie, if you keep skipping school, breaking the law, and going through life as though there are no consequences for your actions, then you better get used to life behind bars, because that is where you are headed on this current path. I suggest you apologize to your mom, and you better damn well mean it. She's got a punishment in mind for you, and whatever that is, my husband who is a cop, and myself will be making sure you adhere to it. I've heard good things about your mom from the other LPO's, so you better believe me when I say, that not only will she have me for support but all of them too. I hope what you did today was worth it for what you've lost, which is your mother's trust and respect!" I scolded.

Marnie bawled like a baby when the police arrived, and as requested by Melanie, she was searched, handcuffed and taken to the station in the back of a police car. Her sobs could be heard throughout the store as she was led away. One thing was for sure, that would be the last time she found herself on the wrong side of the law. Melanie was devastated, I called Simon who also reassured her that the actions of her daughter, in no way reflected on her.

"Thank you Eliza, I don't know what is wrong with that girl, she gets everything she wants, but I'm also pretty hard on her, ya know," Melanie's voice broke as she gulped back tears.

"Look, it's not the end of the world, we all did stupid shit when we were kids, but it looks like you have a good handle on her Melanie, and you have our support if you need it," I offered.

I told her I'd look into a volunteer program for Marnie that helped with handing out blankets and coats to the homeless in the city, and also a few shifts with a food van that offered free meals to the less fortunate. We hoped that Marnie would learn a few life lessons and that her entitled, self-absorbed, ungrateful attitude would have a serious adjustment. The police called to say they were ready for Melanie to speak with the children's unit, so we said our goodbye's and I hit the floor.

CHAPTER 25
RED DEVIL, WHITE ANGEL

Bethany Muller had all the tell-tale signs of a junkie, her pock marked skin, black teeth, and sunken eyes were hidden under a pile of greasy dark hair. She grabbed a shopping cart on her way into the store, sniffing loudly and picking at her face as she walked around selecting items from the home entertainment section. Her cart was full with a flat screen TV, DVD player, several DVDs and two floor rocking chairs with built-in wireless speakers. All she needed was some popcorn and a bag of m&m's and it would make for a great night in!

Initially, I thought she was going to attempt a fire door break out, or a trolley walk out through the self-serve registers, so you can imagine my surprise when she went to the registers and paid for it all. Something still didn't feel right and going with my gut instincts, I followed her out of the store and to the car park, where she emptied the stock into the trunk of her car. As she closed the trunk I noticed she still had the store receipt in her hand, and taking the empty cart, she headed back into the store. I watched as she selected all of the same items that she had just purchased, scratching and picking at her face as she walked around. I called the police unit on their cell, and was a little shocked to hear my husband's voice on the other end.

"Shit...," I said pausing.., "what are you doing down there? I thought you were on the road today?" my voice trailing off as I wondered exactly how this would work. We had been very careful not to be rostered on at the same time when I worked at this store.

"Dan called in sick, and he was scheduled to work this tour with a newbie so I had to cover, what's up?" Roman answered.

"I have a junkie who is double shopping, she put a load of stock in her trunk already, and is now using the same receipt to shop. I have an awful gut feeling about her Roman, I don't want to approach her without you guys," I replied apprehensively.

"Ok babes, don't approach her, we're on our way," Roman responded, then hung up.

As Bethany got to the registers, she grabbed a bottle of coke from the fridge and went through a staffed checkout. She showed the receipt for the shopping cart of goods,

"I paid for all this stuff already, I just forgot a drink ay," she sniffed loudly.

I suspected that the staff member knew something was up, but she had no reason to question her so she allowed her to leave. I expected her to go out to the car park, but instead, she went around to the returns counter and began refunding all of the items in the cart.

Roman and the new recruit Constable Martha Stable arrived, and I explained what she had just done. As Bethany exited the store with the money still in her hand, Roman approached her and told her she was under arrest.

"I've done nuffin wrong ya fucken dirty pig, I had me docket, I paid for all of it but din' wan it no more," Bethany shouted loudly as she edged closer to Roman wagging a finger in his face.

"Look, you either comply with my orders, or I'm going to handcuff you and take you to the watch-house," Roman told her as he reached for his handcuffs.

"Yeah, I'm gonna ave you sacked ya pig dog fuck, I fucken paid for it I told ya," Bethany insisted, her voice was getting even louder.

"What about the stuff in the boot of your car then?" The new constable blurted out.

Idiot! I thought, I was hoping that wouldn't get mentioned until she was in custody. I could tell by the look Roman shot at the recruit, he hadn't wanted to give up that information yet either.

Bethany knew the game was over, she knew instantly that she'd been caught red-handed. As she looked hastily around for a way out, Roman stepped forward and asked her to turn around and put her hands behind her back.

"Fuck you cunt," Bethany literally spat at Roman, and attempted to kick him in the groin, he blocked the kick and sent her spinning to the ground.

As Roman pushed her arms up behind her back, I jumped in and grabbed his cuffs for him. It was almost like a Déjà vu!

"Not this time Eliza, get back. Martha get over here," Roman yelled.

I stood back feeling helpless and a little annoyed, as Roman and a very frightened Constable Stable wrestled with Bethany to put the handcuffs on her.

"LET GO NOW!" I heard Roman yell.

Bethany, in the struggle, had somehow turned herself over and was biting Roman on his forearm. He slammed his body down on her. Bethany now had blood pouring from her mouth and she was attempting to spit it at Roman and Martha. I jumped in again, certain that I could be of some help, and at least hold her legs while they dealt with the business end.

"JESUS CHRIST ELIZA, STAY THE FUCK BACK!" Roman bellowed at me.

I jumped back surprised, what the hell? He'd never spoken to me so angrily before, I knew it was a mixture of concern and adrenaline, but fuck me? I was only trying to help I thought as I stood back and watched the train wreck unfold before me.

"FUCKEN CUUUUUUNNNNT!!" Bethany howled as Roman's grip tightened on her head, pinning her face to the concrete floor, he told her to calm down.

"I gotta get home to my six kids, it's my youngest kids birthday today, they are home alone..., sir, please let me go. I'm pregnant too," Bethany pleaded, using every excuse now to try and get away with what she'd done. But she knew the deal, she knew the only place she was going after tonight's fiasco was jail.

"Martha hurry the fuck up with the cuffs will you, Jesus Christ!" Roman yelled again. He'd completely lost his composure, his face was contorted with rage.

Constable Stable was anything but stable, she was a trembling mess, she finally got the handcuffs on a very irate Bethany, and then helped to hold her down while Roman radioed for back up. Bethany's wails became louder when she realized she was drawing a crowd, people had stopped to see what all the commotion was about, and several people had pulled their phones out and were recording the incident.

She continued to spit blood and scream about needing to get home to her children, and that she hadn't done anything and this was police brutality.

What a lying scumbag bitch, I bit my tongue but I was furious!

"If you want to help me Eliza, start giving people a move on direction, if they don't leave immediately, tell them you're going to take their details. That ought to get them moving along," Roman commanded.

With the help of Cole Warner (who had come out to see what all the screaming was about), we began telling people to move along. I chastised a group of young Mothers who had stopped with their small children in strollers

"Really? You want your babies to see this? Get out of here, you should be ashamed of yourselves," I scolded angrily.

S/C Matilda Berry was one of the first to arrive, and with Roman's help, they lifted a screaming Bethany off the ground. Cole and I followed them out to the car park.

"The cuffs are too fucking tight you fucken pigs," she wailed incessantly.

"Oh are they? It's because they are new," Roman responded sarcastically, as he none too gently escorted her to the back of the police wagon, locking her inside.

"Can you sort her out Matilda, Martha can go with you too, I'm going to head back and clean up and I'll be over in a bit. Make sure they don't release her, because she has property in her car," Roman ordered.

As Roman walked back toward me, I could see he had blood on his arm where he'd been bitten. It was on his hands and also down his shirt. He looked furious. I was angry too, mostly at the scabby bitch for behaving like a rabid dog, and causing such a scene. But I was also mad at Roman for refusing my help when his useless partner should've been right in there. I felt like this was partly her fault too, for opening her damn mouth about the stuff in the car, and because she hadn't acted quickly when she needed to. Her big mouth and hesitation to jump in had resulted in Roman being bitten. Fucken rookie!

"I will see you in a little while ok, let me go sort this shit out," he said gesturing to his arms and shirt. "Oh, and can you see if center security has any footage of this too, coz I'm going to need it."

"Ok," I replied, but he was already walking away.

I called security, they were already in the process of burning the footage. A store owner had called them when things were getting out of hand, but by the time they sent someone to help out, Bethany was being escorted away. I picked up the shopping cart of stock that Bethany had refunded, and photographed it, I burnt the store footage, wrote a very detailed statement and then headed down to the police beat.

As I entered, Roman opened the door. He'd changed into a clean shirt, the smell of Dettol and cleaning products hung in the air. He led me to his office and shut the door, he knew by my face that I was still angry, but before I could say anything he jumped in.

"She has HEP C and is HIV positive Eliza, I've dealt with her before so I knew that. So before you jump on your high horse and have a go at me for yelling at you, think about that ok? I was trying to protect you," Roman confided.

I sat heavily onto the chair, OH MY GOD! She had bitten my husband, drawn blood and spat her own blood at him. I couldn't even comprehend what he was saying beyond that. Seeing the look of sheer horror and panic on my face, Roman knelt in front of me;

"I know exactly what you're thinking Lize, and please stop. I have no open wounds, yes she bit me, but it didn't break the skin..., see?" He said showing me his arm.

I grabbed his arm, running my finger over the area I could see slight indent marks left over from her dirty black teeth, the area was red and the tell-tale signs of bruising were beginning to appear. But he was right, there didn't appear to be any broken skin.

"But I saw blood coming from your arm Roman," I fretted, feeling confused.

"Babes..., it was all her blood, she must've bitten her lip when I did the takedown. Hun, it's going to be ok I promise," Roman tried to sound convincing.

But a small part of me worried, what if he had been infected?

"I have to go get tested anyway, because it's standard procedure," He continued so casually, he may as well have been asking me what we were having for dinner, or how was my day?

I knew now was not the time to be melodramatic, after all, he was still on duty and as convincing as Roman thought he sounded, I knew he would not be completely at ease until he had been given the all-clear. I stood up and hugged my husband close to me, I breathed in deeply, but instead of the familiar scent of his cologne, my nostrils were invaded with the smell of industrial strength sanitizer. I felt sick, furiously I blinked back tears, I clung to him, not wanting to let him go..., wishing that I had never laid eyes on that fucking junkie Bethany Muller, and then as selfish as I knew it was..., I wished that my husband..., my sweet Roman hadn't been the one who responded to the job.

"Babes, go home..., I will try and get this wrapped up as quickly as I can," Roman said, kissing the top of my head.

As I drove home my mind was racing, I knew the next few months were going to be rough. I'd spoken in length, with the spouses of police officers who'd been exposed to various infectious diseases, and while the risk for a positive result was actually quite low, (at least in this situation) it certainly didn't make the agony of the wait any easier.

It changed everything, especially on an intimate level. Roman had told me that he knew of a few marriages irretrievably breaking down because of either fear of passing on a disease, or catching one. Even the way in which an officer interacts with their children, some too frightened to share a drink with them or mend a scraped knee.

I shook my head in disbelief, this was such bullshit! All of this because some low life grub made poor choices in their own life and had zero regard for anyone..., including themselves!

I knew this also meant, that for at least the next three months we would not be trying for a baby. Even though most results could come back in as little as two weeks, Roman and I had discussed this before, and he'd been very clear on the fact that he would want to wait the full three months for complete screening. He did not want to risk having unprotected sex, and potentially infecting me, or our unborn child. I could feel the hot sting of angry tears welling behind my eyes, I felt robbed, cheated, pissed off that this decision had now been made for us. We had been actively trying to conceive since our engagement, but my period had shown up each month like clockwork, all the ovulation tracking, body basal temping, eating a natural diet, and taking vitamins, hadn't done shit, but at least the actual love making had been within our control.

What was worse..., was that someone like Bethany seemed to just trip on a dick and get pregnant. If what she was saying was true, that she had six kids at home and one in the belly, then life really wasn't fair. I could only hope now, that those poor children had someone to take care of them, and as much as I despised her right now, I hoped that Bethany would get the help she needed too.

My biggest concern right now though, was Roman. I knew he'd be putting on a brave front, acting like he wasn't in the slightest bit worried about this, and I knew I'd have to go along with him on that. A Positive attitude, with negative results, that was all we could hope for, and while I wasn't the praying kind, I knew I would be now.

I pulled up in the driveway, and looking at the huge, dark, empty house, I wondered if we'd ever be blessed with even just one child? I couldn't bring myself to go inside, instead, I went to the barn, right to the bar and poured myself a shot of whiskey. I hadn't had a drink since the night of our wedding, the burning sensation in my throat made my eyes water. I poured another drink, this time JD honey on ice. I knew if I started I may not stop, and I questioned myself, if you do this, are you really that different to Bethany? She's just a junkie with a different poison. The thought was sobering, possibly even a reality check? No good would come from this, tomorrow I'd wake up and feel like shit all day. I knew I'd come a long way from the girl who'd used alcohol to numb the emotional pain, but clearly old habits die hard.

Right now I felt like I had one of those little red devil's on one shoulder, and an angel on the other, red devil was telling me to drink it..., drink the whole damn bottle. White angel was shouting NO, NO, NO, you don't need it!

I felt like swatting both those annoying little fuckers off my shoulders, even though I knew there was nothing there. I walked away with the glass in my hand, upstairs to the bedroom, and ran a hot bath, I messaged Roman to tell him I was having one drink, a soak in the tub and that we'd be sleeping in the barn tonight.

***

As I lay back in the tub, sipping on my drink, I made a decision, I was no longer going to worry about what I couldn't control, after all, life could be an absolute bitch at times, then your best friend the next, but as long as you have a few good people in your corner, you'll always come out the other side of any shit storm relatively unscathed.

CHAPTER 26
SEX FINGERS

I woke up in the round bed in the barn with the sun blazing through the huge open windows, I looked at my phone and saw it was only 6 am. Man, it was hot already I groaned to myself.

I rolled over and gently ran my fingers up and down my husband's bare back as he lay sleeping beside me. We'd slept in the barn a lot lately, I was working on a book and would be on the computer until quite late, or until Roman dragged me away. It was easier on those nights to just sleep here, rather than have to deal with those awful fucking cane toads that would jump out of nowhere, and scare the bejesus out of me as I walked back to the house. They were harmless, but I knew I'd never get used to them, creepy looking things, give me a bug or a spider anyday, at least you could splat them with a shoe!

Snuggling back into Roman, I dozed off again. I dreamt we were holding our first baby, a boy. With his dark hair and green eyes, he was a stunning combination of us both, handsome little Logan Jack Beach. I felt suckling on my nipple..., what the...? I stirred from my drowsy state, realizing it was

Roman, who'd obviously woken up aroused. It had been a very long three months, we'd still had sex using condoms, we'd even played with toys, but it wasn't the same for either of us, however this last week we were more than making up for it.

"Good morning you," I grinned sleepily.

"Hey babes," Roman answered with a mouthful of nipple.

His fingers moved down to my pussy, I spread my legs apart as he kissed his way down my stomach, his hot tongue lashed at my clit.

"Let me suck your cock," I murmured, desperately wanting a distraction so I wouldn't cum so quickly.

Roman turned himself around and climbed on top of me, I took his rock hard dick into my mouth and sucked him hard. As I felt him cum in my mouth I swallowed and continued sucking until I came too.

"Wow, what a way to wake up," I beamed at Roman as he climbed off and lay down beside me.

We spoke about my book, our plans for the day and then I told him about the dream I'd been having before he woke me up.

"Logan Jack Beach huh? Sounds good to me. Unfortunately, I don't think you can get pregnant orally though babes," Roman teased.

"I really want to be a mom Roman," I pouted.

"Well you're going to have to wait at least thirty minutes before I try to impregnate you, so how bout you go make me breakfast I'm starving!" Roman exclaimed, still teasing me as he got out of the bed.

I looked around the room, and noticed the high-heel chair was still laying on its side from last night's session. Climbing out of bed, I picked it up and moved it back into its usual position.

"We really shouldn't fuck on these, they might break," I said seriously to Roman.

"Yeah, probably not, but it was fun though, I've never been fucked on a shoe before," Roman joked, he was in a particularly good mood today.

I picked up my coffee cup from the hand-shaped coffee table, but fumbled and dropped it on the edge of the table, it smashed into pieces on the floor.

"FUCK!" I shouted, annoyed that I'd broken my favorite cup.

Alexis had bought it for me as a gift, and given it to me on our final training day together. It said "I run on coffee and cuss words" and of late it had been very fitting.

I went to the cleaning cupboard downstairs to get the vacuum, and somehow my sheer robe got caught on a hook and tore down the side as I walked away.

"JESUS CHRIST!" I shouted angrily as I looked at the huge tear.

Roman came to investigate and told me he'd take care of the cup, I threw the gown on one of the bar stools, and walked naked back to the house.

I needed a strong, hot coffee, so while I brewed a huge pot of Belgian cream I attempted (very poorly) to make a batch of imitation Cinna-stack IHOP pancakes. It was a good thing that Roman could cook, because I was hopeless! I had never bothered to master the art of cooking when I lived in the states because the food was so cheap. It actually cost less to eat out, and you didn't have the mess to clean up after.

Roman often joked that I needed cooking classes, little did he know I'd secretly been taking them when he was on afternoon shifts. Betty Ku, a little Asian customer greeter had been giving me regular private lessons. She had been a cooking instructor and had already taught me how to make the perfect scone, or biscuit as I called them. She was coming over this evening to help me prepare a surprise meal for Roman.

"I've got sex fingers today, so watch out!" I joked, raising my eyebrows at Roman.

"Say what?" Roman laughed, looking confused.

"Well..., I broke the cup, ripped my gown, and just now I dropped coffee beans all over the floor, and you don't even want to see what's going on in this bowl, so..., it's obvious that today I'm gonna fuck everything I touch, therefore I have sex fingers," I declared, giggling as I stirred the batter.

Roman laughed shaking his head, he came closer to have a look at what was in the bowl.

"What is that?" Roman laughed wildly as he looked at the lumpy pancake batter in the bowl.

He burst out laughing, slapping the countertop over and over hysterically when he saw the sorry excuse for a pancake sizzling on the stove.

"Want a closer look smart ass?" I laughed picking up the bowl and pretending to throw it at him.

"Don't you dare Eliza," Roman protested, pointing a finger at me.

But it was too late, some of the batter had practically leapt out of the bowl and onto Roman's bare chest.

"OH MY GOD!" Roman yelled laughing.

"Shit, I didn't actually mean to do that. I told you I have sex fingers," I cackled.

I put the bowl down on the bench and moving closer to Roman, I licked the batter off his chest. I wasn't sure if it were his skin or the batter that tasted a little salty. I felt the cool batter as Roman poured it down my back, I squealed loudly and fought him for the bowl. He held it in a vice-like grip, so scooping some of the batter out with my hand I threw it on him. It was war!!

Five minutes later we were both on the kitchen floor, laughing and trying to catch our breath in a pool of sticky batter. I rolled over and pulled

Roman's boxer shorts off, climbing on top of him I kissed him on his mouth and neck until I could feel the stirring of his erection against my naked body. There was definitely too much salt in the batter I decided smiling. I sat on Roman's cock, rocking back and forth, fucking him at a steady pace. He pulled himself up, turned and leaned back against the island bench, I continued riding him as he sucked on my nipples, I came first, and was about to suggest a change in position when I heard someone knocking on the door.

***

"I'm coming, oh god I'm coming," Roman called out loudly, oblivious to the churchgoer who from the door, could see directly into where we were fucking on the floor.

"Er..., umm, sorry, I'll um..., just leave this here," the old lady stammered, leaving a pamphlet on the chair next to the door she scurried away.

Roman looked mortified, but I burst out laughing.

"Holy shit, I bet she won't be back here again, I didn't even hear a car, what the hell are they even doing all the way out here?" I asked incredulously, I climbed off of Roman and sat beside him, leaning against the island bench.

"I can't believe her timing, we really need to do something about people mistaking our kitchen door for the front door Eliza, it's not the first time someone has seen your naked ass, just last week it was the Telstra guy. We should get one of those alarms for the gate, so we at least have two minutes notice," Roman exclaimed.

"Actually, the Telstra guy got a nude full frontal too, with a runway model pirouette as I turned and ran to get my dressing gown," I giggled, blushing at the embarrassing situation I'd found myself in the week before.

"Well, we are going to Bunnings to get a sausage for breakfast and a gate alarm. I don't want the whole world looking at your beautiful naked ass anymore," Roman winked at me. "But first.., Mrs sex fingers.., we better clean up this mess," he finished, pointing around to the batter all over the cupboards and floor.

It had been such a fun spontaneous moment, but we hadn't given much thought to the clean-up. Roman grabbed the mop and bucket and cleaned the floor, while I wiped down the bench surfaces and cupboards. We showered together, and Roman washed the batter from my hair. After a quick stop at Bunnings for a sausage with onion and ketchup on bread, we purchased a gate alarm, then decided to head out to the beach for a walk and a quick lunch. We ate at our favorite fish and chip shop, Seafood lovers, then we walked barefoot in the edge of the water hand in hand. It was ridiculously humid today so the water was a welcome relief as it lapped at our feet. We were discussing baby names and deciding which bedroom we would use as the nursery when my cell rang, I looked at the screen and saw it was Jessica.

"Hey Jess, how's things?" I asked.

"Eliza, I can't get hold of Rob and I'm in labor," Jessica sounded panicked.

"Oh my god, how far apart are the contractions? And where are you now?" I asked.

"They are ten minutes apart, I'm at the hospital, can you please come..., I don't want to do this on my own," Jessica asked desperately.

"Of course I'll come, we are actually just down the road, I'll get Roman to drop me off and then he can go look for Rob, see you in a bit," I said then hung up.

An hour later, Jessica gave birth to a beautiful little girl, Rob had arrived just minutes before his daughter was born, but they'd insisted I stay for the birth. Roman poked his head around the curtain as I cradled this perfect little newborn in my arms.

"She's gorgeous Jess, congratulations, what's her name?" Roman asked as he looked over my shoulder at the swaddled baby in my arms.

"We've decided to call her Raine, after you Eliza," Jessica said proudly.

"Oh my..., Jess, are you sure? Thank you, what an honor," I gushed.

"We want you and Roman to be her godparents if you'll accept," Rob added.

"We'd love to," Roman grinned.

We left the hospital and I called Adam, Alexis, and Georgia to tell them about the new baby. Holding baby Raine had only reinforced the urge to have a child of our own. Once home, Roman showered quickly and changed into his uniform, when he left I wandered around our huge empty home, deep in thought.

I'd read everything I possibly could online about ways to conceive, laying with your legs in the air after sex, eating or avoiding certain foods and drinks, I'd even cut right down on caffeine and hadn't had an alcoholic drink since the nightcap in the barn after the whole Bethany Muller incident. There was no medical explanation why we couldn't get pregnant, after all, it had happened once already, when we weren't even trying, when it shouldn't have even happened because of my IUD.

I was back to tracking ovulation and basal body temperatures and all that other shit, but none of it was working, each month when my period made an appearance I felt like my body was betraying me, rejecting the very thought of a baby. Because of the three month break, my Doctor didn't feel that we'd given it long enough trying on our own for any type of medical intervention just yet, but it was getting closer to that point. I was becoming increasingly impatient, obsessed even, we were having more sex than most couples, but it just wasn't happening. I knew I needed to stop, that I needed to take a giant step back, enough was enough! I didn't want sex to become a chore, or all about us conceiving. I'd joined an online support group for women trying to conceive, and saw how easy it was to become so obsessed about getting pregnant that it damaged relationships. If we were meant to have our own baby, it would happen, we were still young enough to consider other options, and for now, as much as I longed for the pitter patter of tiny feet, I needed to just focus on my marriage with Roman, and enjoy him in and out of the bedroom without all the pressure.

Betty arrived at 6:30 pm and helped me prepare a meal for Roman, the distraction was just what I needed. She showed me how to make garlic bread bruschetta, and left the instructions on how to put it together once she'd gone. We made Penne Alla Vodka and a fresh raspberry cheesecake for dessert. By 10 pm the kitchen was clean and tidy and Betty had gone home.

I was sitting in the library flipping through an Italian cookbook, sipping on a JD honey on ice when I heard Roman come in. I only hoped he felt the same way about this whole taking a break from conceiving thing. Relief swept over his face as he sat beside me on the lounge, and I told him what I was thinking. He hadn't wanted to tell me I was becoming obsessed, he'd been worried it would upset me, or that he'd come across as being insensitive. We spoke in length about needing to be honest with our feelings, and realistic in our expectations about starting a family. We'd decided to do the, not trying not preventing method, no more peeing on ovulation sticks, or charting temperatures, we'd give it a year, and if nothing happened we'd look at our options.

"I'm starving, did you pick up something to eat or should I make some toast?" Roman asked rubbing his growling stomach.

"Actually, I have a surprise, come with me," I grinned pulling him by the hand to the kitchen.

He sat at the island bench while I heated the bread in the oven, once it was cooked I spooned the diced tomato and herbs on the top and placed it in front of Roman, he eyed it cautiously, and began to eat. I heated the Penne Alla Vodka on the stove top, and served it in fancy pasta bowls that I'd bought when I moved in, but until tonight they had never been used.

"Oh my God, this is delicious, what brand is it?" Roman asked as he shoveled the pasta into his mouth.

"Well, you won't believe it..., but I actually made it. I've been taking lessons," I said shyly.

"Really? Wow..., babe, this is really good," Roman sounded genuinely surprised, "Did you make the bread too?"

"Not the actual breadstick, but the garlic oil and topping yes," I replied grinning. "I even made a raspberry cheesecake for dessert, but you better be a good boy and eat your dinner first."

***

"Next week get her to show you how to make pancakes, our way is kinda messy, and I never even got to have whipped cream on top," Roman winked, then stuffed another fork full of pasta in his mouth.

"Oh…, you can have the whipped cream on top later my dear husband," I purred seductively.

After dinner we had hot chocolate and cheesecake, Roman insisted on stacking the dishwasher while I showered. I was a hot mess from all the cooking, so took him up on the offer. I climbed naked into bed beside Roman and kicked off the covers, it was still far too sticky and hot.

'Pshhhhhhhhhhhhhtttttttttttt…'

"What the fuck?!" I jumped, squealing loudly.

Roman had squirted canned whipped cream onto my nipple.

"You didn't think I'd forget did you?" he said mischievously as he licked the cream off.

CHAPTER 27
DAVID AND GOLIATH

Adam Martin was a monster, standing at almost 7 ft tall and built like a brick shit house, (another Aussie slang term I'd grown to love.) His hands appeared to be the size of dinner plates, and his bare feet were huge! His gargantuan size was what had caught my attention in the first place. Beside him, I looked like an elf.

He was crouched down in an aisle, and I couldn't quite see what he was up to, but I knew by his demeanor he was up to no good. I looked for somewhere to hide, but no matter where I stood, I couldn't see what he was doing. I knew I'd need to get in close, use one of my three sight strikes to get a better look.

So, entering the aisle where Adam was still crouched, I pretended to look at the items on the shelves around him. He barely glanced in my direction, and remained as still as a statue, as if trying to blend in with the fixtures and stock on the shelf. Perhaps if he weren't a giant he may have succeeded?

I could see he had a Stanley knife and glue, but his dinner plate hands and fat sausage fingers covered half of the box he was leaning on. I needed to think quick, and somehow distract him enough to move his hands. I picked up a set of car seat covers and walked up to him.

"Excuse me sir, I was wondering if you might be able to help me. I'm not sure if these seat covers will fit my particular car, and I don't want to buy the wrong ones," I said giving Adam a very friendly smile.

He stood up, whoa he really is enormous! I thought to myself.

I looked past him to the box he'd been leaning on and saw he'd left a pile of barcodes, glue and the Stanley knife on top.

"What kind of car have you got?" He asked as he looked at the covers.

"A 2010 Holden Cruze," I lied.

"Nah, these ones won't fit, maybe go to a proper shop coz they have more variety there," Adam said handing me back the car seat covers.

"OK, well thanks for your help anyway," I thanked him and placing the car seat covers back, I walked out of the aisle.

"Hey, you wanna hook up later?" Adam asked.

"No, I don't think my husband would approve, thanks again though," I shook my head, leaving a grumbling Adam in the aisle.

Now I knew what he was up to it would be easier to hide, I wouldn't have to keep bobbing my head in and out of the aisle to keep an eye on him. I watched through a very tiny hole as he glued fake barcodes on to several boxes. I called the police and asked if they were able to assist with an arrest, even though he'd come across as a gentle giant, and even wanted to 'hook up' I knew that attitude would quickly change as soon he was approached outside under very different circumstances.

I hid behind a rack of clothing near the registers and watched as Adam paid $25 instead of $550 for the items in his cart. If the young lad on the register figured there was something wrong with the prices, he certainly didn't say anything. I couldn't blame him, Adam Martin was doing a fantastic job of intimidating the boy as he glared and complained loudly at how slow the service was, saying he had better places to be than this shit hole.

"Well, you are going to get quite acquainted with the back office of this 'shit hole' shortly," I scoffed quietly to Cole, who was hiding beside me.

I scanned the outside of the store, but saw no sign of the police, I wondered how this was going to go down without them.

"Have you read the story of David and Goliath Cole?" I asked.

"Nah, why's that?" Cole asked looking puzzled.

"Because this shit is going to be biblical," I grinned, "but I feel like even David would need more than just a pouch and some stones to take down this giant, to be honest I'm not even sure a taser would drop the big bastard!"

"I didn't know you were religious Eliza," Cole said idly.

"I'm not, but my father told me the story when I was a child, he was worried that I would be intimidated by people because I was so small, and thought the story would encourage me to always stand up for what I believe in no matter how big the fight. Maybe he was trying to prepare me for this moment, only I don't have a slingshot or stones, all I have is a useless biro, my mouth and you," I finished. Poking my tongue out at Cole I bravely headed for the door before I could change my mind.

"Jeez Eliza, are you going to try and apprehend him then, or wait for the police?" Cole asked sounding worried.

"I have to at least try, it's what I'm paid to do Cole," I replied feeling very nervous about approaching him.

Taking a deep breath, I approached Adam outside with Cole and introduced myself as the store's Loss Prevention Officer. I told him as confidently as I could, that we were going to be escorting him to the back office.

"Like fuck you little slag, I paid for my shit, now piss off!" he yelled angrily as he attempted to keep walking away.

"You know what you did, and you *will* pay for it one way or another," I responded boldly.

"Not my fucken fault if it's got the wrong price on it is it?" he scoffed trying to sound convincing.

"It *is* your fault when you glued the wrong price on there. You didn't think you'd get away with that, surely? Look, you can either come back with me to the office and we can sort it out there, or you can go to the watch-house with the police, who are about thirty seconds away. It's your choice, but I'm telling you now, if you make the police run at this hour of the day, you'll be locked up in the watch-house for at least six to eight hours. So again, your choice, come with me and be home for dinner..., or, go to the watch-house," I bluffed. I had no clue how far away the police were, I just knew..., if he got to the car park any chance of getting him or the stock back were over. Adam Martin stopped walking, in fact, he turned the cart around and headed back to the store.

"You've got some fucking big balls to confront someone like me, I will give you that much. I'm not sure if you're brave or just fucken stupid," he continued walking, and shaking his head as he pushed the shopping cart back into the store.

The truth was, I wasn't sure myself. It took every ounce of self-control I had to keep a steady voice as the adrenaline coursed through my body. I knew when we got to the back office, I would not be capable of taking his details immediately because I could feel my hands shaking, and I was not prepared to let this monster of a man see that he had actually gotten to me.

Once we were settled, I kept my hands busy, shuffling paperwork and bossing staff around while I attempted to calm my nerves. The jitters settled quicker than I expected so I took out my pen and notebook.

"Have you been in trouble with the police before?" I asked him, making small talk as I wrote the details from his driver's license in my notebook.

"Nah, not really..., I'm a good guy you know. So, did you really need car seat covers or are you full of shit?" Adam smirked.

"I guess in your words, I'm full of shit, I was just doing my job," I replied casually, trying to keep the conversation light.

"I bet you're not really married then are you? So, do you wanna hook up later Shorty or what?" Adam grinned like a Cheshire cat.

I didn't respond, instead I held up my left hand, facing my wedding band toward Adam, I smiled weakly, then looked down and continued to fill in forms. The two officers who I hadn't formally met, arrived and introduced themselves as Senior Constables Michael Ridge and Matthew Rhodes.

S/C Matthew Rhodes asked me to step outside so I could give him my details and fill him in on what happened.

"I can't believe you got him back in here, look at the size difference of you and him!" S/C Rhodes looked shocked as he looked me up and down.

"I might be short, but I have a big mouth to make up for it, I can be very persuasive," I laughed nonchalantly.

"Obviously you must be, and as for the big mouth, that isn't a bad thing just so you know, I like a lady who is good with her mouth," Matthew Rhodes said cheekily as he winked at me.

But as funny as I thought his comment was, I kept a straight face.

"Ok, what's your full and correct name?" He asked taking out his notebook.

"Eliza Raine Beach," I replied.

He quickly looked up from his notebook, and giving me a longer than necessary 'once over' he shook his head in disbelief;

"Oh wow you're Roman's wife, no wonder the man is completely whipped, it's a pleasure to finally meet you," he said as he extended his arm and shook my hand. "Roman and I went through the academy together, I've just transferred back from the bush, and he's been telling me all about you the past few weeks. He is clearly besotted with you it's written all over his face."

"Ohhhhh you must be Roady. Roman has spoken about you too. And..., well..., as for him being besotted, the feeling is completely mutual," I smiled.

"Christ, sorry about the comment just before, it kinda seems a bit inappropriate now," he said looking contrite.

"I can appreciate a sense of humor Matthew, no harm done," I grinned.

Once my details were taken, I went back into the office and S/C Rhodes joined us a few minutes later.

"Here's your notice to appear, you realize you are probably looking at a bit of time in the bin for this one, given your long history with the law, and the fact you're out on parole with strict conditions it's not looking too good," S/C Rhodes explained to a very annoyed looking Adam Martin.

"Yeah, I thought as much, oh well I better enjoy my last week of freedom," Adam grumbled. He took the notice to appear in court form, and looked directly at me before continuing, "any chance of us just having a drink then Miss, seeing as I came back in without a fight, might be the last one I have for a while, especially with a good lookin Sheila like yourself. Surely your husband won't mind."

"Like I've told you twice now, I am married. To a police officer actually, and even if I weren't married, I have this rule about not socializing with criminals, so it's a firm no from me," I replied coolly.

"Should've figured you'd be married to the filth, fucken pigs and floor walkers, like birds of a feather you flock together." Adam spat vehemently at me as he walked toward the door.

Adam, had unknowingly slam danced on my very last nerve;

"Filth? Filth? You want to talk about filth? Listen here you piece of shit, trash like you should get off your lazy ass and get a damn job, instead of cruising through life as the world owes you something. Earn what you want instead of stealing it. Also, you fucken stink! You should've stolen some deodorant and body wash, and a hygiene kit for your damn mouth, because the only filthy pig I see, *and* smell in this room right now is you, now get out!" I shouted angrily at him.

SHIT!.., I had completely lost my temper, I waited for Adam to lose his too, and was not at all prepared for the raucous laughter that followed.

"Fuck me sideways you vicious little bitch, no one except me mum has ever had the nerve to cunt me to my face like you've just done. If you were a man, I'd drop you on your plump little arse, but I also have a rule..., I don't hit women, so I'm going to swallow me knob, as me old dad used to say, coz I guess I deserved it," Adam shook his head, turned and walked away. His psychotic laugh reverberated down the hall.

Both Officers stood silently in shock, staring at me as I tried to calm down.

"Fuck..., I am sorry about that. That was completely unprofessional and I should not have let him get to me," I apologized feeling contrite.

"When Roman said you were a little live wire, he wasn't exaggerating was he?" S/C Rhodes laughed, "Michael, this is Roman's wife Eliza."

"Remind me never to piss you off, you tore shreds off him. I honestly thought he was going to go off his brain. You might be a tiny little thing, but our boy Roman sure has his hands full by the looks," Michael added. Laughing he shook my hand.

"I really am sorry, I'm actually not usually like that, honestly..., Roman would go crazy if he knew I'd just done that. He was a big unit and could've caused some serious damage if he wanted to. I shouldn't let my personal feelings overrule my common sense. Thank God for his rule huh?" I shrugged..., feeling relieved that at least Adam Martin had some kind of moral compass.

Adam clearly hadn't gotten over being roasted, and his freedom was short-lived. As he walked to his car, a junkie in the car park abused him for not giving him a cigarette. He beat that guy so badly he ended up in the hospital. It took four police officers and multiple shots from their tasers to take Adam Martin down.

When we heard the call come over the radio for back up, both officers left immediately to assist, I realized how close I'd been to imminent danger, dealing with someone as unpredictable as Adam Martin was definitely an occupational hazard. Before I even began my report I called Roman, I figured it would be better coming from me, than him hearing about the tongue lashing from his colleagues, and for the second time that day, I was surprised at the reaction I got.

"I did tell the boys that you had a quick tongue babe, but I didn't mean it that way," he joked, "now, are we going to BrisVegas tonight, it's been a while? I had planned on you meeting the infamous Roady before now, but it just never happened. I'll ask if he wants to come too."

"Sounds like a plan hun, come home first though, and I'll drive us in. If Matthew wants to stay in the barn tonight, tell him to pack an overnight bag," I replied jovially, feeling relieved that he hadn't lectured me about my 'crazy shit' as he so often referred to it.

A few hours later we had fucked in the shower, dressed, picked up Roady and were sitting in BrisVegas. The boys were catching up on old times over a few beers, and I was on the hard stuff..., coffee!

I really wanted to be back in the barn working on my book, so I suggested to Roman that they finish their beers and we'd pick up pizza and head home. The bar in the barn was stocked, and with none of us working the next day, we could all have a late night *and* a sleep in. After a quick tour of the house and barn, we were sat on the comfy lounges enjoying a few drinks.

"Mate..., you did well with this one hey, good looking, great personality and filthy rich by the looks," Matthew Rhodes rambled on, as he looked around admiringly.

Clearly his filter was broken, or he'd had too much to drink. I thought, shocked at his blatant honesty. Roman, on the other hand, puffed his chest out and proudly and put an arm around me.

"What can I say mate, it was her feisty attitude, and gorgeous green eyes that got me, the rest is just a bonus," Roman winked at me.

I always felt uncomfortable when my money was mentioned, I'd give it all back in a heartbeat if it meant having daddy back again. Roman knew how I felt about it, and sensing my discomfort, squeezed me closer to him. I loved that Roman wasn't driven by money, he never even knew my net worth until just before we married. Against the advice of my family accountant and attorney, I had insisted on no prenuptial agreement this time around. I loved Roman, and didn't even want to consider a future without him in it.

When we'd sat down to talk finances, I'd asked how he felt about having a joint bank account, we both agreed it made sense and set it up. The day he logged in to the online banking and saw five million dollars in the account, he thought there had been a huge error, he was shocked when I told him it was no mistake, and that the money was ours.

Daddy had set up a series of trust accounts too, some I wouldn't be able to access until I reached the ages of 30 and then 35. He'd been concerned that in the event of his death, I'd go crazy (which I did) and completely blow the lot. So, he'd made these arrangements to ensure that no matter what else was going on in my life, financially I'd be secure.

Roman and I led a fairly simple life though, sure we enjoyed nice things, but then again, who doesn't? But we weren't show-offs, and until people felt the need to comment on what we had, we didn't really think about it. I helped people when I could, but had also learned the hard way, that all too often people are either fake or jealous, and only hang around long enough to see what they can get from you. I knew I had more money than I could ever need..., (or spend) in this lifetime, but I also wanted to make sure I had something left to hand down to my own children, (should we be blessed with them).

"Earth to Eliza, hellooooo do you want another drink?" Matthew asked as he headed to the bar.

"No thanks, I'm good," I replied. I looked up at Roman, "If you don't mind, I really want to just go work on my book upstairs. Come and get me when you're ready for bed, you know I'm still scared shitless of those toads, and I can't sleep out here now can I," I kissed Roman gently on the lips and stood up.

"You ok babes? You know he means no harm, he is pretty envious actually. Truth be told..., he said he was going to hit you up for your number until he realized who you were," Roman said the last part with a huge grin on his face.

"Well, that would have been awkward! You definitely better come and get me at bedtime now I know that," I teased, Roman pulled me back into his lap and kissed me hard.

255

"Get a room you two," Matthew said as he put a drink down in front of Roman.

"Sorry Matthew," I laughed as I climbed from my husband's lap, and headed for the stairs.

"Hey Eliza, you do know that's my bedroom up there tonight don't you?" Matthew yelled, "you won't get any complaints from me, but I'm not sure that Roman likes to share."

"Damn straight, I will share my beer, my food even my car, but my wife is strictly off limits. Now shut up you clown, and get ready to have your arse whooped at pool," Roman laughed slapping Matthew on the back as they headed toward the billiard table.

***

I was grateful that Roman was not the jealous type, and was reminded at how much my life had changed. My first husband would have been seething at those comments, even though they were said in jest, I would've paid the price later..., been blamed for having done something to encourage the attention. The thought made me shudder, and I had to stop myself from taking this trip down memory lane, it was over, in the past, left in the dust. Well..., almost, the door to my past would be firmly shut once Michael was sentenced for what he had done, not only to me but to the other women who had now come forward.

There is a reason your windshield is bigger than your rear-view mirror, because where you are going, is far more important than where you've come from. I liked that analogy, it had been my mantra for quite some time.

I sat at the desk, and opened the file for my book, losing myself in the stories and characters I tapped away on the keyboard, only returning to reality when Roman came up behind me a few hours later.

"Let's go to bed baby," he slurred his words a little.

I saved my work and closed my computer. We said goodnight to a very drunk Matthew Rhodes, and walked back to the house. Thank God the toads were a no-show, because the state Roman was in, he wouldn't have been able to carry me if he tried. I tucked my husband into bed, made myself a cup of vanilla and rose tea and retreated to the library to read.

"Come to bed my love," Roman called out a short time later.

By the time I'd rinsed my cup and shut all the lights off, Roman had fallen asleep, resting my head on his chest, I fell asleep listening to the soothing sound of his heartbeat and his very light snore. Life was good.

CHAPTER 28
FACEBOOK

Facebook..., pretty much everyone I knew was on there, and people were shocked when I told them I wasn't. I was not sold on the idea of putting your entire life on the internet for the world to see. Roman and I had discussed it and decided that it wasn't for us. We enjoyed the anonymity of our lives, and didn't feel it was necessary to share our location, or what we were eating for dinner each night!

It only took one mutual friend, and your friends list expanded. With games, groups, memes, and messages, it sucked the life out of you. I called it the Facebook diet, you lost three hours but gained twenty friends!!

I did however, create a dummy account. Just because I wanted our lives to remain private, didn't mean I couldn't utilize this tool to look into other peoples. Simon had recently put out a memo on a recidivist offender that appeared to have gone quiet, and asked us if we had any information or had seen her. Logging in to my Facebook account, I typed "Simone Kelly" into the search bar, I narrowed the search to Brisbane and there she was!

Let's see what you've been up to, I thought as her personal page loaded.

It turned out, the reason she had gone quiet was that she had been arrested and was back in jail, and her girlfriend was not at all impressed, or so I could gather from the post she had put on Simone's wall calling all cops dogs for locking her girlfriend up on her birthday.

There were also some very interesting posts that I saved for Roman to look at, pictures of drugs, and bundles of money, also several references to a string of break-ins where they took "some old bitches jewelry" as one of her friends had bragged.

The best thing about Facebook, was that if people were stupid enough to leave everything public, you could easily skip from friend to friend looking through their pages and photos. It was actually quite entertaining to see how many offenders I had caught were mutual friends, such as Simone and Australia's dumbest criminal Tommy!

Perhaps the funniest thing I stumbled across, was a prolific graffiti gang who had gone to all the effort of covering their heads in bandana's or masks, only to have one of their idiot friends tag everyone in the photo! That was definitely worth a screenshot!!

When I called Simon to give him the update on Simone Kelly, he assumed I'd had Roman look her up for me, and was shocked and impressed when I told him that it had been via social media. I reinforced to Simon, that I would not put my husband in a position where he could be formally spoken with, or worse, stood down for giving sensitive information to me. It was a golden rule and one I would not bend on. Plenty of officers were very helpful when it came to giving up information on offenders, and in earlier days Roman had helped me too, but now we were married it was just a line I wouldn't cross.

With Facebook, most of the information was accessible at my fingertips, and in the comfort of my own home. I shared this tactic with the Loss Prevention team, and soon we were all comparing notes on different offenders.

***

No longer did we have to rely on our sometimes grainy CCTV images (that often looked like every offender you'd ever captured) We now had access to picture-perfect snapshots.

One Thursday morning, I was looking up an offender Chrissy Wheelhouse that I had been profiling for a while, when she 'checked in' at a shopping center that I knew she was banned from. I called Georgia who was working with Melanie, and alerted her that Chrissy was in the center. I sent through her current profile picture via text message, and a few hours later Georgia called to tell me that she'd just apprehended Chrissy with over $500 worth of BONDS underwear.

Facebook was particularly useful for putting faces to names with the refunds, often we only had a name and address to go on, and no CCTV (especially when too much time had gone by). So I often logged on to see if I could get a match.

One particular repeat offender Sherry Bass, who seemed to have a penchant for wallets, (and had returned 100 of them in the space of a month) had her privacy settings on, but I was able to look through her friends list and saw that she was friends with a staff member from one of the stores I worked in.

I had a conversation with Timothy Moore (the staff member) and asked him if I could have a look at his Facebook page, he was more than happy to oblige. I saved a few of her photos to show to Madison who worked the door in the store that she frequented, Madison said she was a regular, and would keep me updated if she saw her. A few days later I was in the store when Madison called,

"Eliza, its Maddy, that lady you showed me the pictures of, she's in the store and heading to the men's section," Maddison spoke quickly.

"Awesome thanks," I responded. Hanging up the phone, I headed to the men's section.

Sure enough, there was Bass, helping herself to a few wallets, as she stuffed several of them into her bag I called the police. Sherry Bass headed toward the door, when she willingly opened her bag for Madison to inspect on her way out, I knew she must have a fake lining in her bag. Bursting with confidence, she even said hello to the police as she walked past them in the mall. I signaled to S/C Michael Ridge and S/C Matthew Rhodes and approached her with them.

"Hi, I'm the Loss Prevention Officer, I'm going to need you to come back to the store with us," I gave her the usual spiel.

"Sure, have I won something?" Sherry asked, trying her best to look surprised.

"Unless you consider a notice to appear in court winning, then no," I said sarcastically shaking my head.

"Court, what for I haven't done anything wrong?" Sherry replied, still trying to sound innocent.

I chose to ignore her until we got to the office.

"Right Sherry Bass, anything you have in your bag that doesn't belong to you put it on the table," I demanded.

"Search my bag I have nothing," She said, "hey, how do you know my name?"

"It's my job to know the names and faces of all the frequent refunders, and you Sherry are on the list," I replied dryly.

Sherry sat back on the chair with her arms folded, Matthew who was searching the bag looked puzzled.

"What am I looking for in here exactly, coz so far all I have is a used lip gloss and a purse?"

Matthew looked up from the bag at Sherry and then me.

"I'm certain if you have a look in the lining of the bag, you will find several wallets, pick the bag up, you'll see it feels heavier than an empty bag should," I suggested while keeping my eyes firmly fixed on Bass.

Sherry had gone the extra mile with the bag, and had Velcro sewn in to the lining. To an untrained eye, the bag looked perfectly normal, you couldn't see the Velcro holding the lining shut unless you really looked for it.

"Ah-ha, here we go!" Matthew exclaimed as he pulled the Velcro open and removed six wallets from the lining.

"I didn't put them in there, they must have come with the bag, or just fallen in there..., honest," Sherry lied.

"Sherry, we have it all on CCTV, do you realize you have refunded over 100 wallets in our stores already? At $30 a wallet that is $3000, plus the 6 today at $180 so how about you cut the crap," I snapped at her.

"I just did it for milk 'n' bread, for my kids..., honest," Sherry continued, "can you just let me go this one time?" she sniffed loudly.

The truth was, Sherry didn't know what the word 'honest' meant.

"Matthew, can I have a word outside?" I asked heading toward the door, we left Bass with manager Stacy Greer, and S/C Michael Ridge.

"She is so full of shit! She doesn't even have kids, a young lad that works here knows her, and he let me look through her Facebook account. She's stealing to support her drug habit," I told him.

"Facebook huh? What else have you got on her?" Matthew asked.

"There are pictures of her partying hard, doing lines in a nightclub bathroom, and at someone's house. She's so stupid she's bragging in the comments about how she "gets her shit for nothing from Jimmy," from what I could piece together from the comments, I think she's stealing his groceries for him in exchange for her fix, and she's also stealing from us and then refunding for the gift cards, which she's probably giving to him too in exchange for a hit. I tracked the gift cards and they are being used to buy gas..., petrol as you Aussies call it," I surmised.

"How do you track where the gift cards are being used? Is there a way to get exact dates and times Eliza, because you could be on to something bigger than just the wallets," Matthew sounded intrigued.

"Yes, I already have all that information too, it's all date and time stamped with the location. Whoever is using them is pretty habitual, it's mostly always on a Saturday night at either one of these two gas stations." I pointed to two addresses in my

265

notebook. "I also called a few of my Loss Prevention contacts in the grocery stores, and they are going to check their frequent refunder lists to see if they can link her to any other gift cards there.

"Wow, you really did your homework huh?" Matthew looked impressed.

"Oh, it gets better..., so because it's a sister company, I was able to get the gas stations to pull up the footage, they have it all on a flash drive and I'm actually meeting with their LP guy tomorrow to pick it up, but from what he told me, it's the same car. A male puts the gas in, and the female pays, and yes..., before you ask, we do have the license plate information," I grinned. "As for Sherry, I have enough footage of her stealing from us, and I have footage of all the refunds, she's clearly not the brightest crayon in the box, so I'm sure if you press her hard enough, she will confess and it should be a pretty easy case," I concluded.

"Ok.., let's get this show on the road shall we," Matthew grinned as he entered the room.

Twenty minutes later, Sherry had admitted to everything, she even confirmed my suspicions of stealing her drug dealers shopping list for him each week. Matthew had called her bluff, telling her he knew all about Jimmy, and that she was looking at doing some serious time, and she needed to start talking, and talk she did..., Sherry would've sold her own mother down the river if she thought it would help her cause, so she had zero hesitation in throwing Jimmy and his wife under the proverbial bus!

Before Sherry was even taken to the watch-house, Matthew had put the call through to the drug squad, who promptly organized a raid.

***

"So Mrs moneybags, Roman tells me you guys just bought a few pinball machines for the barn, when can I come over for a play?" Matthew grinned at me as he headed for the door.

"I'll check with Roman, he's off this weekend I think, you could come then and sleep over, just don't forget your toothbrush," I laughed, "now get outta here, I have some serious work to do..., on Facebook," I poked my tongue out at him.

CHAPTER 29
AN INSIDE JOB

One of the hardest tasks of being a Loss Prevention Officer is the internal investigations. Not only are they time consuming, but they are much harder to prove. When you apprehend a regular shoplifter, they always have the property on them, but with staff, most of the time you are dealing with the offense after the event has passed, sometimes there is little or even no footage and a lot of hearsay. Sometimes it's the people that you least expect that are caught stealing. Someone that you've respected and admired, worked side by side with that bites the hand that feeds them.

In retail we are told that statistically, half of the theft is internal, so you'd think I'd be less surprised when I'm called in to interview and subsequently terminate a staff member that I have a close, professional relationship with. Mostly though, it was new or casual staff, with figures spiking particularly at Christmas, by those helping themselves to a little Christmas bonus, be it stock or money. But sometimes, and much to my horror, I'd find myself across the table from someone who I thought was a friend, such was the case with manager Stacy Greer.

Stacy 43, was an administrative business manager, over the past six months she had confided in me about her broken down marriage. Her husband had been screwing his secretary for the better part of a year, and had recently left Stacy for the girl, who was 20 years their junior.

Stacy had really let herself go, she was in desperate need of a makeover in every aspect of her life, but it would take more than a cut and color and new wardrobe to pull her up out of the hole she found herself in now.

She had worried about how she was going to find her feet financially, and was barely treading water with legal bills and trying to pay her half of the mortgage. Unfortunately for Stacy, she had made the foolish decision of subsidizing her now single income with the help of the company's safe.

$45,000 to be exact! A figure that even Stacy herself was shocked at when I revealed it to her.

I was grateful that once confronted, Stacy had enough respect for me and herself, to admit to the theft and not try to make excuses or lie about her actions. I had hoped that it would play out this way, after all, I had caught her on the tiny camera we'd installed in the safe, stuffing money into her bra, and attempting to fudge the end of day cash count.

It made me sick to my stomach to think that the meals she'd eaten right in front of me when we'd had lunch together, were probably bought with stolen money.

"I didn't think it was that much money Eliza, just a few hundred here and there, I was going to put it back once the house sold," Stacy cried, bewildered at her own actions.

I honestly didn't know what to say, Stacy of all people knew exactly how I felt about thieves, and how quickly I wiped any staff member who thought they were owed more than they were entitled to. I knew this would be the last time I dealt directly with Stacy, and as much as I felt for her situation it was no excuse for her to do what she did.

***

What made me more angry about the whole thing, was that I'd even offered to lend her some money until her house sold. But she had refused my help, saying she was too proud to borrow money from me, I couldn't wrap my head around how she could then just steal it?

As we sat in silence waiting for the police to arrive, I pondered the past week's events.

It had been brought to my attention by the store manager that there was money consistently missing, at first we had suspected the weekend cash office clerk. Simon and I had gone in after hours and installed two hidden cameras in the cash office. The one in the safe, and one above the counter that the staff used to count the daily takings.

I'd sourced the cameras from my old supplier in Vegas, the ones that Simon had been using were huge and outdated. I wondered how they had ever caught anyone using them, you'd have to be completely blind to miss them! The actual camera was no bigger than a biro, and had motion sensors built-in to only record when there was movement detected and could hold up to 100 hours of footage.

I'd suggested to the store manager that we conduct a cash count prior to the cash office clerk and Stacy doing theirs, and then again afterward. We'd be able to pinpoint a more accurate timeline of events and narrow down the suspect list.

After just two days, we'd found a cash shortage. I downloaded the footage and spent the next few hours watching the usual goings on in the cash office, managers came and went, people picked wedgies out of their bums, and I'd even seen a married manager making out with the cash office clerk. Then, at 6:05 pm, Stacy Greer appeared, she did a cash count, and then without batting so much as an eyelid, she took $500 and stuffed it into her bra. She sat at the computer, adjusting the figures on the screen, logged off and left.

Initially, I couldn't believe what I'd seen, and rewound the footage watching it over and over in total shock. Stupid bloody bitch! Unfuckenbelievable! I fumed.

I'd made myself a double shot coffee, and was watching it for the hundredth time when Roman came in behind me and looked at the screen.

"Isn't she the one you were having coffee with in the office last week when I came by to say hi?" Roman asked pointing at Stacy on the screen.

"Yes, the one whose husband left her for the barbie doll," I answered quietly.

It always hit me hard when I knew I would be terminating a staff member's employment, especially when I'd considered them a friend. But that was the nature of the job and the reason we were strongly discouraged from interacting with staff outside of work. I'd always been mindful of that, and other than the Loss Prevention team I didn't socialize with staff, but working closely with them eight to ten hours a day, unless you were a robot or sociopath how could you not form friendships and alliances with these people?

I knew I'd have to keep up the facade of a friend, at least until I had a full confession, but then Stacy would see me in action, and understand the gravity of the situation upon her. I had to switch off my emotions, and paint on a work face. But it really was a bitter pill to swallow, and I cursed Stacy for putting me in this position.

I heard the police radio, and the familiar sound of jangling utility belts, and was immediately snapped back to reality.

As soon as Senior Constable Dan Simpson and Senior Constable Matilda Berry entered the room, Stacy Greer started bawling. A week ago I'd have been out of my chair and comforting this woman, now I felt nothing but anger and annoyance, as she got louder and louder with her gut-wrenching sobs.

***

Throwing a box of tissues on to the table, I left the room with S/C Simpson to explain what had happened.

Stacy Greer was arrested and charged with 'stealing as a public servant' and made to do the walk of shame past the staff, and out of the store to the police car outside. As she was leaving the office Stacy made a final attempt to speak to me;

"I know I've let you down Eliza, I'm sorry, keep in touch hey," She sobbed incoherently.

I couldn't even bring myself to look up from the pile of paperwork that her greediness had created. Deep down she would already know that she had been wiped, that any form of friendship I'd extended to her was now gone.

Staff attempted to approach me and ask what happened, and..., as much as I wanted to make an example of Stacy..., of any staff member who is caught stealing, we are practically forbidden to share any of those details. Instead, I gave a well-rehearsed and polished statement;

"Obviously if police attend, and Loss Prevention are present, and a staff member is then escorted from the store by them, then it's obvious what has happened, if you steal, you will be caught, and you will be terminated and charged, blah blah blah!"

I'd given the same spiel to at least six staff members in an hour. I was drained. I closed the office door to prevent any further intrusion. A few hours later I'd finished my investigation, compiled all the footage and reports and was ready to head home.

With the roof open on my mustang I drove home with the cool breeze on my face, and I cried. My anger had subsided, and I now felt somewhat sorry for Stacy. I knew no matter how long I was in this line of work, I'd never really get used to these inside jobs.

I'd pulled myself together and called Simon to let him know the outcome.

"Hey Simon, it's Eliza..., she confessed to everything. The police have the footage and reports, HR terminated her immediately and her court date is next month, I'll put the full report online tomorrow, but it came out to a little over 45k," I told him.

"WOW, well done, hey listen, when you get done with that one there's another job I need you to do for me..., there's a female manager Margie Rudd, who's been with the company for a very long time, apparently she is stealing vitamins and stock from health and beauty, and has been marking down or writing off stock for some of the younger staff. Given that you don't know her and haven't worked in this particular store, I'm going to send you and

Alexis up the coast to do the investigation. If you get enough on her let me know and you can do the interview and termination. But Eliza..., tread carefully please because the store manager Michael Giles is suspecting there is something going on with Margie's health and it could be the reason she is stealing," Simon finished.

"Ok, I'll call the manager tomorrow and find out her roster and we can go from there," I replied.

Hanging up the phone my heart felt a little heavier..., I knew there was an underlying reason why Simon wasn't doing this job himself, and I suspected that he had some kind of history with Margie and didn't want to do this one himself.

The next Thursday, Alexis and I packed overnight bags and headed up the coast to Maroochydore, Simon was going to organize us a hotel, but I thought I'd treat Alexis and I to something a little more fancy and we booked a two bedroom apartment by the water. We'd decided to extend our stay into the weekend and Roman and Thomas were going to drive up and meet us on Friday night.

***

We reported to Michael Giles on Thursday mid-morning and he filled us in on the peculiar behavior of Margie Rudd. She had been with the company since she was 17 years old and was now in her very late 60's. She had actually been a manager in one of the stores that Simon had worked in, and had at one point tried her hand at being a Loss Prevention Officer. She'd been trained by Simon and back in the day was apparently very good. But after a year, and a few very nasty apprehensions, she'd gone back into stores as a manager and was well respected by all that knew her. Which is why Michael had taken as long as he had in reporting her to Simon, and which was obviously why Simon hadn't wanted to conduct the investigation or do the interview himself.

Alexis and I watched the footage that Michael had saved, and I ran the mark down and write off reports and it was confirmed that Margie was indeed stealing stock as well as conducting fraudulent markdowns and writing off stock for staff.

All up there were six staff members involved, which meant that there was no way Alexis and I would be having the weekend off..., in fact this could get dragged out into the next week.

I called Simon and gave him the updates, he told me that I'd need to handle things because he was going to Sydney for a conference.

I messaged Roman;

Hey hunna, it looks like this thing is more involved than I first thought, both Alexis and I may be working the whole weekend, give me a call tonight ok xo

I began writing up the interview sheets, compiling footage and Alexis had gone to pick up coffee. I was a little shocked when a few minutes later she returned with one of the staff members we were going to be interviewing the next day.

"As I said outside the store, I'm the LPO, so anything you left the store without paying for, put it on the table," Alexis ordered.

Sandy Smith, 21, removed four tins of baby formula from her bag and a packet of false nails.

"Alexis, can I speak with you outside for a minute," I stood up and left Sandy in the room with Michael. "You know who she is right?" I asked.

"No..., should I?" Alexis responded.

"That's Sandy Smith, one of the staff we are supposed to be talking to tomorrow...," I paused, "it looks like we will have to speak to Margie today now too. Possibly even a few of the night staff who are involved if we can get them to come in. Sandy is likely to tell everyone they've been caught out, and I don't want any of them resigning before we speak to them about it."

"Fuck..., sorry Eliza, I just saw her shoving the formula in her bag and then leaving the store so I grabbed her," Alexis rubbed her forehead.

"It's all good, at least we have something else on her now, she can't deny this can she," I said.

We entered the room, and I introduced myself as the Loss Prevention Investigator and within twenty minutes Sandy had confessed to her part, and also given up the names of the other staff involved. I knew then she wouldn't be telling anyone she'd been caught, because she'd have to tell them that she had snitched on them too. Michael called the local police beat and within minutes Senior Constable Steve Salt arrived, I stepped outside the room with him and told him that we were planning on interviewing and terminating six staff in total.

He said he'd need to call the station to see if they could have a few plain clothes officers come and assist with the paper work. In the meantime he arrested and charged Sandy, and going against our usual protocol, Sandy was escorted out the back door. The last thing we needed was for staff to see her doing the walk of shame and it spooking our other targets.

***

We were almost ready to bring Margie in when S/C Salt came back and asked to speak to me privately.

"Do you or your colleague know Sandy Smith outside of work hours?" S/C Salt asked.

"No..., I certainly don't and I'm quite sure that Alexis doesn't either..., why?" I asked puzzled.

"Look, she's claiming that your colleague is having sexual relations with her long term boyfriend, that you knew about it, and that this whole thing is a set up to get her in trouble so that your colleague can take her man," S/C Salt was struggling to keep a straight face.

I knew he knew it was all bullshit, but I was genuinely shocked..., especially because Sandy had seemed very contrite and compliant.

"WHAT?!?!?! That is the most ridiculous thing I've heard in a long time," I laughed at how stupid it sounded.

"She's with the plain clothes crew now and one of the officer's is talking to her about the severity of making false accusations, so let's hope she doesn't want to make a complaint and go full brief, I don't believe it, and I'm certain a judge won't either, but please make sure you guys have all the footage and put together a solid report," S/C Salt advised.

I told him we were going to be bringing Margie Rudd in next and he seemed quite shocked, he knew Margie quite well and agreed that there could very well be something medical going on with her because it was completely out of character. He left and I went back into the office.

"So apparently you're a home wrecking whore who's sleeping with Sandy's man..., what have you got to say for yourself Lex?" I laughed.

"What the fuck? Are you serious? Oh My God..., she really said that? I don't even know what to say?" Alexis shook her head.

Before we could discuss it any further Michael escorted Margie into the office. Margie was around 5ft 6, thin, with grey hair. Her dull blue eyes looked lifeless, and as she walked toward me I could see her hands were shaking, but not from fear..., she definitely looked ill.

"Hi Mrs Rudd, I'm Eliza and I'm with the Loss Prevention department, can you take a seat so we can have a talk?" I asked, pulling a chair out for her.

Margie looked confused as she sat on the chair, but as we began talking and I explained to her why we were here today she began to cry.

"I'm sorry..., I was just trying to help some of these young kids you know? It's like I can't help myself, it doesn't make any sense to you I'm sure, sometimes it doesn't even make any sense to me," Margie paused for at least 20 seconds, "Markus are we having a meeting today? who are these lovely ladies?" She asked grinning at Alexis and I.

We had no idea who Markus was, we could only assume she meant to say Michael. I looked at Michael, he put his head down, I knew he felt terrible that we were even here, but it was clear to me in that moment, that there was something wrong with Margie.

"Margie are you feeling ok? When was the last time you saw a Doctor?" I asked, I noticed her hands were trembling even more now.

"Well Doug..., that's my boyfriend, he took me one day to see one, are you a Doctor love?" Margie asked me.

"Would you like me to get you a coffee or tea Margie," I asked not answering her question.

Regardless of what she had stolen, I didn't feel right interviewing her so suspended the interview.

I left Margie with Alexis while I spoke to Michael, I told him that he should call her husband to see what was going on with her. I needed to call Simon and let him know that I didn't feel comfortable interviewing her until she had some type of medical clearance. After Michael spoke with Doug we found out that Margie had just been diagnosed with an aggressive brain tumor and was going to be seeing the specialist the next week. Apparently her good days were few and far between, and Doug realized he should have spoken to Michael about it, but he was still trying to deal with it all himself. Margie had had breast cancer, and survived that..., but from what their Doctor told them when they got these results, her future wasn't looking good. We asked Doug to come and take Margie home. I left a voicemail for Simon regarding the situation, and we decided not to call the night staff in and to call it a day.

The next day we interviewed the remaining four staff, they all admitted to stealing stock as well as using Margie's manager numbers to mark down or write off stock. They were all terminated and charged with stealing.

Sandy withdrew her bogus complaint about Alexis, and had further admitted to stealing and selling baby formula to students at her university who were then sending it to China.

Simon had decided to let her regional manager and HR handle Margie, I was thankful for that outcome..., because to be honest, I really didn't think I had it in me to terminate a terminally ill staff member.

By Friday night, I just wanted to go home..., to my own bed, to Roman. I called Georgia and asked if her and Mark wanted to drive up and take our room. They had jumped at the opportunity to get away. So I packed my bag and hit the highway for the long solo drive home.

CHAPTER 30
BLOOPER REEL

Viewing CCTV was usually a long, boring and arduous task but it was totally worth it when you stumbled across something funny, or a ridiculously stupid attempt at stealing.

I had been told by Madison on the door, that she had stopped a male who was trying to exit with a very poorly concealed DVD player down the back of his pants.

She couldn't remember the day or time, but thankfully with her shifts only being four hours long, it wasn't hard to find. I'd learned to ask the same series of questions which usually helped with a process of elimination;

Did you speak to anyone about this?

If yes then who?

Do you recall if you'd had a break yet, who covered for you etc? This method had saved me hours, actually in some cases, days of wasted time searching for an event.

I found Mr. X within an hour of reviewing CCTV, he strutted into home entertainment and grabbed the display DVD player that hadn't been secured to the shelf, he then pulled the back of his pants out and shoved the DVD player down the back, pulling his long shirt down to cover it.

As he bent down to pick up his backpack, the shirt rode up, exposing the DVD player to anyone walking behind him. I sat looking at the footage, following him on the cameras, shaking my head and laughing at the reactions of other shoppers as they walked behind him.

Some people! I laughed to myself.

He approached the door and opened his backpack (that he was wearing on the front) he pushed it under Madison's nose, and was sidestepping awkwardly, obviously not wanting her to see him from behind.

Madison (or hawk eyes as I was now calling her) knew something was amiss, she walked around behind him, and I could see the look of surprise on her face when she realized he had an entire DVD player down his pants.

I only wish the CCTV had sound so I could've heard the exchange. Mr. X removed the DVD player and tried to give it to Madison, who promptly took a giant step backward and pointed at the floor. Mr. X bent down slowly, placed the DVD player onto the floor, and ran out of the store. I watched the footage several times, wondering how on earth he thought he was going to get away with it in the first place?

Reading the log book one morning, Alexis and Georgia had left a note for me to look at some footage in the motoring and clothing sections, they were very specific about the times, but gave no clue as to who I should be looking for.

I found the footage and promptly burst out laughing as I saw Alexis and Georgia dancing up and down the aisle. They had borrowed a few mannequins from a display, and were waltzing up a storm until a manager had caught them. Judging by their shoulder shrugging and pointing, they were denying any knowledge of how the mannequins had gotten there. I flicked between camera's following them back to apparel.

I noticed that one of the mannequins was now missing an arm, I clicked to an overview of the camera's and saw Alexis crouching down on one side of a clothing rack.

A young staff member was on the other side tidying the clothes. Alexis pushed the arm through the rack and touched the poor girl's hand, causing her to jump back, and judging by her facial expression scream.

I burst out laughing at her reaction, and at Alexis and Georgia who were practically rolling about on the floor. They repeated this several times to different staff members, all of whom got the fright of their life. It were pranks like this, that kept us from going completely insane on the job.

Perhaps the most disturbing footage I viewed was of a male who would pleasure himself underneath the camera in the garden section, I'm sure he knew that there was a chance he'd be caught, which obviously gave him a thrill. He'd covered his face with a mask, but was clearly too stupid to realize that the entire center had cameras, so we had a perfect mug shot of his face, but he remained unidentified for quite some time. One Thursday late shift the store I was working in was completely dead..., so I thought I'd check out the BONDS and Nike line to make sure they were all hard tagged, I noticed a rack of women's BONDS underwear wasn't, so I took it to the young girl Sasha in the fitting rooms. She appeared quite shy, and very nervous in my presence, but not in a dodgy way..., some staff had very little interaction with us and were just intimidated by our role. As I put the stock on the bench Santa baby began to play in the store. I knew all the words by heart and even had a routine from a performance back in college. I walked past Sasha and into a cubicle pulling the curtain closed. As I ripped it open and burst into song Sasha's face was priceless, she looked a little shocked but soon joined in dancing and singing with me. As the song finished I snapped back into my role and acted like the entire thing hadn't happened.

It was definitely an ice breaker, and I knew that by showing Sasha I was 'human' she would not only feel comfortable around me, but would hopefully also trust me to come to me about any issues. A few weeks later I was walking past the fitting rooms when Sasha asked if she could speak to me,

"Hey Eliza, it's not really a loss prevention thing but Ummm, there is a guy who is Ummm getting himself off in the men's change rooms. Natalia the other girl who works in here has had it happen when she's been in here too..., we call him Jizzem Joe" She giggled nervously, "it's kind of creepy because he kind of peeks out of the curtain when he's doing it," Sasha finished.

"Have you told anyone about this Sasha?" I asked.

"No..., because all the managers in this store are men and well..., it's kind of embarrassing," Sasha grimaced.

Sasha gave me a description and I was pretty confident that it was the same guy from the garden shop, I showed her several CCTV stills of various men, including the headshot that center security had given me of the 'garden shop wanker' and she identified him immediately.

"I'm going to go speak with the police beat about this, but the very next time he comes in, can you or whoever is in here please call the police, and tell them "Joe is here" and they will come right down and deal with him ok?" I told her.

The next day Jizzem Joe made an appearance, the call was put through to the police beat and he was literally caught in the act with his pants down.

Around Christmas time there was always a spike in shop stealing incidents, as well as an increase in fire door breakouts. After four break outs in just two days, (at the same store by the same people) the manager had new doors fitted that would only open in the event of a fire. One of the offenders was almost knocked unconscious as he ran at the door which failed to open. He'd bounced off the door, slipped backward and hit his head on the concrete floor, after a few seconds he got up, rubbed his head, and once he realized he couldn't get out, he'd left the store empty-handed, and probably with a concussion.

Then there was the guy who used one of our fishing knives to cut open a packet, he slipped and stabbed himself right through his leg. I'd been walking the floor when I noticed a pool of blood in the fishing aisle, it trailed off onto the carpeted area and stopped. So I went to view the CCTV to see what had happened, thankfully I did, because the male was passed out in a cubicle in the men's restroom and had to be rushed to the hospital. He clearly wasn't appreciative of the help we'd given him, because a few weeks later he returned, and right under the same camera in fishing, he dropped his pants and shit on the floor, gave the middle finger to the camera, pulled his pants up and left. I didn't know whether to be more disgusted by what he'd done, or the fact he hadn't even wiped his ass!

From punch-ups, to very intimate makeups, you can be sure that CCTV captures it all.

CHAPTER 31
BOYS AND THEIR TOYS

"I don't understand how our shrinkage in toys can be so high, how are they even getting this stuff out of my store?" Marvin Bird the store manager, looked puzzled at the figures I had just put in front of him on his desk.

"Well, that's what I'm here to find out Marvin, I'm going to hang around the toy department today, and have organized for the other LPO's to be here for the next few weeks. So hopefully we can shed some light on this and get your figures down," I replied.

Heading to the toy department I wandered the aisles for well over three hours, when I overheard two little voices in the next aisle.

"I think we should pinch this one Ty, we already got that one last week," one of the voices said.

"Yeah, but then we can both have one if we get this one," the other voice whined.

As I moved to the end of the aisle, I was a little shocked to see two dark-haired little boys, who I guessed would be only about six or seven years old. As I watched and listened to them, I learned that they had quite a selection of the newest transformers and Lego kits all courtesy of our store, the biggest question was how were they getting these items out unnoticed?

I watched the two boys fill their pockets with matchbox cars, and also select a hot wheels race track and a monster truck. The boxes were almost as big as they were. I honestly didn't know whether to laugh or cry at the sad story unfolding before me.

"Hey, I'm pretty sure I've found your culprits, meet me at the front of the store," I told Marvin on the phone.

The two boys walked to the front of the store, and put the boxes on the floor, they pushed them through an empty register. They then went back into the store, and shoved a bottle of coke and packet of chips down their pants and walked out the front door. As they headed back to the empty register to pick up the toys, I saw Marvin watching them, his mouth agape. I approached the two boys outside with Marvin, and told them they had to come back to the store with me.

Harry and Tyson Barclay were brothers, I was right in guessing that they were six and seven and a half years of age, and came from a very dysfunctional home.

"Our Mum drops us off at the park in the morning, and we have to stay there until dark time, but we get bored on the swings so we come in here to get some toys to play with," six-year-old Harry told me.

"Yeah, but sometimes we leave the toys at the park near the slides or in the bushes, but when we go back someone stole them so we come and get some more," Tyson added.

Both of the boys were in desperate need of a bath, their little faces were grubby and their clothes were filthy. Their hair looked like it hadn't been washed or brushed in a very long time, and I wondered whether the scratching they were both doing, was because it was so filthy or if they had head lice. Both boys had bruised up legs, and Harry had the tell-tale signs of a fading black eye. Some people didn't deserve the privilege of having children, this was certainly the case with their mother, Kathy Barclay. I called the child protection unit and spoke with Detective Luke Case.

"Hmmm yes, I know Tyson and Harry quite well, poor kids. I will be there soon," He said.

"Let's play a game of eye spy for a bit," I suggested as I hung up the phone.

Detective Luke Case and S/C Sarah Bartowski arrived, and I quietly asked if I could give the boys something to eat. Luke nodded.

"Would you boys like some lunch? I made too much today," I asked them.

"Yeah, we are starving," Tyson declared.

I gave the boys each a half of my chicken and salad wrap, and left Marvin to dish out the chocolate cake that I'd brought in for him and I to share over coffee. Luke and I left the room, and I

293

explained that we had been losing almost $1000 in toys each weekend. While I wasn't convinced that the two boys were responsible for *all* of that figure, from what they had told me, it would certainly be close. I'd looked at CCTV on several occasions, but had overlooked the boys because I had been looking for adults.

"Their Mum is a junkie and a prostitute, we are aware that she is leaving the boys alone on the weekends, but we weren't sure where. She is seeing men in her home, and often leaves them home alone at night to go get her fix. There have been several reports of violence in the home, on both her and the boys. Surely by now there's enough to get them put into foster care. I'll call their case worker and have her come to the station," Luke rubbed his forehead in frustration.

"Those poor kids, you can see how malnourished they are. They both need a bloody good bath, and I wouldn't be surprised if they both have headlice, because they haven't stopped scratching their heads," I said sadly.

All I could think of was how unfair it was that there were people like myself and Roman, who'd give anything to just have one baby but couldn't. And women like Kathy and even Bethany, had kids but couldn't give two shits about them, worse, they beat them..., and or allowed their blow in boyfriends to do so too. I wanted to take these little boys home with me, to give them the love they deserved. The sad fact was, there were so many children like

Harry and Tyson who were being dragged up instead of raised properly. It got me thinking that maybe Roman and I should consider becoming foster parents.

Detective Luke Case and S/C Sarah Bartowski left with Tyson and Harry Barclay, and I could only hope that the authorities would finally step in and do something to help these little boys before it was too late.

CHAPTER 32
BLURRED LINES

A boring part of being an LPO is the security checks we are required to conduct each week. Physically counting unprotected, unsecured and untagged stock, we compile a report and send it to the regional office. I was minding my own business in the fishing department, counting the rods and reels when an old man came up beside me.

"You have no idea what you're looking for do you?" he asked. "Where are you going fishing love? I will make sure you get the right set up."

"Oh I'm ok, I'm just looking," I replied smiling, hoping that would be a good enough answer for him to leave me alone.

"Are you looking for yourself or for a man?" He persisted.

The banter continued back and forth, until he had convinced me that I really must buy a particular rod and reel, tackle box, lures, squid jigs (basically something from the entire fishing department!) The funny thing was, I'd never fished in my life, but he was so enthusiastic and knowledgeable about it, that for a moment, I forgot what I was doing in the first place, and was now considering buying a bloody boat!

"You should apply for a job here," I joked as I left the aisle, arms laden with fishing gear, rod under my arm and pulling the roll along tackle bag that was now full of fishing shit I knew I would probably never use.

"Want me to help you carry all that to the checkout?" he asked as I walked away.

"No thank you, I will get a shopping cart, I have a bit more shopping to do first," I lied, "but thank you so much."

As I headed to the trolley bay I passed Carlene Brown, an offender I recognized from a bulletin. Carlene was a big lady, heavily tattooed and judging by the smell, at least a pack day smoker. I doubled back and almost bumped into her as I exited an aisle. The large rod I was trying to juggle had almost poked her in the face, and she shot me a filthy look.

"Watch out for fuck's sake!" she growled as she walked past.

CRAP! She had seen me with all the fishing gear so I had no choice but to follow her around with it all now. I mumbled a sorry, and walked over to a price scanner pretending to check prices.

Carlene headed into the DVD section and I saw her select at least a dozen DVDs and place them on the top of the hood of the stroller she was pushing. She met up with Shawn Bugg, (who I also recognized from the bulletin) scrawny looking with a blonde mullet he looked like he had time warped from the 80's. Several minutes later they had also selected a few external hard drives and went to the cleaning section. I followed behind them (my arms feeling as though they would drop off from the weight of the fishing gear) I kept almost poking other customers with the rod as I attempted to keep it from bobbing up above the aisle. Carlene removed a few post-it bags from the bottom of the stroller, and Shawn began stuffing the DVDs and hard drives in them.

Sneaky bastards, I haven't seen this method of concealment before, I thought as I called the police.

"Hey, it's Eliza, I need you..., now," I whispered into the phone.

"Oh really, that kinda sounds like a song..., is it a quarter after one, are you a little drunk?" S/C Rhodes whispered back, quoting a line from a Lady Antebellum song. "What will we tell Roman?"

"Just Shut up and get here," I whispered trying not to laugh, he really was incorrigible. Roman had warned me Matthew was a huge flirt, and with his rugged good looks, it didn't surprise me that women often drooled over him, add the uniform and it was a dangerous combination. I guessed that he was responsible for more than a few broken hearts.

"Ok, I'm coming," Matthew whispered back. He was laughing as I hung up.

Carlene and Shawn headed back to the door where Betty Ku stood, they stopped briefly showing the stroller and asked for directions to the post office. I could see Betty looked suspicious, but there wasn't much she could do. As they left I headed toward the door, dumping the fishing gear by her as I walked out.

"Betty, call Cole and tell him to come find me, oh..., and keep all that stuff for me will you, coz I'm going to buy it later," I called out as I walked quickly after the offenders.

I followed them down the mall until I saw S/C Rhodes approaching, right on queue Carlene poked Shawn and they swapped sides of the mall in an attempt to avoid any kind of interaction with police. Cole arrived, and I stepped in front of them and introduced myself.

"Fuck off Barbie or I'll snap you in two and rip your pretty little face apart," Carlene snarled at me.

"I'd like to see you try you washed up whale," I scolded fiercely, "that would require effort, and by the looks of you, the only exercise you get is flapping your fat trap!"

Matthew and Cole burst out laughing.

SHIT! What the hell was wrong with me? It was like sometimes I had no filter and my mouth reacted before my brain.

"Well, it looks like you've been told. Now you two..., we are going to take a stroll to the police beat, any funny business and you'll both be going to lock up, are we clear?" Matthew said sternly.

Carlene protested all the way, saying she had to feed her baby, and had a doctor's appointment. I had Cole bring down two-lifetime banning notices to serve on them. As he finished explaining the conditions he put the form down for Carlene to sign.

"I don't want to shop in your poxy fucken shop anyway," Carlene cleared her throat and spat on the banning notice and pushed it away, refusing to sign it.

"Let's get a few things straight big mouth, first..., you *steal* not *shop,* and second, now you have your very own letter telling you that you CAN'T come in," I grinned maliciously at Carlene. "Now..., sign below your spit, and you can put that one in your bag."

Matthew bit his lips together trying not to laugh, and Cole who couldn't contain his grin, left to go back to the store.

Christ, I was in a mood today, people like Carlene pissed me off, all talk and no action, she believed that her size and big mouth were enough to intimidate people. The pair were charged and promptly released. As I went through the stock with Matthew, I could sense him looking at me. I was photographing the stock on the table when I noticed the DVD Dumb and Dumber in the pile,

***

"How fitting," I smirked, amused at the irony.

"You're in the wrong job Lize, you should be a comedian," Matthew laughed playfully squeezing my shoulder, his hand lingered for longer than it should've, and as I stepped away his fingertips ran down my arm.

What the fuck is he doing? My mind was reeling.

"Roman really is a lucky guy you know, sometimes I wonder what would've happened if we had met before..." he began,

"Matthew, stop!" I cut in, "look..., I am flattered that you think so highly of me, but please do not go there, don't say or do something that you can't take back. Roman respects you, you're his best mate. I don't know why you seem to have me up on this pedestal like I'm some sort of exotic creature..., or saint, but you shouldn't. I'm not sure what you know about me, but before I met Roman..., well..., when I was in Vegas, I was not really a decent person. I'd probably have fucked you and Roman, heck maybe even at the same time if the opportunity presented, then fucked you off and moved on. Coming here, I turned my life around, and Roman makes me want to be the best person I can truly be, I love him with all my heart, so please, please don't make it awkward between us for fuck's sake," I pleaded.

Once the words were out, I regretted them. Seriously, what the fuck was wrong with me? Why had I just told him all that?

"Shit, I'm sorry, I wasn't trying anything on you, I would never do that, I don't know what I was thinking," Matthew was tripping over his words now.

"Clearly you weren't thinking, well not with the right head anyway," I laughed punching him lightly on the arm, attempting to ease the awkwardness that now hung in the air.

"He's always thinking with the wrong head, that's always been his problem," Roman looked irritated.

Shit..., how long had he been there? As usual, it was as if he could read my mind.

"Don't mind me, I let myself in. It's a good thing you're a loyal lady my love, or I'd be kicking some major arse right now," Roman shot a look at Matthew before putting an arm around my waist, and kissing the top of my head.

"Mate..., I'm sorry..., I didn't mean anything by it, I wasn't trying to hit on your wife..., I, I just lost my head for a minute there," Matthew stammered. He knew he'd fucked up.

"Even if I can't trust you..., my own best mate..., I can trust Eliza. I do get where you're coming from, she *is* fucken amazing, which is why I was determined to be with her in the first place, *and* the reason she's my wife. I can't stop you or anyone from looking..., hell, I would too, but that better be it, are we clear?" Roman spoke firmly to Matthew.

"Crystal, sorry man," Matthew answered contritely.

The room was eerily silent, and I now completely understood the saying 'You could cut the air with a knife' wow this was awkward.

"I thought I'd come surprise you with coffee on my way to work, Cole said you two were down here so I grabbed us all one," Roman spoke first, trying to change the atmosphere of the room.

"Thanks babes," I smiled, taking the coffee.

"Yeah..., thanks babe," Matthew chimed in.

We all laughed. I filled Roman in on the arrest, and while I still felt a little awkward, I hoped that Matthew had learned a very valuable lesson about blurred lines, and I was certain that he would never confuse, or cross them again with me.

"Do you have time to walk me back to the store before you go to work?" I asked Roman as I packed up the stock.

"Yes, I'm parked down that end anyway so let's go," he replied.

"I'll drop a statement and footage down later," I said to Matthew as we left the police beat.

**

"You know I love you so much more right now babes," Roman said as we walked along, "Casanova in there could charm the knickers off a nun," he laughed.

"Well, as you are aware dear husband, I'm not in the habit, pardon the pun..., of wearing knickers, but honestly babes, you have nothing to worry about ever, because the only person I'm interested in being charmed by, is you," I winked at Roman.

"I can totally understand the attraction Lize, you have a wicked sense of humor, and you don't know how beautiful you are, which is a massive turn on. I don't know what the fuck he was thinking, or what he thought was going to happen, but I'll be having another conversation with Roady, because today he over stepped and I'm not having it," Roman stated, looking annoyed.

"Hello Mr police man," A little boy called out to Roman.

"Hey mate, have you been a good boy for mummy?" Roman asked as he crouched down to speak to the little boy. The mother adjusted her top pushing her boobs up, trying to get Roman's attention as I stood back amused.

"Yes, umm well, I was a bit naughty before, but I'm being a good boy now," he said truthfully.

Roman pulled a sticker from his top pocket and handed it to the boy, scruffing the top of his head as he stood up.

"Here you go then buddy, that's for telling the truth..., bye," He waved to the little boy as we walked away.

"Do I get a sticker for behaving, and being honest too?" I joked as we continued down the mall.

"Well, I think you were a little too honest if I'm being honest..., Lize, you don't owe anyone any explanations about your past. It really is no one's business, I don't care that you told Roady all that, but you didn't have to," Roman pulled me into a staff only corridor and kissed me, brushing the hair from my face he pulled a sticker from his top pocket.

"I know, I can't believe I even said what I did..., I guess I just didn't want him to keep thinking I'm so perfect when I'm not, no one is," I smiled weakly.

"You might not be perfect, but you're perfect for me," Roman grinned, kissed my lips and then pulled a sticker from his pocket.

"So.., you can have this..., or..., I was going to offer you something else," He said mysteriously.

"Oh yeah, what?" I asked inquisitively.

"How would you feel about us getting a puppy? One of the guys at work has these gorgeous Siberian Huskies that were rescued from a backyard breeder. He fosters dogs, and is looking to rehome them in a few weeks. I thought we could get one," Romans grin matched the one that was spreading across my face.

"Seriously? Yes!" I squealed with delight.

We walked back to the store to return the stock, I picked up the fishing gear and headed to the registers.

"Ummm what is all this?" Roman asked looking puzzled.

"It's a long story," I laughed, "I'll fill you in later."

We walked to Roman's car, while he loaded all the fishing equipment into the trunk I looked at the pictures of the puppies on his phone, we agreed to go choose one on the weekend. As I kissed him goodbye, I felt the familiar overwhelming rush of affection course through me, I held him tighter.

"I love you my wild..., unpredictable..., sassy..., sexy wifey," Roman kissed my lips with each word.

"I love you too, you're my everything," I blew him a kiss goodbye as he drove away.

CHAPTER 33
BANDIT

We had picked up the new addition to our family, and Roman and I had spent the better part of our long weekend building a kennel to go in the yard we'd had built for our boy. With a black mask across his eyes, and feisty personality we'd named him Bandit.

Roman had snuck him into our room and let him sleep on the bed the first night (instead of in the laundry room in his basket) and this was now a nightly occurrence. During the day he was in a doggy day care, but now the yard was complete with the kennel, we were going to start leaving him at home for a few hours until he was a little bigger. As Roman tightened the final screw, we heard the gate alarm sound, looking up we saw Liam's car coming quickly down the driveway.

"Something must be wrong, he never comes without calling first," Roman frowned.

I had a sinking feeling in my stomach, feeling my pockets I realized I'd left my cell phone inside.

"Dad's had a heart attack," Liam called out as he got out of the car, "we've been calling you both but it goes to message bank."

"I think both our cell phones are inside," I explained. I began to shake, memories of my own father's death flooded back.

"He's stable, and he's in good hands. I think they are going to run some tests and maybe operate, but we will know more later," Liam explained as he bent down to pat Bandit, who was jumping around excitedly at the new visitor.

"Does mum want us to come up to the hospital now?" Roman asked, the shock of the news was finally setting in.

"She said she will call me in a few hours once the Doctors have been, no point being up there now with them all poking around. He's a beauty Ro, what's his name?" Liam asked picking Bandit up.

"We called him Bandit," Roman answered, then added, "so dad will be ok then?"

I could sense he was still rattled by the news, and unsure whether he should just go to the hospital anyway.

"I'll go in and get our phones, Liam is right, there isn't much we can do right now, but if you want to go to the hospital anyway we can?" I suggested, trying to reassure Roman as well as myself.

"No..., I will wait for mum to call. Do you want to hang out here with us Liam?" Roman asked.

"Yeah, that would be good. While I'm here you may as well show me these new pinball machines you've been bragging about," Liam grinned.

"I'll meet you two in the barn, I'm just going to take a quick shower and I'll bring down some lunch," I said hugging Roman who still looked a little dazed.

"Ok babes, hey are you ok?" Roman asked concerned as he looked at me.

"Yeah, probably a little shocked..., I'm sure you are too," I hugged him close before I headed back to the house.

"C'mon Bandit," Liam called as the two brothers walked toward the barn.

An hour later, we hadn't heard from Jill, and we all decided that while there was nothing we could do to help, we could be there for support. So we made our way to the hospital to visit Phillip. He still looked a little gray, but the Doctors reassured us that with bed rest, and after the bypass he should be ok.

I insisted Jill and Liam spend the night at our house, I felt so relieved that Phillip was going to recover, daddy had been a few years younger when he'd had his heart attack and died.

I vowed to myself that I'd make sure we spent more time with the Beach family, we really only saw them every other month, or for special occasions.

Phillips heart attack had again reminded me just how fragile life was. You never truly know what is around the corner, and should not take it for granted that you can have a conversation or a moment with

311

someone at a later time. Because in the blink of an eye, your entire world can be ripped out from underneath you, and nothing is ever the same. We got back from the hospital late in the evening, Roman was in the barn having a drink with Liam, and Jill and I were sitting in the library talking over a cup of tea.

"Roman told me about your own father love, are you ok?" Jill asked with a concerned look on her face.

"Yes Mrs. B, I was a little rattled earlier, but I am fine, I'm sorry you weren't able to reach us right away, we were out in the yard with Bandit," I apologized.

"It's ok love, so a puppy hey? Not quite the pitter patter of tiny feet I thought you'd be getting. Roman said you two are considering fostering? You are going to keep trying for your *own* baby though aren't you?" Jill pried. But before I could even answer she continued, "I mean, why would you want to do that to yourselves? Look after someone else's children and then have them taken away again..., if you're still having trouble getting pregnant, I will ask my friend Barbara the name of the fertility specialist her daughter used." She finished.

I shifted uncomfortably in my chair, it really wasn't a conversation I felt my mother in law needed to be a part of..., or anyone for that matter. In fact, I was fed up with unsolicited advice from well-meaning people about how to get pregnant.

But given the current situation with her husband, I knew I'd need to tread lightly with my answer.

"We haven't ruled anything out or made any decisions yet," I answered bluntly.

"What does that mean? Personally I think that it would be a huge mistake for you both.." Jill began.

"Jill," I cut in, "I just said we haven't made any decisions yet, but I'm sure when we do that Roman will no doubt let you know."

Bandit scratched and whined at the door, giving me the perfect opportunity to avoid any further personal questions. I excused myself, telling Jill that I was going to take Bandit outside to pee, and then go to bed.

By the time I came back inside, Jill had gone to the guest room. I went to my bedroom and closed the door, changed into my Pj's and pulled Bandit into bed beside me. He laid down with his head nestled in the crook of my arm, and we fell asleep. The next morning I woke up to the playful sounds of a puppy, as I rolled over and looked on the floor, I saw Bandit had been busy. He'd chewed up two of my left high heels, a cushion and was now munching on one of Roman's work boots. I jumped out of bed, and straight into a fresh pile of shit!

"SHIT! LITERALLY SHIT!" I cursed as I hobbled to the bathroom to wash my foot.

I'd woken up in a bit of a mood, I wanted to talk to Roman about keeping our personal life a little more personal. I knew his mom meant well, but I

313

couldn't help but feel irritated at the look of pity she gave me every time she brought up the topic of us having a baby, and I didn't feel that she needed to be involved in any kind of decision making regarding us becoming foster parents. But I also knew that it probably wasn't the right time to have this conversation with him today, so I'd just have to swallow the ill feelings I had right now.

I fed Bandit and put him outside in his yard, cleaned up the mess he'd made, showered and had left before Roman or Jill woke up.

I drove to the beach and ran along the sand, I ran until I couldn't run anymore. Then I sat at the edge of the water, right where the waves met the shore, the familiar serene feeling washed over me, here..., as always, I found my Center.

I heard my cell beep in my pocket, taking it out I saw that Roman had sent me a message.

Babes, where are you?? Is everything ok?

It was out of character for either of us to just get up and leave with no note, or message. I'd been distracted with Bandit and my own thoughts that I had just forgotten. I messaged him back;

Sorry hun, I'm down at Redcliffe, I needed to go for a run and clear my mind. I'll pick up breakfast and come home x

Roman messaged back;

Mum made breakfast for us already, she wants to go back to the hospital soon to see Dad. She asked if Liam and I could spend the

night at her house with her but I told her to just stay here with us. I took today off too, let me know if you want me to wait for you before we leave?

I read the message several times, and wondered what the fuck Jill's problem was? I hadn't been rude to her last night, short maybe but not rude? I'd opened my home to her, and would continue to do so because she was Romans mom, but I didn't feel it was right that she was trying to stick her nose into our personal business, or that she was asking Roman to spend the night away from me to be there for her. I knew I'd have to bite my tongue because the last thing I wanted to do was fight with Roman over his mother, especially while his dad was in the hospital.

You go with your mom, I'll see you later at home. Please give my best to your dad. X

Several hours later Roman came home alone. I tried to act like nothing was bothering me, but he knew me too well,

"Ok Lize, what's going on? What happened between you and my mom?" Roman asked.

"It doesn't matter, honestly it's not even important right now," I answered.

"She told me you got mad at her when she was trying to give you advice about starting a family. What exactly did she say?" Roman prodded.

"I didn't get mad! I *was* annoyed, did she tell you that she thinks we are making a mistake if we

315

foster children, that we should try to have our own kids first and that she knows of a fucken fertility Doctor that we should speak to?" I fumed.

I hadn't wanted to talk about it, I hadn't wanted to open this can of worms right now..., and now I was feeling like someone shook a champagne bottle and was about to pop the cork! Roman pulled me close to him, his silence told me he knew how overbearing his mother could be.

"Lize, I'm sorry, I'll tell her she needs to back off and not bring it up again unless you do first," Roman lifted my face and kissed my lips.

***

"I know you're close with your parents babe, but please..., can we keep this part of our private life private..., at least until we know what it is that we are doing?" I pleaded with him.

Roman said the two words that most women only dream of hearing from their husbands,

"You're right!"

CHAPTER 34
LOVE THE FALL!

The rumor mill was buzzing with news that the entire Loss Prevention department was about to collapse, that life as we knew it was coming to an end. The company of course denied it, stating that they were looking at doing things differently. Their corporate PR people were trying to convince everyone that this change would be beneficial to the company as a whole, and to all of its employees. They used buzzwords like 'new opportunities' and 'collaborative thinking' which really meant the loss of jobs, and a 'my way or the highway' mentality. They could dress up their emails with as many fancy words as they wanted, but we could all smell the bullshit.

We were all summoned to attend a meeting, where we listened for over an hour to the newly appointed head of department prattle on about this exciting new chapter in our lives. I sat there fuming as he dribbled on and on, never once answering any questions properly, just talking in circles. If I'd had a pen and paper I'd have drawn him a map so he could get to the fucken point.

Prior to the meeting, I'd overheard an investigator from another region saying he would just sit back quietly like a church mouse, and hopefully fly under the radar and into a new role.

Gutless coward, I thought. How about standing up for what's right and telling these pompous pricks that they were making a huge mistake? I knew it really wouldn't matter what we said, the decisions had already been made, and the jobs had probably been filled long before they even told us what was going on. They just had to make it look like they were doing the right thing by asking for our input.

The whole lot of them couldn't lie straight in bed if they tried, and there was no way I was going to just go away quietly, because I knew that even if I were offered a job I wouldn't want it anyway. I genuinely loved my job. I was passionate about it, and felt a strong sense of obligation to every store manager and staff member who I'd worked with to make sure their concerns were heard. With theft on the rise, stores needed more Loss Prevention Officers not less. Without LPO's on the floor, there would be no one to catch the thieves in action. Staff and managers didn't have the time, or proper training to deal with offenders, which would mean that they would either turn a blind eye or find themselves in situations out of their control.

Shoplifting statistics would rapidly decline, well.., at least until the first stock take! Once word got out on the street to the grubs that the floor walkers were gone it would be a total free for all. It made about as much sense as pulling the support beam from a big top full of people, mind you the entire restructure *was* a complete circus with two clowns running the show. I stood up and asked all of the hard questions that they had hoped we would all be scared of asking.

How many people were going to lose their jobs?

What would happen to those who didn't get a job?

How would redundancy pay outs be structured?

Are you planning on replacing us with contract companies?

When were all these changes expected to take place?

***

Not one of my questions was answered satisfactorily, instead I'd basically just painted a massive bullseye on my own head, but I couldn't care less. I knew already there was no place for someone like me, they wanted people who kept their mouths shut, who went with the flow, and who wouldn't question anything that they were told to do..., and that didn't sound like me at all. I felt sorry for Simon, he was the captain of a sinking ship, and people were bailing left and right.

Roman and I had decided I'd ride it out until the end, we'd had several deep conversations regarding our future family. We both wanted nothing more than to have a baby of our own, and were booked in to have further testing to see why we couldn't conceive naturally.

We'd also met with families who fostered children, to get some inside information on the process, and to speak about how it can affect you emotionally when it was time for the children to be placed back with their parent(s). We met with long-term foster families, and both Roman and I agreed that we would be much more suited to that level of commitment. I wasn't sure if we would emotionally be able to handle having to give a child back, to a parent like Kathy Barclay or Bethany Muller.

Three days after the meeting, we got word that Simon had jumped ship too. No email, no phone call, not so much as a thank you or even a goodbye. He had accepted a position with one of Australia's largest security companies as a national manager, no one could blame him for not hanging around, but we were all a little shocked at his abrupt departure.

His temporary replacement was an obnoxious asshole called Brian, he was an investigator from Sydney, brought in from head office to oversee things until the last day. We were all expected to carry on business as usual until the next update.

I knew that no matter what happened, lifetime friendships had been forged between Alexis, Georgia, Jessica, Adam and myself and no amount of time or circumstances would change that. Or would it? As the situation unfolded, it was bringing out the worst in people, I was hearing stories of coverts throwing their co-workers under the bus in an attempt to retain a position. No longer were loyalty, integrity and honesty core values, well at least not for some. I was reading the latest email from Brian regarding our new schedules when Alexis called.

"Hey, did you see the email from that douche canoe Brian about our new rosters?" Alexis asked.

"Where do you come up with these insults?" I laughed, storing douche canoe in my vocabulary bank for later use.

"I dunno, it just spews out of my mouth sometimes. You should know by now I have no filter, if I'm thinking it, chances are I'm saying it," Alexis paused, "anyway, I'm not sticking around to get fucked over, I heard a covert got sacked yesterday down in Melbourne for a false apprehension, shit's going down Eliza, and they are looking for any little reason to sack people, probably so they don't have to find us jobs or pay out redundancies. So..., I'm throwing in the towel. I got offered a job in a cash office at Pinewood and I'm gonna take it, I start on Monday," She trailed off.

"Are you sure? I mean..., is that what you want?" I asked sounding a little shocked.

I knew it was inevitable that my co-workers would soon have to look at real options before the final date came down, but I just wasn't expecting Simon and Alexis to be gone the same day.

"Well Mrs money bags, it's not really what I want, but my bank account doesn't look like yours so I don't have a choice do I?" Alexis' voice broke and she began sobbing down the phone.

My eyes filled instantly with tears, Fuck!

"I'm sorry Lex, I really am..., I don't even know what to say?" I could feel the lump forming in my throat and I gulped down hard.

***

The store manager Max had entered the room, so I told Alexis I'd call her back.

"You LPO's are acting like it's the end of the bloody world, at least us managers are offering you jobs in our stores, *and* we have to suck up the cost of your over inflated wages, do you know what that's doing to our store budgets?" Max sniffed arrogantly.

"Fuck you Max, I'm sooooo sorry that us losing our jobs is such a fucking inconvenience to ya'll, but unless you've gone through this you don't know how it feels, so how about you show a little compassion. You're worried about your budget huh? Well, let's see how your stocktake looks in a year's time with us gone hey!" I shouted angrily. I clenched my mouth shut so hard my jaw hurt.

"Eliza, I understand but...," Max started to speak but I quickly cut him off.

"Actually Max..., NO..., you don't!" I fumed, "so you're telling me that if your regional manager and HR came in right now and said they no longer require your services, and then offered you a shitty job somewhere else in the store that you'd be ok with that? Because I don't think you would, so unless you've got something supportive to say then shut the fuck up and stop running your damn mouth."

I angrily snatched up my bag and keys and stormed out of the office. I was done! Well at least for today. As I climbed into my mustang I could feel the heat rising in my face, I was raging. I put the top down and turned the radio on, pulling out of the car park I could see Max in my rear view mirror, waving his arms like mad trying to get my attention. I didn't give a shit what he had to say, I knew I was out of line for cursing at him so much, but he deserved it.

As I picked up speed, the cool wind whipped my face, I turned the radio up as loud as I could and heard the guy announce the next song;

"Here's a blast from the past its Michael Paynter and The Veronica's with, Love the fall," he said dramatically as the song began.

Catchy I thought as I tapped the steering wheel in time with the beat.

"What if I dive off the edge of my life and there's nothing beneath? What if I live like there's nothing to lose just to die on my knees? At least I know I've walked the dark, I took the scars and risked it all, and learned to love the fall."

323

As I listened to the lyrics, I could feel the sting of tears welling in my eyes. I quickly switched channels.

"Crashing from the high, I'm letting go tonight, I'm falling from cloud nine... I'm wide awake."

As the rush of tears came, I turned the radio off. Thank you Katy Perry! There was no avoiding it, no matter what I listened to I was sure it would feel like the words were ripping through my very soul. I'd come undone, everything I'd been holding in was finally pouring out, I cried angry frustrated tears for myself, for Alexis, for Georgia, for everyone in this shitty situation. The floodgates were opened, and the tears so intense I had to pull over. I cried hard on the side of the road for the job I loved that would soon be gone, for the friendships that had blossomed into my own handpicked family.

I cried for everybody's unknown futures. Because even though the HR robots spoke to us all about these fabulous doors of opportunity, for most of my co-workers, it felt like they'd been pushed into a black corridor and were stumbling around in the dark looking for a way out. There was no sugar coating it, the entire thing was fucked, and the way the company was handling things was appalling!

I knew we would all be ok..., eventually, that everyone would move on to something else. It was inevitable, but it wouldn't ever be the same. Years of loyalty and service meant nothing, there were men and women who'd reached their 20-year milestones, and it meant shit! They were just another employee ID number when it came to the crunch.

Pulling myself together, I drove home and poured a JD on ice. I knew it was foolish to drink even just one in this current state of mind, but tonight I didn't want to think about any of this. As I walked around my home, I pondered what I'd do with myself in the time between the job ending, and hopefully having a baby. I could always concentrate on my writing? I also had my investigative skills to fall back on and had spoken with both Alexis and Georgia about starting my own Private Investigation business, similar to the one I'd owned in Vegas.

By the time Roman arrived home I was drunk, well..., if I'm honest I was absolutely legless. I had not been this intoxicated in a very long time, and I knew with each drink I poured I would regret it tomorrow but right now I didn't care, it seemed like it would be worth it.

"Oh my God woman, what on earth are you doing?" Roman laughed as he entered the kitchen, where I was attempting (very badly) to make dinner. No amount of cooking classes from Betty Ku could save the cremated mess in the oven. I staggered toward him laughing.

"Jesus Eliza, this is not fucken funny, how much have you had to bloody drink? You should be in bed, not the kitchen cooking..., fuck!" Roman sounded concerned, but he was also more than a little annoyed.

I started crying again, this time I couldn't stop, and he held me as my body was wracked with gut-wrenching sobs, I was so drunk I made no sense as I tried to explain what I was feeling. Up until this point I'd been ok, holding it together, the shoulder for everyone else to cry on. I was crying like someone had died, the grief felt similar, or maybe I was so drunk I was just confused? Roman picked me up and carried me to bed, he returned with a big bottle of water, a banana, and 2 Panadol.

"What you going to do with that banana?" I giggled.

"I heard if you eat a banana it helps soak up some of the alcohol, I don't know if it's true but it's worth a try. Eat some babes, then take these Panadol, your head is going to be banging in the morning," Roman kissed the top of my head.

"No banana..., it will make me sick," I slurred, "I love you, you're my everything you know that?"

I lay back against the pillows, the room was spinning faster than a theme park ride, I closed my eyes tightly and fell asleep.

The next morning I woke up feeling like someone had literally stomped on my head, and my mouth was drier than a desert.

"Oh..., I'm never drinking again," I groaned as I rolled toward Roman.

"Famous last words," Roman laughed at me, "babes..., you know you drank almost an entire bottle of Jacks last night don't you? and I'm sure that empty bottle of Moscato wasn't on the sink yesterday either," he said looking worried.

"Christ, no wonder my head is pounding. I'm sorry hun, yesterday was a really bad day, and I think it finally hit me that soon it will all be over, I feel so bad for everyone, and well..., it's almost like some people think I shouldn't be sad about it because financially we are ok..., but it still hurts so much Roman," my voice cracked, I knew I was going to start crying again.

"Babes, I'm really worried about your emotional state, I don't want you coming home getting pissed like that, I don't wanna bust your balls, but do you think you should maybe give Anthony a call? I mean, I'm here for you too, and you can always talk to me about anything, but he's a therapist, and he might be able to talk you through this," Roman spoke quietly, hugging me close and kissing my head.

It was my turn to say the two words that most husbands only dream of hearing from their wives...,

"You're right." I whispered.

"Oh can I get that in writing?" Roman joked.

"Ha-ha wise guy, I can admit when I screw up..., I will email Anthony later today to set up a time. I really am sorry Roman, I know I shouldn't drink like that. I won't do it again I promise. I was doing ok until I heard two songs on the radio, and the lyrics just hit me you know?" I looked up at my sweet caring husband.

"Those soppy meaningful songs are why I listen to Triple J," Roman joked as he moved the hair from my face, "you know you are going to be ok, don't you? I think you should focus on writing your book, hey..., maybe you could even start a new one about your time as a loss prevention officer, it would be a bloody good read, especially with all your funny stories, you never know, it may even be a bestseller."

"Hmmm, you just never know," I grinned.

A little over two weeks later, the job was finished. All trace of our existence within the stores was shredded and disposed of like we had never existed. We truly were like the Lochness monster, nothing more than a tale, a myth.

That evening I invited the entire team to the ranch for a dinner. As we all sat around the barn discussing our futures, it was clear..., everyone was changing, evolving, making new plans, moving on to new chapters in our lives. I was still uncertain about what I was going to do in the future, however one thing was for sure that I would eventually learn to love the fall.

CHAPTER 35
NEW BEGINNINGS

"**R**oman come on, we are going to be late!" I called up the stairs to the bedroom in the barn.

The renovations were finally completed on our office in Fortitude Valley, and today was move-in day. Next week we'd officially be open for business in our own private investigation firm.

While I waited for Roman, I pondered all the changes of last year.

I'd flown back to the US a few times to speak with detectives regarding the ongoing case with Michael. It seemed that I wasn't his first, nor his last victim and due to my report, he'd been investigated and found to be heavily involved in underground sex trafficking clubs, using women and children as young as 13 years old for sexual gratification and torture. The case had made national headlines, and several high profile people had also been arrested in connection with the investigation, "Operation Red Rock." I knew at some point, I'd have to go back and testify, but for now, I was trying to just get on with life.

I'd taken what Roman and I had joked as a 'gap year' from any kind of paid work, and spent most of the time at home in the yard, planting herbs and vegetables in the garden beds that we'd had built. We planned on becoming as self-sufficient at home as we could be, with a variety of fruit trees already on the block, and now the vegetable and herb gardens the only fresh produce we had to buy was meat and dairy.

After a few disasters with Bandit getting used to the chickens, the hens were now laying eggs. They had a mutual understanding of each other, that being.., Bandit stays the fuck out of the hen house or Red, the Rooster will peck his eyes out.

We'd purchased the ten-acre block behind our home, and had hired a team of landscapers to come in and clear a walking track through the forest of trees, to a clearing where we'd hung a huge wicker pod from a giant eucalyptus tree. It was our little love nest in the woods, a tranquil place where we could make love outdoors, enjoy the wildlife, especially the adorable Koalas who could often be seen in the trees, and where I could escape to write.

I had finished my first novel, and was in the process of self-publishing. The yard was complete and there was nothing else to update or decorate at The Ranch, so it was time to jump back into what I loved doing..., Investigations. And so, Fox Investigations was reborn. I wanted to honor my father, carry on his legacy, and rebuild the business I'd dismantled and then sold in Vegas.

We'd spent quite a lot of money setting up the business, buying the office, redecorating, purchasing all the equipment and even buying advertising space. It was a gamble, but then again.., I was a Vegas girl at heart, sometimes you have to lay all your cards on the table, bet big and pray for a good return. I was more than confident that with the team I had, this business couldn't be anything but successful.

The office was perfect, prime location with some off-street parking, and close to the train station. It had needed a lot of work inside, and we'd spent the better part of six months having it redecorated and fitted out. But it was worth every dollar we'd spent.

"Sorry babes, I'm ready," Roman broke my train of thought as he bounded down the stairs.

"Let's do it!" I said excitedly. We locked Bandit in his yard and headed off.

I'd given Georgia and Jessica the task of setting up the kitchen, we'd no sooner unlocked the doors when the two women came bursting through with boxes full of stuff. Cups, plates, bowls, cutlery, a microwave, kettle, toasted sandwich machine, and regular toaster, it was a good thing I'd left them in charge because otherwise, we'd be living on Starbucks!

"Wow, did you max out the card I gave you?" Roman laughed as he took a large box from Georgia.

"Almost, we were going to put a coffee machine on there too, but thought we better check first," Georgia answered.

"It's ok, I will order one online now," Roman said as he set the box down on the bench.

I really hoped the business took off, because we were discussing Roman resigning from his job and coming on board full time too.

"Helloo, anybody home?" Adam called out as he and Alexis walked through the corridor down to the kitchen.

It was obvious my new employees were keen to get the show on the road.

As we walked around the office, I showed everyone their new work space. There were two large offices on the right as you walked in, and then eight decent sized cubicles dividing up the rest of the floor space. The kitchen and bathroom were down the back, and outside was a fully enclosed courtyard, that we already planned to turn into a BBQ area.

"Now you're all here, I have a few announcements to make. Roman can you pour the wine please, I'd like to make a toast," I beamed.

Roman handed out a glass of Moscato to everyone.

"Firstly, thank you all for being here, not just as my new employees, but as my very dear friends. Thank you all for taking a giant leap of faith with us, for leaving your jobs, and for believing that dreams really can come true. I'm sure you all noticed the two big offices to our right here, the first one will be our boardroom, for team meetings, and somewhere to meet with new or potential clients. My office will be out here with you guys, not to check up on you, but because I want to create an equal work environment. Finally, the second office is going to be transformed into a playroom/nursery. Jess is going to need to bring Raine to work with her sometimes, and I will also need somewhere for our baby to sleep when he or she is born, because I'm 12 weeks pregnant, so cheers!" I grinned, raised my glass of Moscato and then placed it down on the table beside me without taking a sip.

After the excited congratulatory hugs and kisses, and a series of toasts, everyone got busy with setting up their office spaces. Roman came up behind me and put his hands around my waist, he caressed my tiny belly.

"I'm so glad everyone knows now, it's been so hard to control myself from touching your belly when everyone's around," he said as he kissed my neck. "I still can't believe we are going to be parents Lize, you are going to be one hell of a yummy mummy."

"Oh yeah? Well, you're going to be one hot dad," I turned and kissed his lips.

By 8 pm everyone was finished setting up, we ate pizza in the boardroom and discussed possible new business. As I looked around at my friends, my new team, I felt blessed. It was surprising how quickly life could change. How just a year ago we'd all stumbled in the dark, trying to find our new door.., thankfully through my father's hard work, and then my own, I'd been able to build not just a door of opportunity, but an empire.

CHAPTER 36
TEAM GREEN

Five months later the business was picking up, Adam had successfully landed four major clients, all with ongoing workers compensation claims. Alexis had also been marketing her ass off, and we were now the number one go-to company for internal theft investigations. We'd even outsourced a few LPO's for various companies who had identified shrinkage issues within their stores.

Jessica's (now husband) Rob, lost his job through a company restructure and was working part-time with Thomas as a personal trainer, as well as looking after Raine, so Jess was pretty much working full time in the business. Everything was finally falling into place, as my stomach rounded and I felt the heart-warming kicks of this little life growing inside me, I knew it would soon be time to step back, and hand over the reins (at least for a few months) to Adam. He was looking forward to the added responsibility and leadership that I was entrusting in him, and I'm sure he would welcome the pay raise.

Roman couldn't get enough of me even now, although our love making was much gentler now, and *most* of the toys had been packed away. I'd tried (unsuccessfully) to convince Roman it was still safe for us to play, but he wouldn't hear of it. Even though my growing breasts were getting far more attention than usual, and while I was loving every minute of my pregnancy, there was a tiny part of me that couldn't wait to have my body and uninhibited husband back completely. He had become obsessed with decorating the nursery, even though I'd insisted that this little bundle would be sleeping in our room with us for at least the first year. He'd decorated the walls a very light gray, with a pretty teal colored crib, a large set of shabby chic white drawers and matching change table and huge padded rocking chair with ottoman for night time feeding.

We had decided to be 'team green' and not find out the sex of the baby. It didn't matter to us whether we had a boy or a girl, we were just grateful to be blessed with this baby at all. The nursery/playroom at work was something to be admired too, Jessica and Roman had decorated it beautifully. It had large animal alphabet pictures on one wall with a wooden table and chair set underneath, the bookshelves were stuffed full of books, toys, and games. A mini climber jungle gym was in the center of the room, and behind large vibrant privacy screens was a toddler bed and crib.

I'd had another miscarriage shortly after being made redundant, and I was convinced we would never have a baby of our own. But this little one had snuck up when we least expected it. Although Roman is giving some credit to the fertility statue that he made me touch at Ripley's believe it or not.

"Babes, are you ready to go home?" Roman asked as he brushed the hair away from my face.

"I must have dozed off," I yawned, sitting up and stretching my arms above my head.

One thing was for sure, this pregnancy was kicking my ass, I was getting so tired, no matter how much sleep I'd had or what vitamins I took.

"Here let me take a look," Roman said sliding my chair out of the way. "OooOOOooh is someone being naughty?" He laughed as he looked at the file marked infidelity on my desk.

As he sifted through the mountain of florist, motel and lingerie receipts his eyes shifted toward me;

"Cheating bastard! Promise me we won't ever get like these people Lize, no matter what happens," he said glumly.

Looking at my husband I wanted nothing more than to reassure him that we'd never be like this. That we'd never cheat, lie, or hurt each other. But can you ever really promise all of that?

I hoped with all my heart that we would never be these people, that we would always love and respect each other, and be truthful and loyal. But sadly sometimes people change, situations change. I knew neither of us would ever intentionally fuck up what we had together. Marriage required not only commitment but effort, from both parties. It seemed that people gave up on relationships in general, they wanted that fresh 'new' feeling that couples have in the first few months of dating. The hunger, lust, rush of something brand new. Instead of watering their own lawn, they wanted to check out the greener pastures somewhere else.

"Never stop dating each other, and talk often about your own love story," Roman's mother had told me the night before my wedding. Even though she could be an absolute pain in the ass, her advice held so much truth. We reminisced a lot about our early days, and the closeness we felt afterward was enough to keep our own 'lawn' evergreen.

"No judgment remember Roman, you can't personalize this type of work. People have affairs for all different reasons, but the common denominator is, that *all* of them feel there is something missing in their relationships, some need is not being met. It doesn't necessarily make it right, but it doesn't mean they are all bad people either. No one really knows what goes on in someone else's marriage. But as far as you and me, I promised to be honest and loyal to you, and I meant it. Our marriage is strong, we are both great communicators, our sex life is very healthy, and as long as we work through problems as they come up I think we are good," I kissed Roman's hand, hoping he would let it go, the last thing I wanted was for this type of work to cause issues in our own marriage.

"You're right babes, I just don't get why they don't leave?" Roman sighed.

"Sometimes, it's just not that easy," I shrugged.

This was why I handled most of the infidelity cases, because through my own experiences I'd learned to look at it objectively, and not get attached, lay blame or personalize the case. Nothing was black and white, and you couldn't just label the cheater as the asshole.

I'd been cheated on, had cheated on, *and* been cheated with. It was easy for an outsider to lay blame, but if you dissect each situation, you'd see that at least 80% of the time, all parties involved had a hand in it happening in the first place. Cheating was not just about sex, the variables involved were often complex. I'd worked on several cases where spouses had thought their husbands/wives were physically cheating, but all investigations had led to the conclusion of an emotional cheater. I'd spoken with several spouses afterward, who'd said they wished I'd found proof of physical infidelity, because knowing that their spouse was having their emotional/intellectual needs met elsewhere, stung worse than any kind of sexual act.

"You're so open-minded Eliza, it's one of the many traits I admire in you. Maybe one day I'll look at this all objectively, but not tonight, right now I'm starving, and you look buggered, let's go home," Roman begged.

"Sure hunna, but I need to bring this home with me, I think I'll work from home tomorrow so I can just chill out a bit," I yawned, picking up the file I put it in my briefcase with my laptop.

"Night guys," Adam yelled out from his cubicle giving me a fright, I'd forgotten he was still here.

"Night mate," Roman called back.

"Goodnight Adam, I'll call you tomorrow," I said sleepily.

As I climbed into the passenger seat of my mustang, I wondered how I was going to adjust to driving a family car soon. With the business doing well, we'd decided to give everyone a company vehicle, after test driving several cars, we'd all decided on the ford territory. Roman had also decided to sell his car too, and would now be using the Mustang to go to and from work. I knew it made sense, that it was practical for me to have the family car, but I'd be lying if I said I wasn't slightly jealous of this arrangement.

When we arrived home, Roman let Bandit out of his yard while I put a lasagne in the oven. I took a quick shower and threw on my bathrobe, I was relaxing in the library when Roman came in. He quickly showered and then joined me.

"Come and lay down here babes," Roman patted the space next to him on the shag pile rug.

As I lay down beside him, my gown slid open revealing my swollen belly and plump breasts.

"You're even more gorgeous now than you were before.., do you know that?" Roman purred,

his eyes twinkled as he licked his lips and looked at me.

"To be honest, I feel fat and frumpy," I pouted.

"No way, you are such a yummy mummy already," He kissed my stomach, and ran a hand over a very sensitive nipple.

I hadn't believed it could be possible to be more aroused, or the need for sexual contact greater during pregnancy, and while some women craved all kinds of things during pregnancy, I craved my husband. Roman removed his boxer shorts and lay back beside me, stroking my stomach with his fingertips, his face in awe at the changes in my body.

For the first time ever, I felt self-conscious about my body. I enjoyed our baby moving inside of me, and loved tracking the progress of growth in the book I'd bought. But I wasn't sure I would get used to the changes I saw in my body in the mirror each morning. The first tell-tale sign of stretch marks, so far only a few long, angry red lines, but it had been enough to reduce me to tears. It didn't matter what potion or lotion I rubbed on every inch of my body, they were still there. Georgia had assured me that the minute I held the tiny little bundle, every ache, every mark, every bit of pain would all be forgotten and totally worth it. I hoped she was right.

Kissing my stomach tenderly Roman worked his way up to my breasts, tweaking my right nipple while he bit gently on my left, his lips moved up and over my breast, along my neck line until his mouth was on mine. One hand wandered down my body, tracing a line to my pubic mound where his fingers parted my labia, he found my clitoris, rubbing it faster as his tongue entered my mouth finding mine, we kissed deeply while he rubbed me until I came. Roman grabbed a pillow and placed it underneath my ass, spreading my legs wide he entered me, thrusting in and out slowly.

"Would it be too uncomfortable if I fuck you from behind?" Roman asked as his thrusts became faster.

"We can try, but we may need more pillows," I laughed, "actually, lay down," I ordered.

Roman pulled out and lay down on the floor. Facing away from him I lowered myself down onto his cock. I rocked back and forth, fucking him slowly at first, and steadily increasing my pace, lifting up so his shaft would be seen entering and exiting my pussy from his position on the floor.

"Oh fuck..., oh God..., I'm gonna cum," Roman groaned loudly as he came inside me.

As he recovered on the floor, I got up to retrieve my bathrobe.

"You know, when you were riding me like that, you didn't even look pregnant," Roman laughed. "But honestly babes, you're so sexy now. I love touching your big boobs and beautiful round belly."

"I'm glad you're loving it," I chuckled as I left the library to check on dinner.

We sat on the floor of the library eating our meal, talking about work, just enjoying each other's company. Baby B was obviously enjoying the meal too, and began to move about and kick wildly, a little foot protruded from the side of my stomach, I squirmed and rubbed my beach ball belly.

"Is the baby kicking?" Roman asked moving his hand onto my stomach.

"Yes, check out the little foot," I showed Roman where what appeared to be a little foot was still protruding out the side of my belly. "I think we have a soccer star in the making with all the kicking that Baby B is doing lately."

"You know you're going to have to slow down soon hun, let Adam take over. I'm thinking about going part time too, so I can help out a little with work and this little one," Roman stroked my belly.

My blood pressure had been a little high, and I was extra tired lately, but I had planned on working until at least 38 weeks in the office and then from home until Baby B arrived.

"Just one more month and I will step back babe, I promise. I'm in the middle of a few cases that I'm hoping to finish first," I said stubbornly.

"Two more weeks in the office Eliza, and that's it. I know you're planning on working from home anyway, but you really need to pull it back. It's not healthy for you to be working such long hours right now. The whole reason you gave Adam a promotion *and* pay raise was so he could step up, you need to let him," Roman said firmly.

I knew he was right, my Doctor had been concerned at my last prenatal appointment and wanted me to modify my work schedule, and I had..., well..., a little.

I woke up the next morning feeling exhausted, I slept most of the day with a pile of pillows strategically placed around me. I called Adam and told him I was going to spend at least the next few days at home. Roman insisted on me seeing my Doctor for a check-up the following day, because I'd been complaining about a severe headache. I had the early stages of preeclampsia, and was advised to rest for at least the next week.

At 37 weeks pregnant my waters broke.

"Roman," I called out from the library to the kitchen, "I think my waters broke."

Roman and Matthew rushed in, both looking a little stunned at the news.

"Are you sure? Is this normal? We still have a few more weeks right?" Roman questioned me. But before I could answer him, my body was gripped by a ferocious contraction. Crying out I leaned forward and held on to the chair beside me. As the first contraction eased, I went to the bathroom while Roman packed my hospital bag. I could hear them talking through the closed door.

"What do you want me to do mate?" Matthew asked Roman.

"Umm.., I don't even know what I'm doing, can you just go sit with Eliza and see if she needs anything," Roman answered.

"Mate, she is in the toilet," Matthew laughed, "how about I go bring the car closer and I can drive you guys to the hospital?"

"Yes good idea, geez I'm glad we hadn't had a beer yet," Roman was sounding more flustered by the minute.

As I got to the bathroom door, my body was wracked with another contraction, much stronger this time. SHIT! I wasn't as prepared for this as I'd thought.

"Roman, I don't think I'm going to make it to the hospital, I think the baby is coming now," I called out, my voice shaking a little.

"Babes, are you sure? Doesn't it usually take hours with your first one?" Roman asked.

Another contraction ripped through my body and I yelled loudly in pain.

"Roady, fuck the car, call an ambulance!" Roman shouted out to Matthew who had been heading to get the car.

I stood holding on to the bathroom door as another contraction tore through me, the pain so excruciating I felt like I was going to pass out. As the contraction subsided, I threw a bunch of freshly rolled towels onto the floor and sat down.

"Baby, do you want to lie up on the bed instead? It will be far more comfortable," Roman suggested as he came into the bathroom.

"No way, I just changed the sheets," I laughed.

But my attempt at a joke was short lived as another contraction peaked, this time I felt it in my lower back and stomach, and felt the urge to push. Roman sat on the floor beside me, he held my hand as I attempted to breathe through the next contraction.

"Do I need to get hot water and some more towels, or is that just some bullshit they do in the movies?" Roman asked me seriously.

If I hadn't been in the throes of yet another back ripping contraction, I'd have laughed at him.

"I don't know, this is my first time too you know," I panted as Matthew returned.

"The ambulance is on its way, but the dispatcher told me what to do in case they don't get here on time. Roman are you cool with me being here, or do you want me to just stand outside the door and tell you what to do or...," His voice trailed off.

"I can't think of anyone else I'd rather have here right now mate, I'm freaking out honestly, so get in here and help me deliver my baby," Roman grinned.

It really was true what they say about labor, even the most modest of women couldn't have cared less at who was in the room, or how many people stuck their hands up your vagina, as long as they were assisting with getting the baby out, and stopping the horrendous fucking pain of these awful contractions. Several minutes, and multiple contractions later, the Paramedics arrived. They set up quickly, knowing there was no way I was going to be delivering anywhere but the bathroom floor.

"I see a head," the paramedic declared.

"Pull it out, pull it out," I groaned in pain.

"You're doing great, just breathe, just a few more pushes and your baby will be here," the second paramedic said encouragingly.

Several quick contractions and what felt like an hour of pushing, our baby was born.

"It's a boy!" Roman exclaimed proudly, his voice cracked and his eyes filled with tears as the paramedic showed him where to cut the cord.

Matthew, who was sitting beside my head, leaned down and kissed me on the cheek,

"Well done Eliza, you know that pedestal I have you on..., well I'm fairly certain you just moved to the crown in the Statue of Liberty because you are truly amazing," he grinned.

I laughed, would the man ever learn?

"Here son, meet your Mummy," Roman spoke gently, as he kissed our babies head and placed him on my chest.

"Congratulations bro," Matthew exclaimed, slapping Roman on the back before pulling him into a hug. "Your wife is awesome, having a baby at home *and* even leaving enough time before the big kick-off," he joked.

"I don't think I'll be seeing much of the game tonight. You're welcome to stay here though, after all, there is plenty of beer and pizza. And mate..., thanks so much for being here with me man," Roman returned the slap on his back.

As the Paramedics packed up and prepared to transfer us to the hospital, Roman and I were left alone.

"I never thought it was possible to love you more than I already do. I'm so proud of you Lize, you are amazing..., and as for this impatient little guy, wow, I can't believe he's here already, I love him so much too," Roman beamed, he stroked the mop of black hair on our sons tiny little head.

"So, are we set on Logan Jack Beach?" I asked, looking down at our handsome son who was sucking gently on my breast.

"Yes, ever since you dreamt that I've looked forward to this moment. I can't believe it all happened so quickly. How are you feeling babes?" Roman asked.

"Not too bad I guess," I replied as the paramedics returned.

An hour later I was laying in the hospital bed on the ward, Logan was sleeping soundly in the little see-through bed beside me.

"Yep, six pounds five ounces, he is a little beauty Mum wait til you see him," Roman boasted proudly on the phone to his mother, "I think they are coming home tomorrow all going well, I will call you in the morning and let you know what's going on."

We'd already made it clear to our friends and family, that we wanted the first 24 hours to bond with our baby without visitors. I intended on breastfeeding, and didn't want the interruption of people coming and going while I was trying to get the hang of it. Our phones buzzed with messages of congratulations as the news spread about Logan's early arrival. I lay back on the pillows, feeling exhausted, Roman lay beside me not wanting to go home. Other than the occasional night shift, we had not spent a night apart since we married.

"You and me against the world my love," Roman murmured sleepily.

I shed a few silent tears for daddy. He would have been the most amazing grandfather, and would have been so proud of how far I'd come. It always surprised that Roman used that saying in times where I really needed to hear it. I had never told him that it was something daddy had often said. I

351

preferred to believe it was a sign, some divine intervention to let me know he was still around.

The following day, Roman secured Logan into his car seat in the back of our car. He fussed over me as he helped me into the car, and I wondered for the millionth time..., how on earth had I got so lucky?

The first few nights at home were rough, Logan screamed almost all night long, until Georgia told me about 'white noise', which then became our new best friend. I was completely unprepared for just how sore my boobs would be when the milk came down. The cluster feeding was a total nightmare, and several times I contemplated giving up breastfeeding altogether. But instead, I just cried in the shower and wondered what the fuck I was doing wrong? No one warned us that this parenting thing would be *this* hard. I cried even harder when I realized that we were just getting started, and that we still had to get through teething and the terrible twos! I was an emotional wreck, my hormones were all over the place, and so was my hair which had decided to start falling out and an alarming rate. On the fifth day, things were a little better, and I was craving the normality of adult conversation. I invited our friends and family to come for dinner.

Jill and Phillip had already been to see us once, I could hardly tell them they couldn't, after all, it was their grandson. I'm certain that Roman warned his mom not to overshare with advice, because for once she actually kept quiet, and had just spent the time fussing over her first born grandchild.

Everyone arrived by 6 pm, we'd decided to just order in so that we could both relax. By 7:30 pm we'd all eaten, and while Logan was being passed around and fussed over, I gestured to Adam to follow me to the library.

"How's business?" I asked.

Just because I wasn't there, didn't mean I had to be out of the loop. I hadn't yet spoken about it with Roman, but I planned on going back to work in a few weeks. Only a few mornings each week, and I would take Logan in with me, after all, it is why we made the nursery there in the first place.

"Jess got on to the people whose accounts were outstanding, and either got full payments, or at least half, with the rest to be paid up by the end of the month. We also picked up six new clients this week, I think we are going to have to hire another full-timer to keep up with the workload," Adam suggested.

I knew my instincts about Adam were spot on from day one, he was hardworking and dedicated, and as passionate about the business as I was.

"Hmmmm..., it looks like you're running a tight ship, I will leave the hiring to you or Jess, do you know anyone who might be interested in coming on board?" I asked.

"I'm glad you asked, I'm not sure how you feel about working so closely with family but I'd like to bring Liam in," he paused momentarily, watching my facial expression closely before continuing, "I don't know if he has said anything to you guys, or to his parents yet, but he wants to leave his job, and I think his expertise could really help us build and expand the business."

Adam finished, and looked relieved at the grin that was beginning to spread across my face.

"No, he hasn't said anything yet. He is probably worried about what Phillip and Jill will say, they paid for a huge chunk of his University. I'm sure once they get used to the idea they will be ok with it. Draw up a contract and we will get him in ASAP to brief him on his role, and Adam, thank you..., I'm lucky to have you," I thanked him and squeezed his hand fondly.

A few hours later everyone had gone home, and I was cleaning up the kitchen. Roman came up behind me, as he pulled me into a hug I could feel him becoming erect as he caressed my stomach and ran his hand up over my breasts.

"I can't wait to make love to you again babes," he murmured in my ear as he kissed my neck.

"Me either, but we have to wait hun," I replied.

I was feeling so turned on as he kissed and nibbled my neck, but the thought of actually having sex made me shudder. Turning me to face him, Roman gently lifted me off the ground, I wrapped my legs around him and we kissed.

"Just because I can't get any doesn't mean I can't pleasure you though," I winked saucily at Roman.

"Can you possibly be any more perfect Lize?" he said as he lowered me to the ground and removed his shorts.

His anticipation was short lived though, because no sooner had his shorts hit the floor, Logan woke up and began to wail.

CHAPTER 37
PANDORA'S BOX

I'd been back at work three mornings a week, for a little over six months. Roman was actually quite supportive of my decision (I think he'd finally learned the meaning of the saying choose your battles.) Logan slept most of the morning anyway, and on the odd occasion that he was restless, he settled quite quickly on my lap while I worked. With his gorgeous green eyes and dark hair, he wooed everyone who came into his orbit, and I was never short of an extra pair of hands to help with him.

Roman was a very hands-on dad, spending every possible minute he could with his new son. We were seriously talking (again) about him either resigning, or going part-time so that he could help with the expanding business, and just have more time with us in general. We'd also been approved as foster parents, but had decided that we'd wait until after Logan's first birthday before we took on any more responsibility. We had had a few overnight emergency stays, and on those occasions, I wondered again if we were cut out for the 'foster life' because I hadn't wanted to give those sweet children back.

Liam was now with us full time, his parents had initially hit the roof when he told them he was leaving his job, but once they knew he was going to be working with me, and that his education would be put to good use they came around. It also meant that they could drop in when they liked to see their sons and grandson. Jill would often take Logan in his stroller and go for a long walk or out to lunch with her friends.

Life couldn't have been any more perfect. As I sat at my desk, I looked around with so much pride, and love for all these amazing people I'd been blessed with, and for all that I'd achieved. Our futures were secure, and I looked forward to experiencing new adventures with them all, in the unwritten chapters of our lives.

I opened my laptop and logged in to check my emails, my eyes were immediately drawn to an email with the subject;

LOOKING FOR RELATIVES OF THE LATE, ELIZABETH MARY FOX-NEE MILLER

I frowned, and staring at the screen I wondered, what on earth could this be about. My mind drifted to the unopened box of documents that were on the top shelf of my walk-in closet. Roman had asked once about it, and I had told him I didn't really know if I wanted to delve into my mother's past. I was curious sure, but I was also apprehensive about what I would find. I was content with just looking at her pictures occasionally, and having this idea in my head about what she was like.

***

I clicked on the email;

> *Hello, my name is Sebastian Lopez,*
>
> *I was put up for adoption at birth, and according to my birth certificate my Mother was Elizabeth Mary Miller.*
>
> *If I have the correct contact information, then I am your brother.*
>
> *I am truly sorry to contact you like this, but when I found out through the private investigator I hired, that you were in Australia and with me being in New York, this seemed like the only way.*
>
> *I'm not sure what you know about me, or if you even know about me? But I hope to hear from you soon.*
>
> *Kind regards*
>
> *Sebastian*

Closing the laptop I picked up my keys..., reeling in shock I called out to Jessica,

"Jess, can you watch Logan for me for a few hours, I need to step out," my voice was trembling, and my hands shaking as I walked out of the office.

As I headed toward home, toward the box in the cupboard…, I already knew what I was going to find…, I knew it had to be true. I wasn't an only child after all…, I had a brother. But why was it kept a secret? I'm sure daddy knew, why hadn't he told me?

But with both my parents gone, would I ever really know the truth?

11657066R00217

Made in the USA
Middletown, DE
14 November 2018